AF338179

Pix of Me and You

George Kayde

CR&C Studios
Toronto, Ontario

Copyright © 2018 by George Kayde.

All rights reserved. No part of this publication may be reproduced, distributed or transmitted in any form or by any means, including photocopying, recording, or other electronic or mechanical methods, without the prior written permission of the publisher, except in the case of brief quotations embodied in critical reviews and certain other noncommercial uses permitted by copyright law. For permission requests, write to the publisher, addressed "Attention: Permissions Coordinator," at the address below.

George Kayde
CR&C Studios
Unit 1021
20 Minowan Miikan Lane
Toronto, Ontario M6J 0E5
www.georgekayde.com

Publisher's Note: This is a work of fiction. Names, characters, places, and incidents are a product of the author's imagination. Locales and public names are sometimes used for atmospheric purposes. Any resemblance to actual people, living or dead, or to businesses, companies, events, institutions, or locales is completely coincidental.

Ordering Information:
Quantity sales. Special discounts are available on quantity purchases by corporations, associations, and others. For details, contact the "Special Sales Department" at the address above.

Pix of Me and You / George Kayde — 1st ed.

Get Your Free Starter Library!

Sign up for the no-spam Reader's List and get **TWO** free books, and lots more bonus content, all for free.

Get started by visiting: http://georgekayde.com/free-books/

Chapter One

Brittney felt more like an Instagram account than an actual person.

Her smartphone quacked like a duck; a notification for a new comment. She'd only just posted the photo of her modelling the beige crop top that Guess had sent her to promote its upcoming summer wear. Not even ten seconds had passed and already someone had seen the photo and liked it.

Not just someone, but her fans. One of over 300,000 followers.

She switched off the Instagram notifications. While the likes and comments put food on the table and a roof over her head, she didn't need to be notified of every single thumbs-up or heart. The first twenty were a good dopamine hit, but anything more and it was like someone tapping her on the shoulder a hundred times.

Derrick, lying in her bed, rustled awake. Smiling to himself, he cracked his eyes open, then stretched and swallowed a yawn.

"Sorry," Brittney said, "did I wake you?"

"What time is it?" Derrick said, lifting himself up on one elbow. His hair stuck up in the back. Messy, but cute.

"Quarter to eight."

"You let me sleep in?" he said, pulling the covers aside. He swung his bare legs off the bed and stood. He wore nothing but a pair of black boxer shorts. His jeans and shirt were strewn on the floor. She stared at him for a moment. Not an ounce of fat. Not crazy muscular either. Just right. Here was a man she could wake up to every morning and never get tired of it.

She flung open the curtains to let in the sunlight. Snow covered the streets of downtown Toronto. Thankfully the snow had stopped before morning.

"Babykins." Derrick said. "Those aren't your pajamas."

"Obviously." She kissed him on the lips. "This is the new crop top from Guess. Just posted a candid while you were sleeping." She probably had twenty likes by now, five comments, something like that. She turned to her right, then to her left, arching her back. "What do you think?"

Derrick's eyes focused on her cleavage. "I like it," he said, his hands on her hips. "But you're not wearing any pants."

Nope. Just the crop top and the pink granny panties she wore to bed for maximum comfort. "It was a body shot. Nothing below the belt."

"You sure there, babykins?"

"Positive," she said. "Not making that mistake again." Like that time she posted a candid of her wearing a blouse and blazer sans pants. She'd placed her makeup mirror behind her, and the photo showed not only the business attire supplied by Burberry but also Brittney's naked behind supplied by her mother. That had been mortifying. Image equaled life, and that was not the image she wanted to showcase.

"Good," he said, the corners of his lips twitching into a half smile. He tapped her butt cheek. "Burberry bottom."

She slapped him playfully. "Not funny. It was one time." She wiggled out of his grip.

He reached out to her, but she flitted away, escaping into her walk-in closet. Once inside, she slipped off the crop top and put on a pair of skinny, dark blue jeans and a black sweater, along with a pair of wool socks to keep her pedicured feet warm against the January cold. A red bag, nearly stuffed to the brim, sat in the corner of the closet next to her laundry basket. She brought the bag and the crop top to her bed, opened the bag, and stuffed the crop top inside.

"You're not going to keep that one?" Derrick said, doing the buttons of his white shirt.

"I never do," she said, digging her hands into the bag and moving the clothes around. Shirts, pants, underwear, socks, a pair of boots. All new, and all clothes she modelled for different clothing brands.

Derrick plucked up a lacy bra by the strap. "You gotta keep this one."

"Nope," she said, snatching the lingerie and stuffing it back in the bag.

Derrick sighed, shaking his head. "All this free stuff. Gone."

"Not gone. But sent to Goodwill."

"To people you don't know and who haven't earned it."

"To people who need it more than I do."

Derrick raised an eyebrow. "Like who?"

"Like a single mother needing a blouse for her next job interview so she can feed her kids." She checked her phone: thirty likes and counting on the crop top photo. "Or maybe a wife who wants to look and feel sexy for her husband but can't afford a pricey piece of lingerie from Victoria's Secret. Well, now she can."

Though she wouldn't take it to Goodwill herself. She had the concierge downstairs make arrangements to have it delivered. She couldn't go. It reminded her too much of how life had been after her father left, and her mother had to take care of her alone. Money had been tight. There'd been no walk-in closets or Burberry bottoms then.

"None of the other models are as selfless as you," Derrick said, grabbing his camera and placing it carefully in a pocket of his messenger bag. He worked for one of the big photography studios in North America, though the name of it escaped her now. He stepped close to her. "I had fun last night."

She put her arms around his neck. "Thanks for dinner."

"My pleasure, babykins," he said, pulling her into a hug, her cheek resting on his chest.

"It's been, what? Two months?"

"Really? Feels like I've known you all my life."

Cheesy line, but Brittney couldn't help but smile.

"That's, like, the longest relationship I've ever had."

She pulled back, staring up at him. "Does that mean we're in a relationship?"

"Sure."

Her shoulders sagged. So much for enthusiasm.

"I mean, of course we're in a relationship."

She smiled again. "So what do you like about me?"

"You're pretty."

"And?"

He paused a moment. She raised an eyebrow.

"You're *very* pretty." He grinned, clearly proud of himself.

"Is that it?"

The grin fell from his face, eyebrows knotting together. "Noooo…" He said it softly, slowly, and without much conviction. "There're other reasons."

"Like what?"

His expression went blank.

"Never mind," she said.

He pulled her in again, wrapping his arms around her tightly. "You're the prettiest girl on the planet. Isn't that what every girl wants?"

"Yup."

There was more to her than her looks, wasn't there? She wanted to be more than just a photograph on Instagram. More than the clothes she wore or the makeup she applied. Why couldn't a guy see her for what was underneath? Maybe her brain? She had one of those and used it every day.

She could do more than just model.

She bit her lip.

Probably.

#

Rob Ackerman was a clean-shaven, clean-cut sort of guy, always dressed in a navy suit and black tie with black shoes and belt to match. He was also Brittney's manager. His black hair was slicked back and shiny with gel. Pale skin like a vampire. Sometimes Brittney and Derrick referred to him as "Count Drackerman." But instead of sucking blood, he sucked twenty percent of Brittney's earnings per photo shoot.

"New Year's is over," Brittney said, sitting in a plush chair across from Ackerman's desk. A sign reading "Happy New Year" hung on the wall opposite the floor-to-ceiling windows. Pieces of gold and silver confetti stuck to the carpet's thick fabric, and the office still reeked of spilled champagne even three days after New Year's Eve. Thankfully, she and Derrick had decided to stay in that night instead of attending the agency's party.

"I'll get Katie to take it down later," Ackerman said, putting papers into folders and moving the folders aside. "I saw you posted a new photo today. How many likes so far?"

"Over two hundred likes and thirty comments." She hadn't read them yet. Probably just the usual—stuff like *OMG you're gorgeous*, or *OMG you're sooo beautiful*, or *OMG I need that top*! Her girl fans usually commented on her makeup and clothes while her guy fans usually commented on her makeup and tits.

Ackerman loaded a spreadsheet on his computer screen. "I got you another shoot today at two p.m. Can you make it?"

"Sure. Who's it for?"

"Calvin Klein."

Hopefully not underwear again.

"With who?"

"Derrick."

She sighed. "Okay."

"You and Derrick break up?"

"No."

"Have a fight?"

"Uh-uh."

"Then?" Ackerman said.

"It's nothing." Nothing was right. She was nothing to Derrick but a pretty face. He was as bad as the commenters on her Instagram. Or maybe he just thought that was what she wanted to hear. But it wasn't. Not even close. She'd been told she was beautiful all her life. She made a living out of it. But no one ever looked beyond her big blue eyes, blonde hair, and smooth skin. She wasn't *that* pretty. Photoshop and filters did most of the magic.

Ackerman placed his elbows on his desk and leaned in. "We've worked together since you were sixteen years old. I know when something's bothering you and something is definitely bothering you."

"It's nothing." Nothing to Ackerman at least. "Really."

"You said the same thing when your father left, and that certainly was something instead of nothing."

She bit her lip, crossing her one leg over the other, and lowered her head, hands tucked in her lap. Like she wasn't already feeling bad today. Any mention of her father would make it worse. "Any word from him?"

Ackerman sighed. "I wish, sweetheart, but no."

She nodded. Nine years of modelling, over 300,000 followers on Instagram, and still her father hadn't reached out to her. Not one phone call, text message, or even a heart on one of her photos. What was she doing wrong? Maybe her father had no respect for her because she sold her beauty for money. She'd heard that criticism from people before. Sometimes trolls on her Instagram would comment on how snapping photos wasn't a real career, that she ought to consider herself lucky for being born beautiful because there was no way she'd ever manage to get a real job or do anything of substance. She didn't think that, though. Modelling wasn't about her showing off her looks or to bolster her self-esteem. It was about inspiring women to look their best, to see themselves as beautiful and to feel sexy.

"If he called, you know I'd tell you," Ackerman said. "Let me get you a printout of the job." Ackerman typed away on his keyboard.

Portraits of the models Ackerman worked with hung on the wall. Female and male models, all younger than twenty-five years old. A portrait of Brittney at seventeen, clad in a prom dress and a smile showing all her teeth, was captured in a black frame. She looked so happy, hopeful. Like becoming a famous model was the only way to get her father back. Famous was the key word here, the word that made her father leave all those years ago. He'd dreamed of becoming an actor, someone on the big screen and sitting across from Late Night TV hosts. But a search on IMDB showed he hadn't been cast in anything at all. He used to take Brittney to movies and plays all the time and he'd been rapt by the performances on stage. Tabloids were his bible, all the gossip of people everyone knew about. He craved that kind of attention, no matter how good or outlandishly bad. Fame and image had been more important to him than his wife, than his daughter.

Image equals life. Her father had said that to her before he'd left nine years ago in search of his own fame, his own image.

"What if…" she started, biting her nail.

"Hm?" Ackerman said, glancing at her. "Hey, don't bite your nails! You'll chip the paint."

So? Her nails were acrylic anyway. Which made typing a text message a Herculean task.

"What if I stopped modelling?"

Ackerman's jaw dropped. He went even paler than usual. White as French tips. "And what would you do?"

"Go back to school?"

Ackerman chuckled, leaning back in his chair. "You barely passed high school."

"Because I was modelling so much."

"And why would you want to leave all this? You've got a good living here."

"I know." Her hands shook; she tucked them between her legs. "I'm getting older, though. Most models my age quit by this time. Do something else."

"Seriously, sweetheart, don't bullshit me. What's up?"

What's up? The fact she was a shiny object to Ackerman and Derrick. Something to show off and make money from. A means to an end. And when she was too old to model, she'd be replaced and forgotten. Thrown out like the clothes she gave away to Goodwill. Except no one was going to pick her up, appreciate what someone else had thrown out, and make something out of her. She had to do that herself.

"I want something more out of my life," she said.

Ackerman leaned back in his chair, studying her. Had he heard this line from other models before? "And what, pray tell, are you going to study at school?"

"Business."

Ackerman barked with laughter. He pressed print on his computer screen. The printer next to his desk whirred, shooting a sheet of paper out. Ackerman laid it flat on the table. "Give me a break, Brit. Who ever heard of a model going into business school? Maybe you can make clothes and sell them on eBay."

If she was going to start a business making clothes, she'd have her own store with her own employees, not sell them online on eBay. She was smarter than that. "There are lots of things I could do," she said with an edge to her tone.

"Well, sweetheart," Ackerman said, "you gotta dig deeper than that pretty surface of yours if you want to quit modelling. In the meantime…" He slid the piece of paper to her. "Here's your next shoot."

The shoot was in a studio in Yorkville, one of Toronto's upscale neighbourhoods.

"You want my advice?" Ackerman said. "Stick with what you know. You're not cut out for business." He chuckled, shaking his head. "Go take pretty pictures. It's what you're good at."

#

"Hello?" Brittney called, poking her head into the old Victorian brick house, the location that Ackerman sent her to meet with Derrick. She had tried knocking a few times with no success before the cold winter forced her to try the door knob. Finding it unlocked, she let herself in.

Synthesizers of electronic dance music boomed from the upper floors. Derrick was waiting for her. She smiled to herself. Maybe Ackerman was right. What did she know about business anyway? She was a model, had been for nine years. This was all she knew.

She unzipped her black Canada Goose coat, loosened her patchwork scarf, stomped her snow-covered boots on the welcome carpet, then climbed the creaky steps to the second floor.

Murmurings. Derrick was with someone.

"Why couldn't you stay with me New Year's Eve?" A woman's voice, half-whiny, half-husky.

"You know why." Derrick's voice. "I was too drunk."

Brittney cocked an eyebrow. No, he wasn't. They'd had one glass of champagne that night after the ball had dropped. She skulked toward the music and voices at the back of the room.

"You could've texted me to wish me a Happy New Year's." The girl again, now pouty rather than husky.

"I did. In the morning."

"You should've done it sooner."

"I'm sorry, babykins."

Brittney's chest seized. Did Derrick just call this girl *babykins*? Forget stealth, she marched down the hall.

"I'll make it up to you," Derrick said.

"What the hell is this?"

"Brittney?" Derrick's eyes widened.

"Who's she?" the other girl said. She looked no older than nineteen and clearly a model with a body that could only be achieved through eating bland salads every day, and hair and makeup done with fake nails and fake eyelashes. She wore pink panties but nothing else, no bra, and Derrick's hands were around her waist. They stood as close as Brittney and Derrick had been that morning.

"You piece of shit," Brittney said.

Derrick let the girl go. "It's not what you think."

"Oh?" Brittney crossed her arms over her chest. "Then why're your pants around your ankles?" Not to mention his obvious hard on.

Derrick raised his hands. "I can explain. Just let me explain."

"Fuck you," Brittney said, emotion catching her throat. She whirled around and ran down the hall.

"Wait, babykins!" Derrick called out to her. "Please!"

"Uh, babe, I'm right here," said the other model, clueless and as model-stupid as it got. "Why you calling that old lady babykins?"

Old lady? Brittney had half a mind to go back and slap the blush off her.

Derrick called after her again, but Brittney didn't stop. She stormed down Hazelton Lanes and caught a cab at Yorkville Avenue. She sat there with fists on her knees and a clenched jaw.

Once inside her apartment, she tore off her coat and slammed it down on the floor, kicked off her boots, and yanked the scarf from her neck. Then she plopped down in front of her laptop and checked her phone.

Eight missed calls from Derrick. Twenty text messages, the last one reading, *I didn't think we were exclusive.*

Three missed calls from Ackerman and one text message all in caps. *YOU MISSED THE SHOOT. WTF.*

She tossed her phone on the bed. Forget them. Then she loaded up her Instagram account. The candid photo she'd posted that morning had gotten over eight hundred likes and seventy comments. The comments were all the same.

WOW. Gorgeous!
Beautiful! :)
Love that top on you!
Ur on fire, grrl!
Bangin bod!
#hawt

She didn't need this anymore. She was more than just *hawt*. More than some guy's plaything.

She went on the Delete Your Account page. Under the drop-down menu for *Why are you deleting your account?* she selected the one that most applied to her: trouble getting started.

She clicked on the *Permanently Delete My Account* button.

A window popped-up. *Are you sure you want to permanently delete your account?*

She clicked *Yes.* And if she could, she would've clicked *Hell Yes.*

Chapter Two

Guy Moraine stood in front of the two-storey building. A sign reading Collar Gallery, in artsy block lettering, was plastered over the main entrance. This was the place, right here in the West Queen West neighbourhood, in the middle of the Art and Design District of Toronto. He took a breath, the below zero weather turning his breath to fog.

He slapped the beige folder with all his photographs on the palm of his hand. All he had to do was get the director, Helene Collar, to agree to showcase his work in her gallery. It'd take some convincing, some selling tactics, some of his boyish charm and practiced smile. And all this before his boss noticed he was missing from the office.

Simple.

He went into the building, finding himself in a small but bright foyer. Framed art pieces hung on the wall—some photography, others paintings and intricate sketches. Each image told a story. A black-and-white landscape photo of a meadow with ominous, thick clouds in the background. A tree with books hanging off the branches. A winding corridor of what looked like a building under construction.

One day he'd have his own studio, and *his* photographs would decorate *his* walls.

The click of heels on the hardwood floor caught his attention, followed by voices.

"Who told you to throw your whole life away with the click of a button?" said a woman, her voice mature, her tone exact. "You can't pay rent if you're not making money."

"Clearly I wasn't thinking, Mom," another woman's voice said, this one younger and rash. "But I can't go back. I can't!"

"Didn't you save any money?"

The clicking heels grew louder.

"I live in a luxury condo in downtown Toronto. The rent alone was half my earnings."

"*Lived.* You *lived* in a luxury condo in downtown Toronto. Now you'll live with mommy." The voice was friendly, the words weren't.

"So you'll take me in?"

"Of course I will. Oh!"

A woman emerged from the gallery, and Guy smiled tightly at her. He hadn't meant to overhear that heated, emotion-filled conversation. He cleared his throat and realized his blazer poked out of the bottom of his leather bomber jacket. God, he was a fashion disaster. Not his fault he didn't own his own suit and had to rely on a hand-me-down from his father. Guy was an artist, the struggling kind. Appearances didn't matter. Talent did. He wouldn't have even worn one if his roommate Josh hadn't made him.

He scratched the back of his head. "Hi, there."

The woman gave Guy a once over. Brow furrowed, she glanced at her watch. Guy had come here at ten after nine in the morning; the earlier he got here the better chance he had of getting back to the office before anyone missed him.

"I'm sorry," she said, approaching Guy with her hand extended. "I wasn't expecting anyone. I'm Helene Collar."

Guy lit up. Jackpot. He shook her hand eagerly. "My name's Guy

Moraine." She wore a navy suit with a white blouse. Her blond hair hung in curls around her shoulders. In black high heels, she stood eye level with Guy, but her bearing made her seem twice as tall as his five feet ten inches. She stood straight, shoulders back, chin up. Not in an arrogant way, but in a way that made her regal. Guy swallowed the lump in his throat. He couldn't afford to wuss out now. He shot his shoulders back, puffing his chest out. Show confidence, Josh had told him. "I'm sorry it's early. Is this a bad time?"

"Do you have an appointment?"

"No, I don't," Guy said. All the books he'd read about selling yourself and your brand recommended the cold drop-in, which showed how passionate you were about your chosen career path. All successful people were go-getters. "I'm a local artist in the area, trying to get my foot in the door with a gallery. I walk by this place every day on my way to a desk job from hell"—it was true, no use dancing around his desk-job life—"and finally today had the courage to come in and show you what I've got."

Helene's lips twitched into a half smile, and her expression warmed. "Come on in, let's see what you've got to show."

Guy blinked. "Really?" He cleared his throat. *Confidence, Guy. Confidence.*

"Mom!" the other woman's voice boomed from the back room.

Guy flinched. "Sounds like you're busy."

Helene waved her hand. "My daughter. She just quit her job and is in a bit of a crisis of… well, of everything. She just needs to have a little freak out and she'll be fine. She's not usually this bratty." She sat down behind the front desk in the foyer. "That folder for me?"

"Yes, it is," Guy said, passing her the folder. He had to commend Helene on her calm demeanor while her daughter was falling apart in the back. Either way, none of his business. "This won't take long, I swear."

"So what do you do? Paintings? Drawings?"

"Photography." He unzipped his leather jacket, revealing the camera hanging off his neck by a black strap. "Fine art."

"Really? Is your studio around here?"

"Not really." Meaning that the closest thing he had to a studio was the computer folder he had cleverly entitled GUY'S PHOTOS.

"What am I going to do with my life?" Helene's daughter said, her freak out still in play. Footfalls sounded in the back, as if she walked in a circle while contemplating the pursuit of life, love and happiness.

Helene rolled her eyes, taking Guy's folder. She opened it in front of her. "We'll figure it out, honey," Helene yelled over her shoulder. "Don't worry. I support you one hundred and ten percent."

Guy leaned in. "Sure this isn't a bad time?"

Helene shook her head, lips mashed together. "Quitting was the best thing you ever did," she yelled back to her daughter. "I never liked that Vladackerman."

"Count Drackerman!"

Helene sighed. "I apologize. This isn't very professional of me."

"No, that's okay," Guy said. He didn't care if there was a banshee screaming bloody murder in the back so long as Helene reviewed his photos.

"Now, let's take a look," she said.

Guy bit his lip, watching as Helene sifted through his work with scrutiny, like she was studying for an exam in art history. Though this was what he'd wanted, he couldn't shake the sinking feeling in his chest and wiped his clammy hands on his suit pants. The best part about being an artist was doing the work. The worst part was showing it to someone.

That her daughter was here and yelling at the top of her lungs about the sky falling didn't help either.

"Not bad, right?" he said, a little too squeaky for his liking. He cleared his throat. He pointed to the photograph she frowned down at. "See what I did there? The colours of dusk reflecting off that church. Gorgeous. Not touched up at all." He picked up the next shot—a micro image of a bee, all in black and white except for yellow eyes—and passed it to her. "One of my finest and artsy-est."

Helene's nose crinkled, her mouth twisted. Not a good sign. Not exactly the beaming smile or the oh-la-la he expected for his artistic genius. She flipped through the portfolio and stopped at a very specific and very vulnerable photograph, and chuckled. Guy snatched the photo before she could pick it up. "That shouldn't be in there." He folded the photo, stashing it in the inside pocket of his leather jacket. Heat rose in his cheeks. "Sorry about that."

"That one I liked," she said.

How could she? Nothing interesting about a shot of Guy in a stained undershirt and long johns, a Blue Jays baseball cap on his head, eating cereal with a fork.

"My roommate took it," Guy said, a roommate he was going to murder when he got back home for slipping that embarrassing photo in Guy's portfolio. "Of me. To prove a point."

"That you're out of spoons?"

"That he thinks I should be doing fashion photography. Portraits."

"Why don't you?"

"It's not real," Guy said. "Not genuine."

She lifted one of his digitally-enhanced photos, a burning tree in a snowy field. "And this is?"

Good point. "No, but it has a message. It says something."

"What?"

Guy paused, stumped. Sweat beaded his brow. "It's art. I'm just the photographer. The viewer interprets it."

His nerves settled. Good comeback.

She leaned forward on the desk, eyes studying him. "Why take these photos? What do you want to *say*? What story are you trying to tell?"

"Uh…" That he was an awesome fine art photographer?

"You have to go deeper than this. Find your message." She pushed the folder back to him. "These photos don't mean anything."

Her words dug a hole into his chest, scraping away at the confidence he'd built up in his heart. He stood agape, but no words came out. What could he say? That there was meaning in meaninglessness? That his photos were just pretty images, and that was it? That he wanted to show off his editing skills with Photoshop?

That was it. He was done for. Career over before it had even begun.

Footsteps again. Coming from the back room. Pounding steps. Each one banging in Guy's head, ringing in his ears.

"What do you think is beautiful?" Helene asked, a question no one had asked him before, a question he had never asked himself.

The pounding footsteps stopped. A young woman stood at the door's threshold. Helene's daughter. Long, straight blond hair parted in the middle. Sparkling green eyes, like lime juice with ice. Round pink lips. Heart shaped face. Black shirt with tight dark blue jeans and black boots—elegant but understated. Guy couldn't look away, his gaze bordering on staring.

What did he think was beautiful?

Her.

She blinked at him. "Didn't know someone was here. Did you hear—"

"Everything, honey," Helene said. "He heard everything."

Her cheeks reddened. "Sorry about that. God, I'm so embarrassed."

"No worries," Guy said. If working with Helene meant more

exposure to her daughter, he'd do everything in his power to impress her. But that didn't start with his stupid, old suit. Helene's daughter looked like a fashionista. Her outfit matched, her hair and makeup impeccable.

"Guy, this is my daughter, Brittney," Helene said.

"Nice to meet you," Guy said, extending his hand. "I've been in a crisis or two myself. One averted, the other one still underway. My advice? Bob and weave."

She smiled at him, the natural light beaming from outside illuminating the fine creases around her mouth. They shook hands. "I knew those Tae Bo lessons would come in handy."

"Guy was just showing me his work," Helene said. "He's a photographer."

With those words, Brittney's expression darkened, and she squeezed down hard on his hand. Guy winced. She tossed his hand aside like it was trash. Guy stretched his fingers, then closed them in a fist, loosening the joints in his knuckles. A grip like a heavyweight champion. Maybe she wasn't kidding about the Tae Bo.

She glared at him. Openly. He retrieved his folder and hugged it to his chest like a protective shield.

"Looks like you guys are done here," Brittney said to Helene. "Can we go home? I've got to start unpacking."

Helene nodded. "I'll reschedule my morning appointments for the afternoon. Grab your stuff. Meet me in the back."

Without a word to Guy, Brittney spun on her heel and stormed off. When she was gone, Helene shrugged. "Like I said, crisis of everything."

"It's all right. I should probably go, anyway. Thanks for reviewing my work. Sorry to disturb."

Guy started his way back to the main entrance.

"Come back tomorrow."

Guy stopped. "Tomorrow?"

"Yes. Bring your work in tomorrow. I'll give you some tips."

"Like mentoring?"

Helene laughed. "Maybe I can help you go deeper with your work." She stood up. "Tomorrow. Let's say around six o'clock?"

"Perfect. I'll see you then."

It wasn't an exhibit in the gallery, but it was a start. Anything helped at this point. Maybe if he worked with Helene on his photography and he proved himself a hard worker, she'd offer to exhibit his work. So long as Helene's daughter wasn't around to derail it.

That glare. She must have a thing against suits.

#

Brittney stared out the window of her mother's car as they drove back to the house. Once she got all her stuff back in her old room, she was determined to sit down, crack open her laptop, and figure out her future. Going back to school was one idea, and one she liked. There was lots of opportunity in business. She could always start a business helping women dress for success. Like an image consultant. Didn't matter that Ackerman didn't think she could do it, because she knew she could and would prove him wrong. After all, her mother was a successful businesswoman so why couldn't Brittney be? Same genes, right?

"The gallery looks good," Brittney said. Tall buildings loomed over either side of the street. Sky high superstructures encased in glass. The models of the city.

"A lot better now than the dump it was when I bought it," Helene said. "I'm getting more client, too. High calibre. Some even from outside of Toronto." She stopped at a red light. Students from the University of Toronto crossed the intersection. "I think the website helps."

"That's great, Mom. I'm happy for you."

The light flashed green.

"So," Helene said. "You going to tell me what made you want to give up everything you worked so hard to build?"

Brittney readjusted her seatbelt that felt like it was choking her. "Just wasn't fun anymore."

Helene snickered. "If that's your criteria for a job you like, you're in for a world of disappointment, honey. What's the real reason?"

Brittney sighed, shoulders sagging. Hiding something from her mother was like hiding something from God. Even if they hadn't talked as much these past couple of years, her mother still knew Brittney inside out. "I got sick of being used for my looks." That was as close to the truth as she could get.

Helene's hands tightened on the steering wheel. "Who was using you?"

Everyone. Ackerman. Derrick. Her fans. The clothing brands. None of them ever wanted to know who was the real Brittney under the mascara and the lipstick. They wanted to see cleavage and thongs and pursed lips and fake eyelashes. "I'm not saying I didn't enjoy modelling, but I'm more than just a pretty face."

"Who said you were just a pretty face?"

"Mom, please. You're turning into the Incredible Hulk."

"Sorry, honey, go on."

They drove past Yorkville, and it reminded her of the last time she saw Derrick. She stood up straight in her seat. Forget that cheating bastard. He'd been part of a life she'd buried. She had a new life to look forward to.

"I want to be a normal girl with a normal job," she said, then reconsidered. "No, a career, not a job. Something I can be proud of."

"Like what?"

That was the scary part. She had a goal in mind and a plan

percolating. "I think I want to go to university."

"You hated school."

Brittney flinched. That sounded like something Ackerman would say. If she could sit still in front of a mirror while a makeup artist applied makeup and fussed with her hair for several hours, she could handle a lecture where at least she could scratch an itch on her nose. "When I was a teenager, I hated school. But back then I really did think all I needed was my pretty smile and blue eyes." She had Dad to thank for that one. *Image equals life.*

Helene nodded. "What'll you study?"

"I was thinking a degree in business."

Helene glanced sideways at Brittney. "You could always work for me at the gallery."

Brittney shook her head. "I gotta figure this out on my own. Be my own person."

"You were your own person until you flushed away your Instagram account."

She gave her mother a flat look. "The world of social media will live with one less girl posting half-naked photos."

"Some of your photos showed a little too much skin."

"Don't think I wasn't offered to show more. And don't think the pay wasn't worth thinking twice about."

Helene narrowed her eyes at Brittney. "Start researching universities."

They drove in silence the rest of the way. When Helene pulled onto a residential street, Brittney's heart pounded. She took a breath, let it out slowly. Nothing wrong with being twenty-five and moving back in with your mother. It would only be temporary.

They pulled into the driveway of the bungalow where Brittney had grown up. Snow covered the front lawn and the bungalow's flat roof. No Christmas lights decorated the house, unlike the other houses on the street. Dad had hated having lights up. He thought it called attention to a house he was never proud of.

"We're home," Mom said, pulling the car into park and undoing her seatbelt.

"Thanks, Mom," Brittney said. "I don't know where I'd be without you."

Mom rested her hand on Brittney's knee. "You can stay as long as you like and for as long as you need."

The inside of the house smelled of paint like it always did. The den was full of her mother's paintings, ones that were done and ones that were still unfinished. When she was a kid, Brittney used to watch her mother paint, admiring the creation of beauty from a blank canvas. Dad never liked any of the paintings, thought it was a waste of time. Who bought art these days? Who knew any famous painters nowadays?

"Things haven't changed," Brittney said, poking her head into the quaint kitchen.

"Didn't have time to change anything," Helene said. "I spend most of my time at the gallery." No doubt her mom also didn't have the money to change or renovate the house. Whatever money she had went toward improving the gallery. "Speaking of the gallery…"

"You're heading back?"

"I'll let you get settled in." Helene smiled. "I'll see you tonight."

With Helene gone, Brittney felt the heavy weight of loneliness fall on her shoulders. It was quiet. An agitating quiet. A lot of memories flooded Brittney's mind, most of them over the fights her mother and father had.

Brittney opened the door to her old room. Suited for a high schooler. Pink walls, blue ceiling. Her old desk where she had pretended to do homework still had the framed pictures of her with her high school friends. She didn't keep in touch with any of them anymore. Before she'd even graduated, she was already off making a couple grand a month from her modelling.

She sat down on the bed, the springs creaking. She rested her head in the palm of her hands. What had she done? How could she throw away everything for this? If only she'd thought this through a little more. Too late for that. Her account had been deleted. Permanently. Not that that deleted her photos. She had the rights to her Instagram account, but all the photos she took she'd sent to Ackerman, and he had distributed them to the various clothing companies. Better that than violating any contracts and ending up in a legal battle.

She jerked when her smartphone quacked with her duck ringer. Before yesterday she couldn't get the thing to shut up with all the notifications and text messages she got. Now it was all but quiet. She checked her phone.

No text messages from Derrick. Zero notifications. One text from Ackerman. "Got one last cheque for you."

Brittney shook, her breaths coming in short, panicked gasps. That word "last" set her on edge. Her eyes stung, but she wouldn't cry and let the tears ruin her mascara, her image. It was the only thing she had left, even if she wanted to change it.

She couldn't bring herself to text Ackerman back and tell him to mail it to her old home address. She didn't want him to know where she lived now. My, how the pretty had fallen.

She turned her phone on silent and left it on the bed. Then she opened her suitcase and pulled out her laptop. She flipped her laptop screen up and went on the internet. Her home page was Instagram, asking for her log-in info, which she didn't have. Force of habit.

She gave a trembling breath and shook her head. Focus. She could fix this. She didn't need Instagram or modelling. It was a dead-end career anyway. She would've gotten to this place eventually, whether she liked it or not. She had to make something out of herself, for herself. But she also had to do it for her mother, too, and not disappoint her. She had to better herself one step at a time. Make her mother proud of her.

And with the help of Google, she'd do just that.

She typed *business schools in Toronto* in the search bar and found Rotman School of Management at the University of Toronto. Reputable school. One of the tops in Canada, if not all of North America. Hadn't some of her high school friends desperately tried to get into U of T? It was their first choice. Well, maybe not *their* first choice, but definitely their parents' first choice. Attending U of T brought bragging rights to the parents. If Brittney could get in to that school, it would make her mother proud.

She clicked on the website, found the *How to Apply* section. A link below led to the application form.

Aha. She printed it out, grabbed a pen, and started scribbling.

Name and address? Easy.

High school transcripts? A slight obstacle but no harm in taking a trip down memory lane to her old high school.

Personal statement?

Huh.

What are you most passionate about in business?

Double huh.

She typed a new search item: *how to write a personal statement for business schools.*

Google found 9,980,000 results and in a third of a second. Brittney smiled. *Thanks, Google.*

She started reading and, for the first time in her life, she felt like she was doing something more than pose for a camera.

#

Guy picked up the empty pizza boxes one by one off the kitchen counter and started breaking them apart and folding them up for recycling.

"Are you cleaning?" Josh asked, poking his head out from his room.

"Yeah, so?" Guy said.

"First time I've seen you clean."

"It won't be the last either." Something sparked in Guy when he walked into the apartment. He smelled the dirty dish rag smell, saw the piles of dirty dishes in the sink and piles of clothes left on the floor, and couldn't stand it anymore. He'd managed to score a meeting today with a gallery director, and it wouldn't do for a rising star photographer like himself to live in a pigsty. It worked when he was in university, but it was time for him to grow up and take responsibility.

"Where've you been anyway?" Josh asked. He still wore his work clothes, the tie loose at the collar.

"Out. Snapping photos." He picked up his shirts from the floor and dumped them in the hamper. "Thought I'd take advantage of the dusk light." No better time to snap a photo than at the crack of dawn or at the coming of dusk when the natural lighting took on hues you couldn't ever imitate artificially.

"Any good ones?" Josh called from his room.

"A few." He flipped through them on the LED screen. Helene's words popped up in his mind. What did these photos mean? What did *any* of his photos mean? He'd never thought about it. He just saw what he thought was cool and snapped the photo. The actual message and meaning behind his photos would present itself eventually. Maybe when he had a big enough portfolio. A collage of his photos was taped up on the wall next to his futon bed. He stared at them, but no message from on high barrelled down on him. He'd taken competent photos, even some excellent, professional looking shots, but none of them had any real depth.

Not that he'd admit that to anyone but himself.

"How'd your meeting today go? Get a showing?"

"No showing. But I got another meeting tomorrow with the gallery director."

"That's progress," Josh said as he came out of his room, dragging a suitcase. A backpack hung off his shoulder.

"Oh, no," Guy said, groaning. "Say it ain't so."

"It's time, pal."

"You don't have to move in with her."

"Vanessa and I are engaged now. Moving in together is the next logical step."

"Stay here till after the wedding."

"You'll be fine," Josh said, rolling the suitcase to the front door.

"But what would Harvey say?" Harvey, boasting a kaleidoscope of colour, was a ceramic goat's head mounted on the wall. They'd picked it up at some street vendor's when they had moved in together as roommates in university. They thought it was the funniest thing they'd ever seen and gave him a name.

"He'll be fine, too," Josh said. "He knew this day would come. Think about it. The pad's all yours now. Freedom. Privacy. You can put your photos anywhere you like. You can have my room."

Guy plopped down on the futon and winced when his ass hit the almost rock-hard mattress. He might as well sleep on the floor. "That does sound good. And I do like your bed, but I'll miss the camaraderie."

"I will, too." Josh leaned against the kitchen counter, sniffing. "Won't miss the funky smells, though."

Guy grimaced. "How can I make you stay?" The two of them had been living together since undergrad, now Josh was getting married. Unbelievable.

"You can't. Maybe you should start thinking about how to move out of here yourself."

"I like it here."

Josh snorted. "You hate it here. Besides, I'm not going away forever. I'll be back tomorrow to pick up more stuff."

"I'll hate it more now that you're no longer here."

"We'll still see each other every day. We work together." He slipped into his winter boots, then shrugged into his coat. "Which reminds me, make sure to set your alarm for tomorrow. You can't afford to be late with Donaldson gunning for you."

"I'll be fine." Donaldson was their boss, the CEO of SI Financial, and Josh was his protégé. Guy, on the other hand, was more of a liability to the company than anything else. He'd only been hired because Josh, being the true friend that he was, had begged Donaldson to put Guy on staff. Being unqualified for a job in a cubicle, Guy was sentenced to a job of filing and mail delivery.

"No more Operation Sneak into Work Late," Josh said, pointing at Guy.

"Donaldson has never seen me come in late. It's all good." Guy couldn't remember the last time he was on time for work. When he wasn't out taking photos in the morning light, he had Josh to wake him up. At this point in time, he'd become a professional at sneaking into work at ten or eleven in the morning, just like he had today after his meeting at the Collar Gallery. But Josh was right—Donaldson was getting suspicious. The mail still got delivered, though, just a little later in the day. No biggie.

"One day he's going to catch you, and I won't be there to save you," Josh said.

Guy waved dismissively. "You worry too much. I'll be there bright and early tomorrow. Promise."

Josh left, leaving the apartment quieter than a darkroom. Guy stood up from the futon and pulled Helene's business card from his pocket.

Helene Collar, Gallery Director. She'd asked him what he thought was beautiful. Buildings. And landscapes. Things that caught his eye and held his attention. But what did those things mean?

He mulled over his photos in his portfolio and found the one of him that Josh had taken. How ironic the one photo Helene liked was the one Guy hadn't even taken. He smirked. Truth was, he used to take photos like these. Photos of people. He'd watch his friends and catch moments of their lives. Moments when they were happy, or sad, or in love.

Actually, come to think of it, he still had those photos in a box somewhere. He searched around and found the box under the futon. He opened it up, and the first photo was one he'd taken of Josh and Vanessa when they had started dating. Guy could've sworn this photo captured the candid moment when the two of them had fallen in love.

There were others, too. More of Josh and Vanessa, and some friends Guy had gone to school with but had since lost touch. The photos were pretty good. Maybe Helene would like these. Digging farther, he came across a photo of his parents. He caught only a glimpse of it, but it was enough for him to yank his hand out of the box and shut the lid.

Not every photo showed truth, though, and Guy's parents were the perfect example. How many photos had the two of them posed for Guy, showing how happy and in love they were while all the time they'd been signing divorce papers? Love could be faked. So could happiness and sadness. He didn't want to be fake. It was why he had chosen fine art photography in the first place, where reality was expected to be bent and reshaped. Anyone would believe in the happily ever after by looking at the photos of his parents, photos he himself had taken.

And they'd be wrong.

No. That kind of photography wasn't beautiful either.

#

Brittney's head hurt. She'd read article after article about personal statements. What you should say. How you should say it. What format you should use. How long it should be. How many paragraphs. How many words. It was all too much, and even equipped with this newfound knowledge, she found herself stuck. Her fingers hovered over the keyboard. The cursor on the new document blinked, waiting.

A snack. She needed a snack.

She got up, stretched her back, shoulders, and neck and went into the kitchen. Her stomach grumbled. She was a lot hungrier than she'd thought.

And it was dark outside. The clock on the microwave read half past eight.

Her mother was late, and her mother was never late. They were supposed to be cooking dinner together just like they used to do when Brittney was a kid and it was just the two of them. Those were some of Brittney's favourite childhood memories. She'd be in the kitchen stirring spaghetti while telling her mother about her day.

But tonight wasn't like how she remembered. For starters, where was her mother?

Brittney had texted her around six o'clock, asking when she would be home and if she should get started on the salad or potatoes. But there'd been no reply.

This time she called.

"Hi, you've reached Helene Collar …" Voicemail.

She ended the call. To calm herself, she made some tea. Leaning against the kitchen counter, arms crossed, she stared at the kettle and thought the worst. Maybe her mother's schedule had changed? Maybe something came up at the gallery? Some artist emergency or whatever? Yeah, maybe, but she would've called, too.

Twenty minutes later her phone quacked. The display read an unknown number.

"Hello?"

"Is this Brittney Collar? Is your mother Helene Collar?"

"Yes. May I ask who's calling?" What was with the formalities? Her heart plummeted to her stomach, and she felt like she was choking.

"I'm calling from—"

The kettle whistled, sounding like tires screeching on pavement.

"Sorry, can you repeat that?" Brittney said, lifting the kettle to shut it up.

"I'm calling from Saint Michael's Hospital. I'm afraid I have some bad news. Your mother was in a car accident."

The phone slipped from Brittney's grasp.

Chapter Three

"Do you know what time it is, Mr. Moraine?" Donaldson asked, a hint of a smile on his face, as if he'd been waiting for this moment to finally catch Guy.

Guy had woken up late. Josh had even warned him the night before, but bad habits died hard. He'd forgotten to set an alarm, having taken for granted all the times Josh used to wake him up. Now Guy sat across from Donaldson in his office, preparing for the worst. He shuddered; it was freaking freezing in here.

He cleared his throat, made a show of glancing at his watch, and cursed every passed minute. "It's eleven, sir."

"Two hours late for work." Donaldson shook his head. "Two hours."

"I'm sorry." The silence in the office was total, blocking out all the chatter and typing on the floor. Soundproof door and windows. Guy could scream, and no one would hear him. He hoped to catch a glimpse of Josh, but Guy's knight in shining armour was nowhere in sight. "It won't happen again."

"You bet your ass it won't." Donaldson gave Guy a measuring, eagle-like stare. Guy squirmed in his seat.

"Am I d-dismissed?" The cold made him stutter, shivers racking up and down his spine.

"Yes. You are. Pack up your things and get out of my office."

"I'm fired? I was late one time." Countless times, actually, but Donaldson didn't know that. "I'll make up the two hours."

"It wasn't one time." Donaldson picked up the remote and pointed it toward his office television. "Security brought this to my attention." He turned on the TV. A video showed a montage of all the times Guy had been late. Crawling on the floor military-style, hiding behind cubicle walls, checking to see if the coast was clear. The video was on repeat.

"I can explain," Guy said. Then again, Operation Sneak into Work Late was about as self-explanatory as you could get.

"Mr. Moraine, you've been coming in late and leaving early for months." Donaldson smiled. Firing an employee was supposed to be one of the most difficult tasks an employer could do. Not true for Donaldson. He was probably taping this whole thing so he could watch it over and over again. "I'm afraid I can't keep someone so unreliable and untrustworthy on staff with me anymore."

"I need this job." Needed it badly. How was he going to afford the rent? He probably had enough saved up for two or three months, and then? Nada.

Donaldson shook his head. "If you did, you'd be here. But you don't care about this place. You have no respect for it. I've seen you come in wearing sweat pants. You don't care about how you present yourself. I'm not even sure you care about yourself." Guy opened his mouth to defend himself, but Donaldson stopped him with a raised hand. "Do you really even think I need a mailman? The only reason I kept you around was because of Josh. I gave you every opportunity to work your way up in this company. But no, that wasn't what you wanted. And if this isn't what you want, then you should go out there and find what it is you do want." He stood up and pointed to the door. "Now get out of my office."

#

A brace was wrapped around Brittney's mother's neck and an IV stuck out of the back of her hand. Black covered both her eyes like the worst mascara job ever and there were red bruises on her cheeks and nose as well as a split lip. The car's airbags must've done that. Brittney's heart broke to see her mother like this. Feeling like a deflated balloon, Brittney sat on a chair next to the bed.

Helene took a deep breath and her eyes fluttered open. Her gaze landed on Brittney. She gave a small smile.

"I'm okay." Her voice was raspy, hoarse. Barely sounded like her mother.

"Can I get you anything?" Brittney put a hand on her mother's arm. "Water? Food?"

"More morphine?"

Brittney started to stand up. "I'll get the nurse."

"I was joking, sweetheart." Helene chuckled, then winced. Her ribs were broken, and she couldn't laugh without feeling pain. "Any more morphine and I'll be on another planet." Brittney sat back down and sucked in air between her teeth. *Keep it together, Brittney. Mom was fine.* "This wasn't your fault," her mother said.

"I know, but…"

"I'll be okay. So no tears."

Brittney sighed. It was just a stupid car accident. Her mother would be fine and back to her superwoman self in no time. "When can you come back home?"

"I'll be here for a few more days."

"That's it?" That didn't sound like a long recovery at all. Two days of hospital food didn't sound so bad.

"Home for bed rest," Helene said, "and pain meds for at least two weeks before I start physio." She shut her eyes tightly, then she let out a slow breath and opened her eyes, her face softening. "Doctor says it could take a few months before I'm up and moving again."

"I'll take care of you." Brittney grabbed her mother's hand gently.

"I'll be fine. That's not what I'm worried about."

"What are you worried about then?"

"Someone's going to have to manage the gallery."

Brittney let go of her mother's hand. "Me?" That hadn't even crossed her mind. Her mother must be joking. She didn't know the first thing about managing a gallery. The galley would just have to be closed until her mother could go back to work.

"We can't afford to close it down while I recover. No work, no money. No money, no house."

"You want me to be gallery director?" It made no sense. It had to be the morphine talking.

"Yes." Tone resolute. Final. No sliver of question or doubt.

"Why can't Emily do it?" Emily was the girl that worked with Helene at the gallery. She was an art student, but had been working at the gallery for the past year, making her the far better candidate over Brittney.

"She's only part time. And she's nineteen. She wouldn't know the first thing about running a business."

"And I do?"

"You want to learn, don't you?"

She did, but not like this. "This is all happening so fast." Too fast. First, she quit modelling, then her mother ended up in the hospital, and now she had to step up to the gallery plate. It was crazy.

"How much money do you have left over from modelling?"

"Some."

"Enough to pay the house mortgage and the gallery rent?"

Definitely not enough. Especially since she wanted to use most of that money for university. Even if she didn't use it for tuition, she still didn't have enough for more than two months. She may have been making nearly a hundred thousand dollars a year as an Instagram model, but with a pricey condo and an expensive lifestyle, she might as well have been living paycheque to paycheque.

"But I don't know the first thing about running a business." She was no better than Emily. Only older. But not wiser. At least Emily was in university.

"There's no better way to learn than to actually do it. And I'll be there to guide you every step of the way." Her eyebrows hopped. "When I'm not high on morphine, that is."

"But I don't know anything about art." Another problem. All Brittney could see were problems. Lots of negatives, barely any positives. It'd be nice to use the gallery to gain some business experience, sure, but if she screwed it up, what good would that do any of them?

"You were a model. Just pick the artist and their work that you think is most beautiful and display it. You might not have my art degree, but you have my eye for beauty. Always have."

"But—"

"No more buts. Will you do it?"

Could she do it was the real question.

"You trust me that much?"

Her mother smiled, and Brittney could tell it caused her pain. And it was a beautiful, bright smile, banged up face and all. "You're my daughter. I believe in you."

Mom was giving her an opportunity to prove herself, to take something seriously. Besides, if she had any questions, Helene would be a quick phone call away. She did need the experience, and what better way to get it than to run your own business? Way better than folding clothes at the mall or depositing people's cheques at a bank.

Brittney stood up straight, chin up. "I'll do it."

Chapter Four

The next morning, Brittney unlocked the door to the gallery and took her first steps in as gallery director. The door closed behind her, and the silence of the place was so total it made her feel like she was breaking and entering. She wasn't, of course, but try telling that to her brain. She'd been so busy with her modelling that she hadn't come to the gallery as often as she would've liked. She'd come by only because she'd have a lunch date with her mother. She'd peeked at the exhibits but never paid much attention to them. That would change in the next few months.

This place was hers for the time being, and it was a long way away from Instagram modelling.

When she stepped forward, her heels clicked against the wooden floors. Her outfit for her first day as gallery director consisted of clothes taken from her mother's closet. Her own clothes seemed too childish, not professional enough. So she'd put on her mother's white blouse with a gray pencil skirt, pantyhose, and high heels. Good thing it wasn't supposed to snow today. She'd straightened her hair and tied it back in a bun like her mother sometimes did. She even toned down on the makeup—just some eyeliner. Everyone always told her she looked more like her mother than her father, so hopefully dressing like her mother proved that to be more true. Now she wasn't just breaking and entering, but impersonating, too.

Fraud. She'd only just arrived at the gallery and already she felt like a fraud.

In the back room, she flipped the switch by the wall. Fluorescent lights rained down on the gallery. Several columns stood in the centre of the big open space. Hanging off the walls were different pieces of art. She caressed the canvas material, wanting to make a connection with something she knew absolutely zero about. It all seemed kind of cold. Distant. Must have been the quiet, or the fact that she'd be the one to put new art on these walls and—gasp!—sell it.

She took a deep breath. The gallery smelled like her mother's perfume. That calmed her down a bit.

In the back was an office with a phone, computer, and more folders and paper than Brittney knew what to do with. She surveyed the gallery space again, hands on her hips. "So," she said to herself, "this is my life for the next couple of months."

The front door opened, ringing the chime.

Emily, footsteps pounding, bounded from the foyer to the gallery. She had huge headphones on her ears, blaring some kind of punk rock music. She wore knee-high black boots and had black hair with blue streaks. Everything on her was black except for her pale white skin. Her eyes were down on her smartphone, typing away with her thumbs. She marched right past Brittney. Must've been her daily routine. She probably could do it in her sleep. She took her coat off, exposing a black T-shirt underneath that showed the tattoos running up and down her arms, and hung it up on the clothing rack. She turned, shot her hands up in the air, arched her back, and yawned like a lioness. When her eyes landed on Brittney, she jerked, brows knit together.

She took her headphones off, letting them sit on her shoulders. "Who…" She paused, eyes narrowing. "Who are you?" She had such a soft voice, Brittney probably would've missed it if not for the extreme silence in the room.

Brittney and Emily had met on numerous occasions before. She must've looked unrecognizable in her mother's clothing.

"I'm Brittney. We've met before. Helene's daughter."

Her face broke out in a pretty damn cute smile, giving a bit of sparkle to her green eyes. "Oh, hi!" Her tone jumped, and she put a hand over her mouth as if to quiet herself. She even had tattoos on the backs of her hands. Brittney didn't know many people with tattoos. Models never had them since most clothing companies thought the tattoos would distract from the modelled clothes. Some models used tattoos as a niche, a specialty. "Where's Helene?"

Brittney sighed. She must not have gotten Helene's voicemail. Or she did, but hadn't listened to it yet.

She told Emily about the accident and her mother's condition.

Emily's face paled whiter than it already was. Her breath came in quick gasps, and her chest rose and fell.

"She's okay," Brittney added quickly, reassuring Emily, who seemed on the verge of a panic attack. Emily had seen Helene every day at the gallery so they must've spent a ton of time together. "Just banged up. She'll be good as new in no time." Hopefully sooner rather than later.

"Are we shutting the gallery down?"

Brittney shook her head.

"Then who's in charge?"

"Me." Said with just the right amount of denial.

Emily's eyes widened. "Oh, boy." Even she could see how bad an idea that was. "I'm sorry, that's not what I meant." She managed a smile. "You're going to do great."

"Are you sure? I don't feel like I will. I don't know anything about art."

"It's pretty easy. I'll teach you."

Brittney noted her tattoos. "Well, you do seem like an expert."

"These?" Emily lifted her arms, as if seeing the ink on them for the first time when she obviously saw them every day. "What can I say? I'm an art major and I love it."

No kidding.

"So then, what happens now?" Brittney asked. "What do I do? What do you do?"

"Let me check Helene's schedule." Emily took her smartphone out and started scrolling through it. "Huh."

Brittney perked up. "Huh? What's huh?"

"Today you've got a meeting with an artist."

Oh, no. A meeting already? No prep time allowed? Wasn't that the cardinal rule of meetings? No, not her. Because this wasn't technically her meeting. It was her mother's, except that her mother was locked down in a hospital bed. Ten minutes here, and already she was in the lion's den. She should call her mother. She had told Brittney to call at any time with whatever questions she may have. She had a slew of them now. "When's the meeting?"

The front door chimed.

Emily scrunched her face up. "Now."

So much for prep work.

Her impromptu meeting was with Harold, a successful artist that Brittney imagined her mother dealt with daily. Manicured fingers, clothes that matched perfectly, hair long and swept to the side, a five o'clock shadow. They sat in the office in the back. Brittney sat with her legs pumping up and down under the desk. She hadn't any expectations of what this meeting would entail. She was about to learn by trial by blazing, all-encompassing, make-it-or-break-it fire. Harold, on the other hand, sat calmly, one leg crossed over the other, hands resting in his lap. One brow was arched inquisitively. "Where's Helene?"

"I'm sorry to say,"—her tone sounded small and tight, like a child's—"she was in a car accident last night."

Harold's eyes bugged out. "Is she all right?"

"She's at the hospital now, recovering."

"So long as she's okay." Harold rested a hand over his heart. His movements were deliberate, graceful. An artist's hand. Each movement a brushstroke. "That's what really matters. And you are?"

"Brittney. I'm Helene's daughter."

"The model?"

The corner of Brittney's lip curved up. Felt good to know her mother talked about her to her clients. Sign of a proud mother. "I stopped modelling."

"Wow." Harold sighed. "I suppose Helene and I can't plan the exhibit anymore." He rose from the chair.

"Was that what you came by for?" Brittney blurted out. She needed him to stay. She was in charge now, and she couldn't let a client just waltz out of here.

"Your mom and I were supposed to sit down and review my artwork. Figure out which pieces we wanted to exhibit. Figure out the logistics. Pricing, scheduling, that sort of thing." He waved a hand. "No big deal. How long we'll she be at the hospital? A week?"

"Yeah, but…"

Harold lifted his briefcase off the other seat. "I'll reschedule in a week when she's back."

He started to turn around, and Brittney shot up, her chair rolling back and hitting the wall. The sound made her flinch, but at least it stopped Harold from leaving. "She'll be out of the hospital by the end of this week, but she won't be back in the gallery. She's got at least a few months of physiotherapy before she's up and running again."

Harold's eyebrows arched. "A few months?" She could tell by his tone that he didn't like that at all.

"Her doctor told her she needs to take it easy. She shouldn't be pushing herself."

"Is the gallery going to be closed?"

Brittney shook her head. "It'll still be open and hosting exhibits." Which exhibits and how many were a mystery at this point.

"Who's in charge, then?"

Brittney spread her hands out. "Like I said, I'm not modelling anymore."

"You?" Harold looked her up and down. She was used to that stare, especially from photographers, but this was different. He measured her capabilities, or lack thereof, not her appearance. "But you're just a kid."

Brittney pulled her shoulders back, raised her chin. "I—" she started, and that was as far as she got. The only "Art" she knew was the name of a designer at Gucci. And she really was just a kid. Twenty-five years old, whereas her mother had been thirty when she opened the gallery, and with a Master's degree in Art History under her belt.

"It's okay," Harold said, offering a soft smile. "I wish Helene a speedy recovery."

He made his way out of the office.

"Wait." Brittney went after him. She'd cling to him like fungus, do whatever she could to make him stay. "Please don't go."

Harold paused, then turned back around, but his face held an annoyed expression.

"We can still have your exhibit here," Brittney said.

"I don't know." Biting his lip, Harold surveyed the gallery. "Have you ever done this before?"

"Not exactly."

"Ever helped your mother?"

"Not once." She was honest, at least. Let the record show that.

"Do you know anything about art?"

"I know enough. Plus my assistant, Emily, is an art major." She gestured to Emily standing by the corner, her hands clasped together in front of her. "Right, Emily?"

Emily's face whitened, her eyes widened. Then her gaze fell to her feet. What was that? The girl just shut down.

"Look," Harold said, scratching his forehead. "I've been working with Helene for more than five years. I love her dearly, and she does amazing work. But I need my artwork shown in the next month."

"We can make that happen," Brittney said.

To her credit, Emily nodded vigorously to that. Had she burned her tongue on coffee, and that was why she couldn't talk right now?

Harold glanced at Emily, then at Brittney. "I'm not so sure. No offense. I need someone who is going to take my artwork seriously. Who will give it a critical eye and link it to potential buyers who'd like my kind of art. Do you even know Helene's buyers and their tastes?"

She didn't know there was such a thing as a list of buyers. If only her mother had given her training before taking this job. But last night after their conversation, Helene had fallen fast asleep. She needed to recover, not go over every little detail of her business plan.

"I didn't think so." Harold put a hand on Brittney's shoulder. "Tell Helene I said hi, and when she's back on her feet, we'll definitely work again. But until then, I need to take my artwork elsewhere."

"I'm a quick learner."

"I'm sure you are. I just can't take the risk with someone green."

"It can't be that hard, right? Art is either beautiful or it's not."

Harold chuckled. "There's more to art than just beauty."

"Okay, that was the wrong thing to say. Can we start over? Please?"

"Sorry. Really, I am. Best of luck."

He turned around and was gone.

Brittney spun around to Emily. "What was that about? You could've backed me up."

"Didn't Helene tell you?"

Great, another missing piece to the puzzle. "Tell me what?"

Emily shrugged. "I'm shy."

"No kidding," Brittney said, rubbing her temple.

"No, I mean, I suffer from social anxiety. Particularly with men."

That morning Brittney lost two other clients. Both well-established artists, both having worked with the experienced and talented Helene Collar before but not at all interested in working with ex-model-now-vanilla-gallery-director Brittney Collar. Both had pointed it out to her, too. *Sorry, but if you don't know anything about art, I don't want to work with you.* Or, *Sorry, but you're just too new in the business for me to work with you.*

Brittney dropped down in the chair in the office. She put her elbows on the table and rested her head on the palms of her hands. How was she supposed to do this? She needed advice. Someone to help her and tell her what to do. To spur her on.

She called her mother.

"I'm failing," she said. "Miserably. I'm a big fat failure."

"It can't be that bad, sweetheart." Helene's voice was, as always, soothing.

"I met with three different artists. All three of them walked out on me. They didn't even give me the time of day. What am I doing wrong?"

"Nothing. I've worked with some of these people for years. They trust me. They've seen my track record. Seen what I can do and how I can bring them success."

"They don't see success when they look at me," Brittney said.

"They see a huge risk." Brittney couldn't blame them. If she was an artist, she wouldn't go with herself either.

"Build their trust. There's artwork in the gallery that still needs to be sold. Why not start calling people from my buyers' list to see if they'd be interested? If you go on my computer, there's a spreadsheet where I've listed all my buyers, their contact info, and what sort of art they might like."

Brittney tucked the phone between her ear and shoulder, then typed away on the computer. "It says I need a password." Nothing today worked out for her. Just once she'd like for something to go her way.

"It's your birthday."

Brittney typed it in. "I'm in. Where's the spreadsheet?"

"Check under the folder called Contacts. Should be on the desktop."

Brittney searched with her mouse, and double clicked the folder then the spreadsheet. "Got it."

"Good."

Not good. The spreadsheet had hundreds of columns filled in. She scrolled down. "There must be a thousand people on here. You want me to contact all of them?"

"No one said running a business would be easy, honey."

Brittney sighed.

"It's okay. You'll learn, and you'll get better at this."

True. She had more than 300,000 followers on her Instagram account, and that was way more than Helene's buyers' list. If she could reach out to her audience when she was a model, she could do it now as a gallery director.

Still, one problem remained.

"I don't even own art, and now I'm trying to sell it."

"I once knew a car salesman," Helene said, "who cycled every day to work, even in the winter months. You don't have to use the product to sell it. You just have to believe in the product. Believe in the art. Trust your gut instinct. When you see a piece you really like, it'll speak to you on a deeper level than just what's encased in the frame."

"There's got to be an easier way."

"You could always try bringing in new talent. Build your own client base instead of trying to convince my clients to work with you. Work with a new local artist. Take a chance."

The front door chimed.

Brittney pulled the phone away from her ear. "Emily, could you get that?" she called.

"Seems like you have a knack for bossiness."

#

All it had taken was one partial interview at Taco House for Guy to realize he wanted better. Deserved better. And by God, he was going to have it.

He waited in the Collar Gallery foyer. He had his photos with him all neatly tucked away in a bright yellow folder he'd stolen from the office. He wouldn't leave this place until he had impressed Helene, until he had convinced her to take him on as a client. He had to get his own exhibit. He couldn't work at Taco House. Not until he'd exhausted all his options. He'd rather move back in with his father—no, with his *mother*—than work at Taco House. Not that there was anything wrong with the fast food joint, but he couldn't see himself working there, or any job, with any serious work ethic. SI Financial had taught him that. Ever since he'd gotten his first camera as a birthday gift from his parents when he was seven, he'd wanted to be a photographer. He had nineteen years of experience looking through a lens. Now was his time to show the world—or maybe just this little part of Toronto—what it was he saw. To him, it wasn't just an itch he had to scratch but a matter of life or death.

Footsteps. He shot up in the chair, standing straight and proud, and plastered his best smile on his face.

A girl emerged. Someone new he hadn't seen yesterday. A girl no older than nineteen, maybe twenty years old and full of tattoos.

And she was… scared?

Her body went rigid, hands to the side. Face so tense it was almost like she was trying to say something to him telepathically and was frustrated by the fact that he didn't receive the message.

"Hi there," Guy said, cautiously. He kept his smile where it was and infused it with as much warmth as he could. It was almost like he was approaching a frightened deer for a nature photograph and didn't want to scare it away.

Quiet on her end. She sucked her lips in.

"Is Helene here?" Guy took one small step forward, his hand out. "I have an appointment with her." *And I'm not going to hurt you, I promise.*

Nada on her end. More silence. Like hitting the shutter release on a camera that wasn't turned on.

"Can I come in?"

The girl stepped aside.

"Ooookay," Guy said. That was probably the warmest welcome he was going to get. "I was here yesterday. My name is Guy Moraine. Here's my card." He took a card from the inside pocket of his leather jacket and passed it to her. Josh had these cards made for him back at the office. They had his name, address, and contact info.

The girl took the card, but her lips were sealed. Not a peep.

"You all right?"

She nodded frantically. Then took a deep breath from her nostrils.

"You sure?" Sounded like she was in panic mode.

She nodded again, this time slower, and offered Guy a small smile. She was cute. And small. A tiny little thing. He felt kind of fatherly toward her.

Guy lifted both his hands. "I come in peace."

The tension evaporated. That seemed to break the ice.

Another set of footsteps. High heels. Click-clack on the hardwood floors. Someone he did recognize emerged. Helene's daughter, Brittney.

She stopped when she noticed him. Her head tilted to the side, and her eyes narrowed.

"Is your mom around?" Guy asked.

She looked different from yesterday. Yesterday she was like a girl on the catwalk. The kind of girl that had no idea how much a drink cost at a nightclub. Beautiful, no doubt, but snotty. This girl was different. This girl was professional. Her blond hair was straightened. Not so much glossy makeup. She had gorgeous green eyes with long eyelashes. Still beautiful, only now more mature. More in control and serious.

"Do I know you?" she asked him.

"Not officially." Guy extended his hand out. "I'm Guy. I have an appointment with your mom. Is she here?" He peeked around to the back where the gallery was. Didn't see anything. Looked empty. Like Brittney and the silent, tattooed girl were the only ones here.

"No, she's not. She's in the hospital."

Guy blinked. "Hospital?" That didn't sound good. In fact, it was the worst thing he heard all day. Even worse than "you're fired."

"Car accident," Brittney said. Her eyes narrowed on him. "Where do I know you from?"

"Is she okay?" Could this day get any worse? And how could her daughter be so nonchalant about it? As if getting into car accidents was a hobby of her mother's. Just an everyday thing. Nothing abnormal about two cars smashing together.

"She's fine," Brittney said, with a tone that suggested she'd gone through this same explanation of her mother several times today already. "But you won't be able to see her for a few months."

So not a fender bender. Guy's heart sank in his chest. But maybe this wasn't a total miss. Maybe he could salvage this somehow. "Are you the boss here, then?"

She crossed her arms over her chest. A gesture of authority or self-preservation? "You could say that."

Guy lifted his folder up. "Could you take a peek at my work?"

"Uh…" Brittney began. She glanced over at the tattooed girl who nodded her head. Even though she was silent on the matter, at least she was on Guy's side. "What sort of work do you do?"

"I'm a photographer," Guy said. "I was in yesterday, but you were having this crisis-of-everything moment."

Her eyes widened. "I remember you."

Uh-oh. Judging by her glare, it wasn't a pleasant memory.

#

Oh, she remembered who this guy was. The photographer that was asking her mother for advice. The annoying photographer who needed guidance. Would she have to deal with photographers? Did photographers have their own exhibits? Probably. But she didn't want to deal with them. Painters, sculptors, heck, even artists who worked with crayons, were fine. But photographers? Absolutely not.

Photographers reminded her of the superficial life she once led and no longer wanted.

Well, this *Guy* did wrong by waltzing into *her* gallery and demanding she look at *his* photography.

"I think you should leave," she said, deadpan voice—just get out and don't come back.

He blinked. "What? Why?"

"I have another appointment." She wanted to tell him she hated photographers and that was the reason she wanted him excommunicated but she couldn't say that. Her mother probably did work with photographers, but while Collar Gallery was under new management, it would be a photographer-free zone.

Emily, off to the side, gave her a frowny face. She didn't get what was going on, but neither did she have to. Brittney would explain it later. She could take on a different local new artist, one that wasn't a photographer.

"An appointment with another artist?"

"That's right." Brittney lied. "Another artist. Local artist. Someone new." She made herself busy at the reception desk. Tidying up papers. Putting pens in pen holders.

Guy put his forearms on the desktop and leaned forward. "What's his name?" he asked, the hint of a smile on his scruffy face. The bastard was calling her bluff.

Two could play this game. "It's a woman." No way was she about to lose to this woefully dressed and unkempt jerk. He had jeans with holes in them. In January! And that beard—it belonged in the wild jungle. At least his hair and face weren't greasy.

"Her name, then?"

"It's…Emily."

Seriously? Hundreds of thousands of female names out there, and she went with Emily. It'd be okay. Emily's social anxiety meant she wouldn't out Brittney.

"Emily," Guy said, as if tasting the name on his tongue and deciding whether it was good or not. "And what kind of art does this Emily do?"

Brittney stopped fiddling with the desk. "Post-modern?"

Damn it—he had her. What the hell was post-modern? She'd heard her mom say it once.

"I don't believe you."

"Excuse me?"

Guy glanced to Emily, the real Emily. "Is she telling the truth?"

Emily's gaze went to Brittney then to Guy.

"Can she speak?" Guy asked.

"She's fine. She suffers from social anxiety."

Guy's eyebrows rose. "Severe social anxiety."

"Leave her alone," Brittney said, pointing to the front doors. "I think you know the way out. Good day."

She walked toward the hallway. Guy followed her.

"Can't I have a few minutes of your time?"

"I'm very busy."

"With Emily the post-modernist?"

Emily shook her head. Guy caught it.

"Sounds to me," he said, "like there's no one here but you and her. And she may be Emily for all I know."

Emily smiled and shook her head yes.

"Ah ha!" Guy said, fist up to his chest. "See?"

"Traitor!" Brittney said.

Emily shrugged.

"All I need is ten minutes of your time."

"Ten minutes I don't have."

"Why?"

"Because," she said, letting that word sit out in the open. She licked her lips then said, "I don't like photographers."

Guy opened his mouth, but the front door chimed and in walked one of the artists that Brittney had lost previously. Hope sprung up inside her, and she gave Guy a smug expression. Maybe the artist had changed his mind and wanted to work with her after all. The timing couldn't be more perfect. Now she could get rid of Guy.

"See," she said, "I do have someone coming in." She went over to the artist. "You're back. Change your mind? If you come with me to my office, we can—"

"Ah, there it is," the artist said. He walked over to the chairs in the waiting room and retrieved a messenger bag that was under the table. "Forgot my bag. Good luck with everything."

He left, taking her hope with him.

Heat rose in Brittney's chest. Her breathing grew rapid, whistling from her nostrils. Guy came to stand beside her, arms crossed in front of his chest, shaking his head. "Seems like you're not having much luck bringing in business."

"We're doing fine, thank you very much." She spun around. "Right, Emily?"

Emily shook her head slowly from left to right. "We lost three artists today already."

Guy raised his hands in the air. "She talks! Hallelujah. And what beautiful words she sings. Thank you, Emily."

Brittney rolled her eyes. "Yeah, thanks, Emily." To Guy, she said, "We didn't lose those artists. They just had a relationship with my mother and wanted to work with her instead of someone new like me." It sounded pathetic when she said it out loud.

"I'm willing to work with someone new like you."

Her heart fluttered. "I don't think so."

"I'm new, too. And local. And an artist." He counted down with his fingers. "I meet all your criteria. You and I are alike. One and the same."

She raised her eyebrow at him. He wasn't going to win her over, even though she felt some of her resolve relax. "Not even close."

"You need me just as much as I need you. We can work together." The corner of his lips curved up. His hazel eyes gleamed. Derrick had given her that same look. But Guy's was different. Derrick had always been a "me" type of guy, and the words "we" or "together" weren't in his vocabulary.

Behind him, Emily shook her head yes so fast her head might fall off her neck.

Her mother did say she should work with someone new. Someone with whom she could build a client base. She didn't like photographers, but this wouldn't be the same relationship as she had with Derrick. She wasn't planning on getting involved romantically with Guy or any photographer anytime soon. Or ever. This was strictly for business. And strictly for making her mother proud.

"Fine," Brittney said, arms crossed over her chest. "Show me what you got."

Chapter Five

Instead of the gallery, their meeting would be held off-site, preferably at a restaurant where Brittney could not only judge Guy's work but feed her hunger, too. She hadn't eaten anything all day. Besides, she needed to get out of the gallery for a while. That place, though empty and quiet—for now, she kept telling herself—was overwhelming her. She felt like she could be trapped there from morning till midnight and accomplish nothing. Hopefully that feeling would go away, and she could chalk it up to first-day blues.

They went to the Drake Hotel on Queen Street West. Sometimes Brittney forgot it was even a hotel. It functioned like a restaurant during the day, and at night like a nightclub, a bar on the second floor and a dancefloor in the basement. All sorts of events happened here, from comedy shows to art gallery exhibits. It had a classy but hip feel to it. Bookshelves lined the walls, stuffed with novel titles like *How to Save the World in Seven Days,* or quirky like *Butt Anatomy.*

"What'll you have?" the waitress said, a pad of paper in her hand.

"I like the shirt," Brittney said. The waitress wore a white T-shirt with the Drake Hotel logo on it and underneath the words *I love you* written in cursive writing.

The waitress looked down as if she'd forgotten what shirt she'd put on. "We're celebrating the Drake Hotel's upcoming anniversary.

We opened on Valentine's Day so we're prepping for a big party that night. We have this great mailing list you guys can join." She pointed to Guy and Brittney. "Couples get in free."

Brittney shook her head. "We're not a couple."

"Just friends?"

"Just a couple of coworkers," Guy said. He sounded nervous. His hands tucked in his lap under the table, his back as straight as a light pole. "Or misfits."

The waitress put on a smile and lifted her pad up to her chin. "Have you guys decided?"

"I'll have the kale gnocchi." Brittney closed the menu and passed it to the waitress.

"Mmmm, my fav," the waitress said, her smile broadening. "And you?"

"Water's fine." Guy pushed the menu toward her. "Thanks."

The waitress took the menus and gave Guy a lingering look and a half smile before leaving. Did she find Guy attractive? How could she? He was dressed in a sweater that was too big for him and a ratty leather jacket. His hair was too long. He did have nice eyes, though. Brown with flecks of green in them. Only you could hardly see his eyes with all that facial hair. The waitress must have a thing for guys with beards. Didn't everyone these days? Except Brittney. Most male models were clean shaven.

"Not hungry?" Brittney asked, while her own stomach, hell bent on self-preservation, was on the verge of eating the other organs inside her.

"Money is a little tight right now. Let's just say I'm pouring everything I have into this endeavour."

A tingling sensation ran up Brittney's spine. Guy was putting all his eggs in her basket. She hadn't quite agreed to work with him yet, but if she did she had to make it a success. This was not the potential first client she could, years later, turn around and say she gave it her all, even though it failed at the end, but at least she learned what to do and what not to do.

No, she had to do it, and do it right.

Worse—she didn't have much money either and ought to be saving. The Drake Hotel suddenly seemed oppressively expensive. The fancy bar with their fancy bar stools. The beautiful servers. The high ceilings. The intricate lights and chandeliers. They should've gone to Taco House.

Guy tapped the yellow folder on the table. "You ready to see these?"

No way. Not after he dropped a bomb like "this better work or else Guy would be homeless." Did he really have that much faith in himself? Maybe his work was just that good, and she was worrying needlessly. After all, her mom did say for him to come back to the gallery.

"Tell me a bit about yourself first," she said, stalling to give her heart some time to settle before it burst out of her chest like the dinner scene in *Alien*.

"What's to know? My name's Guy. I'm a fine art photographer. And I live just around the corner."

"Hence local artist."

Guy winked. "Exactly." He was warming up, his nervousness sliding off him. "Why don't you tell me about yourself?"

"You already know everything about me," Brittney said, crossing her arms over her chest. She didn't want him to know about her being a model. She saw it as a stigma. Besides, that part of her life was over. Her Instagram account was #flusheddowntheproverbialtoilet.

"Not everything." He paused, thinking. Then tapped the tabletop with the palm of his hand. "For example, what's your favourite dessert?"

When was the last time she even had dessert? Models and desserts were mutually exclusive and never saw eye to whip cream. "Low fat yogurt?"

"No cake allowed in the Collar family household?"

The last birthday cake she had was when she was twelve. The day her father left. After that, she requested no more cake. "Not quite."

Guy pushed the folder to her. "Should we get started?"

Brittney gulped. There was no avoiding this. Part of her new role was reviewing artists' work. Her mother's words replayed in her head, telling her to choose only the photos that spoke to her. Choose the ones she thought were beautiful. If she stuck to that criteria, then she had nothing to worry about.

She opened the folder and started with the first photo: a digitally enhanced, black-and-white image of an old church building in Downtown Toronto with a black background and the stained-glass windows coloured.

The waitress came back, dropping off two glasses of water.

Brittney flipped through the photos, giving each her careful attention. All of them were pretty much the same. All digitally enhanced to give it some "fine art" flair, but missing the key message. Nothing spoke to her. The fact that they were all digitally enhanced was the only common denominator. Otherwise, the photos were all over the place. Photos of green landscapes, photos of moving vehicles, photos of buildings both old and new, photos of the sky. Some microscopic photos of a few insects that, while cool, didn't tug at the heartstrings. There was nothing marketable about these images.

Maybe it was her fault. Maybe she was missing something. Maybe she just didn't get *art*.

But that wasn't true either. She had an eye for what looked good. She was a model after all, and many of her most-liked pictures on her once-upon-a-time Instagram account had been candid ones she herself had taken.

These images simply didn't pop. They didn't sing or dance. And they didn't make her want to cough up money for one.

This was going to be a lot harder than she first thought.

"I can't tell," Guy said, "if your expression is oh-my-God-this-is-amazing or oh-my-God-I'm-going-to-hurl."

She should've checked her facial expressions. One time Ackerman had given her a shirt to model for a top clothing brand, and when she saw it, she had given it the most disgusting sneer. That wouldn't have been a problem if only Ackerman had been at that meeting, but the clothing designer had also been there. "I wouldn't go that extreme," she said.

"You don't like them?"

"They're…" What was the word? "Nice."

She winced. That was definitely not the word.

"Nice?" Guy said, brows raised. "No, no. Nice is what you tell your grandmother after she gets you red and green socks for Christmas."

She had to soften the blow. Give him some credit. "You obviously know how to use a camera—"

"Oh, thanks. I read the instructions."

Her heartbeat raced. "But…" Was this how artists were? Sensitive to criticism. She should've figured as much. Too late now, she was in a field of land mines.

"But what?" Guy snapped. Then his gaze fell to the table. He nodded once then faced her again, as if coming to terms with something limiting him. "Okay, I'm sorry. I'm obviously being a jerk here." He took in a deep breath and blew it out hard. "I have to learn to take criticism, right? It's all part of the process." He pointed at her then at himself. "You and me. As a team."

"Promise me you won't yell?" Brittney chewed the corner of her lip.

"It's that bad?" Moaning, Guy put his forehead on the table.

"None of these are speaking to me."

Guy lifted his head. "But they don't speak. They're pictures.

They're not like…" He lifted one of his pictures up to his face. "I'm a picture. Please like me."

"But pictures say a thousand words. Your pictures aren't saying any words."

The waitress came back, this time dropping off the kale gnocchi that probably cost a monthly mortgage payment.

"Excuse me," Guy said, before the waitress bounded off again.

"Yes?"

"What do you think of these pictures?" Guy asked, spreading out a few on the table.

The waitress leaned her hip into the table, her lips pursed. "Honestly?"

"Brutal truth," Guy said. "Your tip doesn't weigh in on this."

"They're great," the waitress said, a toothy smile on her face.

Guy gave a see-I-told-you-so look to Brittney.

"Would you buy one?" Brittney asked.

The waitress frowned. "Like for money?"

"Dollars and cents."

After a pause, she said, "No."

"Why not?" Brittney asked.

"Yeah, why not?" Guy asked with an edge.

The waitress glanced at them both, then lifted a hand to her ear. "What's that? The order for table fourteen is ready? Okay, be right over." To Brittney and Guy, she said, "Sorry, guys. I gotta serve my other tables."

"And there she goes," Guy said, "with her tip, might I add."

Brittney rolled her eyes. "I'm sure she would've made a lot off a glass of tap water."

"There aren't even fourteen tables in this place." Guy scanned the room. "Tell me. What's wrong with these photos? Do you have any idea how hard I worked on these?"

She couldn't quite put her finger on it herself. "What makes them beautiful?"

"Beautiful? They're art. Art is beautiful."

"They're digitally enhanced images. But that doesn't make them art."

"They're not plain."

She had to try a different tactic. "What are you trying to say in these photos? What do you want your viewer to walk away with? What emotions do you want them to feel?"

Hey, that sounded good. Professional, and like she knew what she was doing. Like something her mom would say. She stood up straight, shoulders back.

Guy's shoulders sagged. "I wasn't thinking about that."

"Okay, then. No problem." Her tone had changed. More confident, self-assured, and soothing. "My mom said that I should look at these photos and see which ones are beautiful to me. What makes these photos beautiful to you?"

"They're beautiful because they're different. They're not normal. They take what is normal and change it. Show it from a different angle."

"But what does that mean?"

"I dunno. I just take the photo and edit them. The viewer interprets it however they like."

Brittney shook her head. "But you're the artist. You're in control. You're supposed to inspire them to an interpretation. Something meaningful. Something deep. These are too…"

"Too what?"

"On the surface." Much like how she had been during her modelling career. Just a pretty face with nothing underneath. No substance. No meaning. No oomph.

Guy scratched the back of his neck. "What does that mean?"

"They don't go deep enough." It was the best way she could describe it. She didn't quite understand it fully herself. That was why she left modelling in the first place. To find out what it meant to go deeper than what lay on the surface.

"What does beauty mean to you?" he asked.

"For a very long time, I thought it was looks." She still did think that. Even now she wondered if she was tired because this was the first meal she had all day, or if the stress was already beginning to show in her eyes and cheeks. She wouldn't admit it though; she didn't want to come off as shallow.

"Look at us. We have no idea what beauty means. We've the makings of a great exhibit here." He ran a hand through his hair. "We're missing something. Something we both can't see. I'm not willing to give up on these photos."

"Maybe it's me. Maybe I don't know what I'm talking about. Maybe they are beautiful. Maybe they are art, and I just don't know any better."

Guy shook his head. "I'm not about to give up on you, either. We're a team now."

Those words shocked her. She hadn't expected them. They left a warm feeling in her stomach. No one had ever relied on her before. No one had ever said that to her. No one had ever treated her like a member of a team. She had to own up to that and contribute as a member of the team. She wouldn't let this fail. "Then we have to figure out what makes them beautiful."

Guy leaned back in his seat, slapping the table. "Well, gallery director, call me Captain Stumps 'cause I have no clue."

Neither did she. She had no idea where to begin.

Her smartphone quacked. It was the first time all day today. It was sort of nice to not be a slave to her phone. Before, the phone had felt like an appendage to her body.

"What is with the duck ringer?" Guy asked.

"I had it since I was in high school." And that was as far as she'd go with that topic. In high school, she'd been the butt of many jokes. Her nickname had been Lanky Doodle because of her long arms, legs, and torso. In grade eleven, when puberty finally caught up with her, she'd been noticed by a modelling agency and transformed from an ugly duckling to a gorgeous swan.

She checked her phone. Emily sent an email to her personal account. Something about an invite to an exhibit for one of the other local galleries in the area. Her mother had been invited to it, but Emily was saying in her email that maybe Brittney could go instead. See what an exhibit was like. Get a taste for art that sold.

It was the perfect idea.

She smiled. "Well, Stumps. Maybe all we need is a sample."

#

For someone who wanted an exhibit for himself, Guy had rarely attended any. The last one he went to he dragged Josh with him and it'd been on sculptures. It hadn't been his thing and he couldn't relate to the artwork.

Electronic dance music, a plain drumbeat with a piano melody, played subtly in the background. The gallery was packed with people, most of them dressed up in suits and dresses. Some in jeans. No one in runners or winter boots. Servers carried plates of wine and cheese and bruschetta. All free, so Guy took as many bruschetta as he could fit in his fingers without spilling any tomatoes on the parquet floor.

"Are you sure we're allowed in here?" Guy said between bites. Either the food was delicious or his hunger was playing tricks on him. They were the youngest people here, and underdressed. Well, Guy was underdressed in his jeans and raggedy boots.

"It's open to everyone," Brittney said. "My mother was invited, and I'm here representing my mother, which means we were invited."

"You mean *you* were invited."

"You're my plus one."

Guy grinned. He liked the sound of that. Not only because it made them more of a team, but because anyone would be happy standing beside a girl as pretty as Brittney. He stood close to her without touching. He didn't want to invade her space. They didn't know each other that well.

But he wanted to get to know her and not just because they'd be working together. She was different than the girl he had met that first day at the gallery. Then she had seemed rash and out of control, but now she was thoughtful and confident. And she smelled good, too. He caught himself leaning to breathe her in, but pulled himself back.

"What do you think?" she asked him.

He thought he'd like her as close to him as possible so he could take her all in. He shook his head. *She means the gallery, Guy.*

He marvelled at the lights in the place, the lights illuminating the photos in the best way possible. The chatter rose to a crescendo in the back room.

"That must be the artist," Brittney said.

Guy followed the direction of her stare and grimaced. The man in question held court with a group of well-dressed patrons. He seemed to be pontificating, his hands moving in lavish gestures. His hair was long and braided, and he wore a puffy shirt like a pirate and a purple tuxedo. His shoes were black and shiny, like something Michael Jackson would've worn.

"I don't have to dress like that at my exhibit, do I?" Guy asked. What was so bad about jeans and a plain black T-shirt? One couldn't argue with timeless fashion.

Brittney gave him a flat look. "I would prefer you didn't."

"He is absolutely frightening." Like something out of Guy's

nightmares. A villain in a superhero comic who had a predilection for art. Artists that dressed up as if *they* were the art were fake to him. Imposters. Posers. Let the artwork shine, not the moonwalking shoes.

"He's an artist."

"His name is probably Art."

"No," Brittney said, grabbing a pamphlet off a side table and reading the front. "His name is…Micah."

Guy snorted. "Bet his real name is Bob."

"So what do you think?" Brittney said, drawing Guy's attention to the artwork on display and for sale. "Seems like our friend Micah here does photography, too." Brittney pointed to a photo of a young, country girl, shaded under the overhanging roof of an old, rusted shed, a tractor next to it.

Guy grimaced. "It's fashion photography. Portrait photography."

"What's wrong with fashion photography?"

"It's fake." Like this girl was a country girl. She barely had a tan on her, and her face was covered in makeup. Not quite the girl living out in the country helping her father's farm by milking the cows. "There's nothing genuine about it."

Brittney raised an eyebrow. "And your digitally enhanced photos are truer than true."

"Take this photo, for example," Guy said, pointing to a different one. This one was plainer, a photo of a dark-haired girl with her lips curved up. "She's smiling but it's fake. She's not really happy. She's just a model, and the photographer told her to smile for the camera. But it's not real."

"How do you know that?"

"Because that's what people do when they're in front of a camera," Guy said. "They pose. And posing for a picture isn't real." He stood next to the photo and pantomimed a model. "Oh, look at me. I'm so beautiful. I'm so happy. Life is so great for me because I'm airbrushed." He pointed to a photo on the opposite wall. "Or how about this one?" He put on his best grouchy face and switched his tone to something deep and throaty. "I'm angry. Look how angry I am. I hate eating. Eating makes my waist go—" He stuck his tongue out and made a farting noise, giving the photo a thumbs down. "It's completely fake."

Brittney examined the price label where a big red SOLD was stamped. "This photo sold for seven hundred dollars."

"Are you shitting me?" Yup, that was a seven with two zeroes behind it. He could understand seven dollars, but seven hundred dollars? No way. "Who would buy this?"

"Apparently, someone. And they paid handsomely for it. For something you think is fake."

Her tone had an edge to it that Guy couldn't quite place. She probably couldn't believe someone had paid that much either. Were these people clinically insane?

"It's definitely not beautiful," Guy said.

She pointed to a photo of a girl in a white robe, lying in a provocative posture. "You don't think this model is beautiful?"

"Even her beauty is fake. That's what models are, fake."

Brittney crossed her arms over her chest and leaned back on one foot. "Oh, really?"

"It's all makeup and fancy clothes." Guy waved a hand, dismissing it. Once, he'd even liked taking photos of people. Like Josh and Vanessa. But his parents had made sure he'd hate it. "It's not real art."

"And you've got real art?"

The edge in her voice grew shaper. Not directed at him, surely.

"I'm an artist," Guy said, pointing to himself, raising his chin. "Bob over here is fake. I mean, look at the way he's dressed."

"Look at the way *you're* dressed." Brittney made a circular gesture, encapsulating all of him. "You're wearing ripped jeans in winter. And your shirt has a stain on it."

Now there was no denying who that sharp tone was meant for. Had Guy been pushing Brittney's buttons this whole time? Idiot.

"No, it doesn't." Guy had specifically chosen a clean, unblemished shirt today. He glanced down and there was a mysterious yellow stain on it. How the hell did that get there?

Brittney dug her finger right below the stain. "Right there. Stain. And your jacket looks like it came from the nineties."

"At least I'm genuine." Guy didn't care about his appearance. It didn't say anything about the type of person he was inside. If that meant he was a sloppy dresser, then so be it. But he wouldn't be a slave to his appearance. Not like his mother or his father.

"Art isn't genuine," Brittney said. "It's supposed to be larger than life. Not an imitation."

"What do you know about art?" Guy said, and now his own tone had an edge to it.

"I've seen your art, and I can tell you right now you'll never be a fine art photographer."

Those words punched him right in the heart. She'd even said them loud enough that some people in the gallery were staring at them. Guy glanced over at the photos of models in different backgrounds, posing to show different emotions that he knew deep down they didn't feel.

Joy? Fake. Sadness? Fake.

What about love? Real?

Why not ask his parents and all the pictures he took of them together, before the divorce?

Fake.

"There's no way I'm going to be fake. Look at these models. *Look* at them. You know what they all have in common? They all lack substance. They're just hair and makeup and skin-tight clothes. They're airbrushed to hell. Products of Photoshop. No one looks this good. It sets up an image that isn't real, a standard that no one could possibly live up to. And those smiles or frowns? They're not actually mad. Or happy. Or sad. Or anything. They don't know what those emotions are like. They can only pretend. There's nothing deep about a model."

Before, only a few of people stared at them. Now everyone gave them their full attention. The chatter had quieted down. Even Micah-Bob had ceased pontificating on art theory or whatever bullshit spewed from his mouth.

"You really think so?" she said softly, not quite a whisper, but not a yell either.

"I know so." Guy let his voice go loud. He didn't care what everyone else thought. Let them hear this before they go off and spend another seven hundred dollars on a piece of fake photography. "Models are all alike. They're con-artists for clothing and makeup brands. You think this model is beautiful? You think fashion photography is beautiful? You're wrong. It's trash. We need less of this fake shit in the world, not charging seven hundred freaking dollars for a girl who poses for five seconds and gets God knows how much money for it."

His breath came out hard and heavy, chest rising and falling. He'd said his piece. There was nothing more to say. He only wished his parents had been here to hear him.

Brittney stared down at her shoes, arms crossed. "Do you really believe that?"

"Yeah, I do," Guy said. "Models make me sick." He noticed that she was hugging herself. In fact, it was like he noticed her for the first time. He'd been lost in his tirade. Why was she getting so upset? He hadn't meant any of those things about her. He put a hand on her shoulder. "Hey, you okay?"

After a moment, she lifted her gaze up to his. Tears glistened in her eyes. "I used to be a model, you fucking asshole."

Oh, shit.

Brittney twisted around and stormed out of the gallery, people jumping out of the way to give her room.

Guy watched her leave, her blond hair trailing behind her, the heels on her boots echoing with each stomp.

"She's right," he said to himself, "I am a fucking asshole."

Chapter Six

Avoid photographers like tacky leopard pants. That had been Brittney's rule since embarking on this new life. The rule was supposed to protect her from getting hurt again.

And Guy had seemed like one of the good ones, too. Slobby dresser, but he'd been saying all those nice things about them working together and being a team. So much for teamwork.

No more photographers. She was done with them. There had to be another local artist somewhere. Didn't anyone paint these days?

The first thing she was going to do was tell Emily that from now on the Collar Gallery was a photographer-free zone.

When she got to the gallery she heard something she'd only ever heard in the movies: a harmonica. It brought images of the countryside to her mind. The sound came from the back.

It was Emily. She was playing the harmonica.

When the melody stopped, Brittney said, "What are you doing?"

Emily gasped, placing her hand on her chest. "Oh, my God." She took a breath. "You scared me half to death." Then she frowned at Brittney. "Are you crying?"

Brittney sniveled, opening her purse and digging for a tissue. "You first."

"I know how to play the harmonica." Emily shrugged. "And I always play it when it's quiet."

"Is it a therapy thing?" Brittney found some tissue, brought it to her nose, and blew.

"It helps with my anxiety. It sounds nice. Calming. So one day I learned how to play." She tucked the harmonica in a box and stuffed the box in her jean back pocket. "Now you. Why are you crying?"

Brittney opened her makeup mirror and dabbed at the mascara running down her cheeks. "I look like a member of Kiss."

"No, you don't. You look fine. Did you go to the exhibit?"

"Yes."

"And?"

"We didn't stay long."

"*We?* You took Guy? So, where is he?"

"Don't know, don't care."

While she cleaned herself up in the washroom, she told Emily everything that happened at the exhibit.

"He really said those things?" Emily sucked in air through her teeth. She leaned against the doorframe.

"Mm-hmm." Brittney flushed the black-marred tissue down the toilet and washed her hands and face. Then she took a fresh towel and dried herself off.

"But not about you. He wasn't talking about you."

"We aren't all like that, you know? Not all models are just dumb blondes who look good in a crop top."

"Why did you quit?"

"Because," Brittney said, "I wanted people to stop thinking I was just a dumb blonde who looks good in a crop top." She sighed and tears threatened an encore. "And I do look fantastic in a crop top."

"No kidding," Emily said. "I could iron a shirt off your flat stomach."

Brittney laughed. She didn't expect the joke, and her laugh forced snot down her nose. She sniffed, grabbed another tissue, and wiped her nose.

"So what now?" Emily said. "What happens with Guy?"

"Nothing. He sucks."

Emily tilted her head to the side. "He's not all that bad. He's cute at least."

Yes, he was. His eyes, even his nose. As messy and uncoordinated as he was, there was a cute factor under all that. "Terrible photographer."

"Is he really?"

No, Brittney couldn't back that up. Not with any real evidence at least. He did know how to take a good photo. He knew how to edit. He just had no clue what art was, what was beautiful. His portfolio was all over the place. No structure, no message, no oomph. "How can I work with someone like him?" She walked out of the washroom and back into the gallery's main open space. "He's not willing to listen. He doesn't care about…about anything."

"So he's stubborn. What artist isn't?"

Why was she defending him? Had she seen something that Brittney hadn't? No, it was that Brittney refused to admit that Guy had potential. "He has no message. No theme. His pictures are just pictures."

"Then *help* him. There's got to be something." Emily waved her hands around the gallery. "Or else we're gonna have to start saving money by eating popcorn and water."

Brittney shook her head. "Crackers. You need a microwave for popcorn. Gotta watch the hydro bill."

Emily grabbed her by the shoulders. "Come on. Guy's a little rough around the edges, but he's a good person."

"How do you know? You met him today." She talked like she'd known him for years, like they were the best of friends. Practically family. "For like ten minutes. You didn't even speak to him."

Emily let her go. "He spoke to me. Most people get weirded out by my social anxiety. But he didn't. He just accepted it."

That was true. Brittney had been there and witnessed it herself. But still—

"We don't see eye to eye. We can't even figure out what we think is beautiful, let alone agree on it."

"Then find out what it means with him. Together."

"I'll find another artist."

"Who?"

Brittney shrugged. "Someone else will waltz in here asking for an exhibit."

"Not anybody new," Emily said. "Collar Gallery is known, and your mom has a list of artists that she works with. She hasn't gotten a new artist in all the time I've worked with her. This is your chance to do something new and build the business with a fresh angle."

It was what Brittney wanted. This was business. This was using her head and making connections. What she did like about Guy was he hadn't bent over backward because she was pretty. He'd even fought with her.

And what had Brittney done? She'd walked away from him. She hadn't fought back like she was supposed to. Like her mother would have with one of her stubborn artists. Brittney hadn't even given Guy a chance before writing him off. She saw him as a photographer and wanted him gone as quickly as possible.

"I hate that you're right," she said.

"Swallow your pride."

Brittney made a face. "I don't have pride. He does."

"You both do. You both are trying to make something of yourselves from scratch and think you know where you're going but don't even have a clue. Go to him."

There was still one problem left. "I don't even know where he lives."

Emily winked. "I do."

#

Guy slammed the door shut to his apartment. He'd slammed it so hard that Harvey the Goat came off its hook and crashed to the floor, shattering into pieces.

"Shit!" Guy kicked his boots off, ripped his jacket off his shoulders, and flung it onto the futon bed. Could this night get any worse? Could he get any more pissed off? Pissed off at the shitty weather that decided it was going to snow right when he left the exhibit. Pissed off at himself for the things he had said to Brittney. And pissed off that a guy like Micah-Bob, Mr. Purple Wonder Tux, could score himself an exhibit whereas Guy had lost his one chance.

Unexpectedly, Josh, still dressed in his clothes from work, poked his head in from his old room.

"What are you doing here?" Guy said as he bent down to pick up the broken pieces of poor Harvey. He hadn't deserved to be the one to take the full force of Guy's ire.

"Good to see you, too. Not so good to see what you did to Harvey." He pointed a thumb to his room. "I came by to grab a few things. And to see how you're doing. You get my messages?"

"Yeah," Guy said, picking up the pieces of Harvey and putting them on the kitchen counter. The messages were warnings about Donaldson, but they were too late to help him.

"I couldn't do anything about it," Josh said.

"You knew?"

"When you didn't show up, Donaldson came right to my cubicle." He ran a hand through his hair. "He wasn't happy. I'm sorry. I tried to convince him otherwise, but he had that video."

"Incriminating evidence. Guilty beyond a reasonable doubt."

Josh shrugged. "You kinda shoulda saw this coming."

Guy rubbed his eyes. "I know."

"Like I warned—"

"I *know*," Guy said. "I'm an idiot, okay?" He sighed. "Today will go down in history as the worst day of my life. I might have to take a job at Taco House."

Josh put his fists to his hip. "What'd you do now?"

Guy told him what happened at the exhibit. How he got Brittney to agree to work with him and then screwed it up by making fun of models.

"You're a colossal moron," Josh said.

"Thanks."

"You had the chance you've been waiting for and you blew it. All in one day."

"Who's a colossal moron?" Guy pointed to himself. "This guy."

"No. You know what your problem is? You don't care. You're stubborn about not caring." He looked Guy up and down. "Is that how you went? I'm surprised she even gave you a chance. You look like you should work at Taco House."

Again with what he was wearing. He was a struggling artist. This was all he could afford. Besides— "Appearances don't matter."

"But they do. You think I like wearing a tie and suit every day? It's uncomfortable, and I can't find a blazer that fits me snug around the shoulders. But you know what? I gotta wear it."

"Because you're a slave to the Man."

"No, idiot. Because how I present myself sends a message."

"Again with this whole message shit. That's *exactly* what Brittney said, too. Kept harping on *the message*." His voice increased a pitch, impersonating Brittney. "What are you trying to say to the viewer? What's the message? Message this and message that." He stuck his tongue out like he was about to be sick. "I'm not a call service. I'm an artist."

"You're not. You're a bum."

Guy glared at him. "Hey, fuck you, too."

"She's right, and you know it." Josh pointed to the collage of photos on the wall. "These photos are a mess. Just like your life." From the floor, Josh picked up the shoebox containing Guy's old photos of Josh and Vanessa and other couples, including his parents. "But you had something real with this."

"Don't." Guy shook his head, pointing a finger at Josh. He should've hid that box after fishing it out under the futon. "Don't you dare."

"You can't beat yourself up forever." Holding the shoebox like it was the Holy Grail, Josh offered it to Guy. "You're great at this photography."

"I don't even know what that photography is."

"It's love."

Something inside of Guy snapped, and he jumped off the bed, grabbed the shoebox from Josh's hands, and tossed it. It bounced off the doorframe and spun around, the photos spilling out and sprawling across the floor. "Love? Give me a break. It's not real. Ask my *lovely* mother."

"She loves you."

Guy barked a laugh. "I haven't talked to her in almost two years. She's probably sun tanning on some exotic island on my dad's money."

"People fall in love. Not everyone ends up like your parents did. What about me and Vanessa?"

"She likes you for your money, too," Guy said, but knew it wasn't true.

Josh picked up the photo of him and her, the one Guy had taken when the three of them were in university. "She doesn't. And you know that, too. That's why you took this picture of me and her."

There was a knock at the door.

"Who the hell?" Guy said. He just wanted this night to end. To get some sleep. And sleep in till well in the afternoon. Those were the perks of the unemployed and the nearly destitute.

He stomped over to the door, turned the handle, and swung it open.

He blinked.

"Brittney?"

#

She couldn't believe she was here. Her heart did jumping jacks, and she clasped her hands in front of her. She kept herself reserved, polite. They had yelled at each other this very evening in the middle of an exhibit. Now she was here, ready to make amends, terrified she was going to make a fool out of herself.

Guy's eyes widened, his mouth hanging open. He wasn't expecting her. Not now. Probably not ever.

"Hi," Brittney said, her voice low and intimate.

Guy's mouth hung slightly open. "What are you doing here?" It wasn't mean, just curious.

"This her?" another man said. He came over to her with his hand out. "I'm Josh. Guy's best friend. Nice to meet you." They shook hands. Dressed in a suit and tie, he was the opposite of Guy, crisp and cleaned up. Even his movements were different. Where Guy's were sometimes floundering, like a kid searching for his favourite toy, Josh's were precise. "I was just leaving." He held a stuffed bag. "Seems like you two have a lot to talk about. Come in, come in."

Had they been talking about her? Of course. Just like she had with Emily. She stepped inside, letting Josh slip past her and out the door.

"I'm not through with you," Guy said to Josh, scowling.

"Later gator." He made kissing noises to Guy, and Guy slammed the door closed on his face. They could still hear him from the other side.

Then silence.

Insufferable silence. Brittney scanned the apartment. She didn't know what to expect. Now she realized there was no other place she could've imagined but this apartment. It matched him: messy, cluttered, with an attitude of I-don't-care. "So this is where you live?"

"Temporarily." He had said it in such a way as though unsure how temporary it would be.

"It's nice."

"Hardly," Guy said. He led her into the den where a futon bed was laid out. "Why are you here?"

Brittney pointed to the door with her thumb. "Do you want me to go?"

Guy raised an eyebrow. "Do *you* want to go?"

She did, but she wouldn't. Now that she'd gone the distance and the hard part was over, she had to see it through. "I came to apologize. For calling you a fucking asshole."

"Yeah, well. I wouldn't exactly say that my behaviour was…" He bit his lip, considering. Then, "Whatever you call the opposite of an asshole."

"Kind? Cordial?" Brittney shook her head. "No, it wasn't."

Guy sighed. "I should be the one to apologize. I didn't mean those things. Would you like some water?"

"Yes, you did. And yes, I would."

"Okay, I did." He took two glasses from the kitchen cupboard. The glasses didn't match, in size or colour. He filled them up with water from the sink. "But I didn't mean them about you." He passed her the water and sipped his own. "If I'd known you were a model, I never would've said anything like that." He slapped his forehead. "I should've realized it."

"Why?"

"Because you're so beautiful."

Brittney gazed at the water in her cup. People didn't usually call her beautiful. Pretty, yes. Hot, plenty of times. Even hawt. But never beautiful. It sounded better than pretty or hot. Like there was more to it than the physical. Like grace. Or maybe she was reading into it.

This whole time they'd been trying to figure out what beautiful meant, and this whole time Guy had meant Brittney.

"Not all beautiful girls are models," she said.

"Especially ones who own a gallery business."

Brittney shook her head. "I don't own it. It's my mom's." She focused on the collage of pictures on the wall. "So this is your work?"

"Itching to start a new fight?" Guy said, eyebrow raised.

"Not a single person in any of these photos. You really don't like taking pictures of people."

"Portraits, fashion." He waved a hand, blew air between his cheeks.

"Why?"

"Like I said. It's all fake." He sighed, coming to stand beside her. "Blame my parents. I used to take photos of them all the time. I'd say, 'Hey guys smile for the camera.' And they would. Biggest smiles you ever saw, for just a snap of a photo. And then they'd go back to whatever it was they were doing."

"Which was?"

"Hating each other."

"I see," Brittney said. "Are they divorced?"

Guy nodded. "Dad's a big shot doctor paying lumps of alimony every month. She married him for his money."

"You don't know that for sure." She couldn't imagine herself marrying someone for money. She would end up feeling too lonely, too empty.

"She never loved him. Gotta blame dad for that one. His fault for marrying a trophy wife."

A trophy wife. Wasn't that how Derrick had treated her? A pretty, shiny, desirable trophy. She shuddered.

"Don't know why you quit modelling. You could've snagged yourself a rich husband."

"That's why I stopped. I wanted to make it on my own." She'd nearly finished her application to business school. Transcripts ordered and first draft of personal statement done.

"Why'd you become a model?" he asked.

"For my father." She shocked herself. She'd never told anyone that. Whenever someone asked her, she always said the same thing: someone saw her, saw she was pretty, wanted her to market the clothes. Rinse, lather, repeat. But while that was how her career began, it wasn't why she started it. "He was obsessed with fame. Left my mother to go become an actor. "

He'd wanted to be a Sean Penn or a Russell Crowe, but she didn't want to let on like it mattered. It'd been more than a decade since her father left and never came back. She refused to show that it still hurt. She didn't want it to matter on the outside as much as it did on the inside.

"What's that got to do with you?"

"I thought that if I became a famous model, he'd come back." She tucked a strand of hair behind her ear. "It was stupid."

"Did he?" Guy asked. "Come back?"

"No." Brittney smiled despite herself. "And I think my mother would kill him if he did."

"Did he become famous?"

Brittney shook her head. The last time she heard from him was when he said goodbye. After that, nothing. Not even birthdays or Christmases.

Guy sat down on the futon. "Look at us. Broken families. Messed up mentalities." He rubbed his eye. "What's the next move, Director?"

She sat down next to him. "I don't know, Stumps. I really don't."

They were at a stand-still. Caught in limbo.

She looked once more at the photos on the wall. She couldn't use them. At least not all of them. They were far too random and, if she was being honest with herself, boring. None of them spoke to her. None of them were beautiful.

She scanned the room. Maybe he had others stashed away somewhere. Her eye caught a pile of photos on the floor with a shoebox turned upside down.

She got up from the bed, went over to the photos.

"Whoa, whoa, whoa," Guy said.

She picked the photos up. Pictures of people. Of couples, specifically. "Did you take these?"

"Put those down." Guy stood up, his finger pointing at her. "I'm serious."

"You did take these." She showed him one of the photos. "This is that guy I just met. Josh. Your best friend."

"*Ex*-best friend," Guy said, glowering.

She pointed at the girl in the photo. "This his girlfriend?"

"Now fiancé."

"They look so…" She knew the word but didn't want to say it. It sounded stupid in her head, but she had no other way to explain it. "So in love. These are really good, Guy. I mean it."

"Don't get any ideas."

"There's a message here." These photos meant something. You could see the relationship between Josh and his fiancé, and they weren't even posing. It was completely candid. Not faked at all. She connected with the photo, connected with the couple. She felt happy for them even if she didn't know either of them. Maybe it was because it was something she wanted for herself. Maybe it was because she wanted to know more about them, how they met, what sorts of things they did or said to each other. "We should use these for the exhibit."

"No, we don't need these. I've got plenty others." He gestured toward the other photos on his wall.

"You've got something here," Brittney said, flipping through the photos. Every single one of them a picture of two people in love. Different candid photos of different types of couples from all ages and backgrounds. They all had the same look as the photos of Josh and his fiancé, that sincere glimpse of the couple's love.

"I should've thrown those out."

"But you didn't," Brittney said. "Because you know. Deep down you know. You know these photos are good. They're beautiful." She came up to him, the group of photos in her hand. "This is your message."

"What is?"

"Love." But it was more than that. She couldn't quite put her finger on it, though. Something about how truthful the photos were. The image, the message, was the same, even if the couple was different.

"It's not love," Guy said. "These are fake."

"Not this one," Brittney said, showing him Josh and his fiancé. "Or this one. Who's this?"

"Some people I went to undergrad with."

"There's almost like a spark between them. Like a love spark. And you've captured it."

Guy gave her a flat look. "Don't make this into something bigger than it actually is. Besides"—he snatched the photo from her—"they broke up."

She grabbed it back. "But in this moment, they were in love."

"I'm not doing it. It'll never work."

"It will." She had an idea for the exhibit. A message. A theme. Something that would draw the attention of viewers and maybe even compel them to buy something.

People would be able to see an honest, true love through Guy's work, and through seeing it, they would believe in it.

"Who would pay to see a couple?"

"They aren't paying for the couple. They're paying to see love."

"It's nonsense."

"Well, it's my gallery," Brittney said. If she couldn't get Guy to agree with her outright, she could always pull the director card. "So if you want an exhibit, you're gonna have to do this. We'll need more photos, but it'll work. Trust me, what do we have to lose?"

Another flat look. "Everything."

Chapter Seven

The two models laughed while Guy snapped a few photos. A man and a woman, both pretending they were a couple.

"Well?" Brittney asked. Again, she'd dressed professionally today, borrowing clothing from her mother. Grey pants with black pumps and a light blue blouse. Her blond hair was tied in a braid, and she wore foundation and eyeliner. A far cry from how she used to dress up with all her glitter and glitz. Guy had dressed differently today, too. Surprisingly so. To start off, a shirt with no holes in it or stains on it and a pair of—did her eyes deceive her?—brand name jeans. He probably had borrowed them from his friend, Josh. He'd even trimmed his beard a little and pulled his hair back behind his ears with product.

"Uh-uh," Guy said, checking the display in his camera.

They'd been trying all day to take a half-decent photo. The models had been friends of Brittney's that she had called in for a favour. If they were going to do this love photography thing—and they didn't have a proper name for it yet—they would need live people to act it out.

And a stage. Brittney, with the help of Emily and Guy, had set up umbrella lighting, a table, coffee mugs and a blue backdrop. Like a date at a coffee shop. That could be one of the background themes, a series of dating locations: coffee shop, fancy dinner, drive-in movie, whatever.

"Let's try something else," Brittney said. She got up from her chair and picked up a blue leather-bound book from the stack of props she had. She gave the book to the woman model, Tina. "How about you have this book open in front of you and you"—she pointed to the male model, Dan—"gaze at her lovingly."

Tina took the book and opened it up in front of her, just below her chin. Dan, on the other side of the table, leaned in closer to her, but his face was turned to the camera, so he gave her more of a sideways glance.

"This isn't going to work," Guy said to Brittney as she came to stand next to him.

"It'll work." Brittney crossed her arms. "Take the picture."

Guy lifted his camera and took a few shots. He got down low, got down to the side. He wasn't talking to the models like how photographers usually did. Brittney did most of the talking and directing. Guy had no idea how to speak to models since he hadn't done much portrait photography.

Once finished, Guy scrolled through the photos.

"How about now?" Brittney asked.

Guy grimaced, shaking his head.

"Didn't we agree," Brittney said, hands on her hips, "that you'd give this a shot?"

"We did," Guy said. "Not a written contract, though."

"Whatever. A verbal contract."

"A begrudgingly verbal contract."

"A contract's a contract. Right, Emily?"

Emily, standing in the corner of the gallery, nodded.

Guy rubbed his forehead. "I find it ironic that the girl who can't talk is agreeing to the validity of a verbal contract."

"Deal with it," Brittney said, and Emily shrugged her shoulders.

"You really think these are good?" Guy said, gesturing to the photos on the screen.

Brittney took a peek and moaned. These stunk. Guy wasn't kidding. It looked really, *really* fake. Almost embarrassing. The models didn't resemble a couple at all. They were trying to get all the camera's attention for themselves. That wasn't the point of this. They weren't even supposed to be *looking* at the camera, but at each other. Looking at each other with freaking love. These photos weren't at all like the ones Guy had done before. Not by a long shot.

Emily came up and glanced at them, too.

"What do you think?" Brittney asked her.

Emily mimicked Guy, pinching her nose.

Brittney sighed. "Let's take a break."

The models stood up and came toward her, their mixed perfume and cologne combination creating a miasma of smells. "We still get paid, right?"

Brittney blinked. "You guys were doing this as a favour for me."

Tina shook her head. "Uh, no. I thought we were getting paid." Her tone was high pitched and annoying. Brittney'd never sounded like that as a model, had she?

"What were you expecting?" She could give them maybe fifty bucks each.

"The usual rate for our time," Dan said.

Brittney raised her eyebrows. Were they kidding? That was a few hundred bucks. "I don't have that kind of money."

Tina tsked. "Don't even, Brit."

"I'll pay you in food, okay?" So much for a favour between friends. "I'll get Emily to order us some lunch."

"The deaf girl?" Dan asked.

"No, she's mute," Tina said.

"She's neither." Brittney's hand twitched; she nearly slapped them both. "She's just shy." She called Emily over. "Can you order some lunch?"

"Sure," Emily said, low enough that only Brittney could hear. "Thanks."

Brittney walked toward the office.

"Nice friends you got," Guy muttered as she passed by him.

"They're very good at what they do."

"Are they, though?"

He had a point. The pictures sucked. At least the clothes suited them well. Obviously, that was all they did: wear clothes. But when it came to taking photos to showcase love? Uh-uh. "Not with this."

"Did you used to be like that when you were a model?"

Brittney crossed her arms over her chest. Here came one of Guy's insults about models. "Like what?"

"Eye-rolling and hair flinging and misusing words, like literally." He mimicked their movements, his lips pursed like a duck's beak. "Every time they talk, the English language loses a letter."

Brittney smiled. "You're insensitive."

"Hey, you're talking to the guy who photographs love." He pointed at himself. "I invented sensitivity."

She almost rolled her eyes at him but resisted, since apparently only models rolled their eyes. "You're enjoying that this is failing."

"A little, yes."

So not only did she have two models who couldn't act, but she also had a photographer who didn't believe in it. "By the way, thanks for trimming your beard. Real professional."

"At least I showered."

She gasped. "It's almost like you care about how you look," she said, sarcastically. She left him and went into her office, closed the door, and called her mother at the hospital, explaining everything.

"Where am I going wrong?"

Helene laughed, a little too loudly. But it was a nice sound to hear, even if it was at Brittney's expense. "You can't expect models to act like they know how to show love."

"They're professionals. They do poses all the time."

"But they don't know how to show love to each other. Even in photos as a couple, their eyes are usually at the camera."

"Obviously. Face the camera. Say cheese. That kind of thing."

"Lovers look at each other. They get lost in each other's eyes. That's real love."

Helene had a point. The other photos that Guy had were in her office and laid out on the tabletop. Each photo had the lovers' eyes locked. They were candid. Not one of them had any of the people looking directly at the camera. It was like lovers living in their natural habitat.

"I'll try it," she said.

"Good luck, honey. I know you'll find a way."

Her nerves settled a bit. At least *someone* believed in her. "How are you feeling?"

"Better."

"Better as in you'll be here to take over by next week?" She crossed her fingers, clenched her jaw.

"Better as in I'll be stuck in bed, and the gallery is yours to run."

Brittney moaned.

"You wanted this," Helene reminded her.

"I know." Brittney said her goodbyes and ended the call. She took another breath and went back into the gallery. "Okay, let's try something different—"

She stopped. Two people, a man and a woman, talked to Guy. The woman wore an engagement ring on her finger.

"Hello again," the man said. Brittney knew him, but had never met the woman.

"Brittney," Guy said, "you remember, Josh. Ex-best friend."

"*Ex*-ex best friend," Josh said, with an airy tone. He was dressed in a plain white button-down Oxford shirt and a pair of dark blue jeans and white Converse shoes. "I'm best friend status now."

"How'd you swing that?" Brittney said, playing along.

"I asked him to be the best man at my wedding."

"Congratulations." And, surprisingly, she meant it. Even though she didn't know Josh or his lovely fiancé. "You must be the fiancé. Or I've just made an ass of myself and you're actually his sister."

She laughed. "No, no. I'm his fiancé." She showed her ring: big diamond. Unlike Guy, Josh seemed to have a bit of money—and taste. "Do we look alike?"

"All the best couples do."

The girl smiled; she clearly liked that. "I'm Vanessa."

"I'm Brittney. Nice to meet you."

Emily walked by, and Vanessa caught her breath. "Emily?"

Emily perked up, like a deer who heard a branch snap. "Vanessa? What are you doing here?"

"So you work at *this* gallery," Vanessa said. Guy raised an eyebrow at Brittney, and she shrugged.

"This is it," Emily said. She had a smile on her face and words came easily when she talked to Vanessa.

"How do you guys know each other?" Brittney asked.

"Family friends," Vanessa said.

Emily nodded. "My mother is planning their wedding."

"Your mother's a wedding planner?" Brittney asked.

"Yep."

"Huh," Brittney said. Who knew? Maybe she could use that information and get a couple of newlyweds in here instead of models. Newlyweds would for sure show love, right?

"I'm so glad we came in today," Vanessa said. "I can't believe you work here. Small world."

"Tiny," Guy said. He nudged Brittney. "You didn't know about this?"

Brittney shook her head. "Uh-uh." But she counted it as something good.

"What are you guys doing here?" Emily asked. She even seemed comfortable around Josh. Not her usual social anxious self.

"Guy invited us to watch," Vanessa said. "I hope you don't mind."

"Not at all," Brittney said. "It's a gallery. Open to the public." She gestured to the artwork on the walls. "Feel free to buy something while you're at it." She winked.

Vanessa held Josh's hand and leaned in closer to him. "We're house buying so we'll need some art to decorate it."

"Then you've come to the right place."

"Do I get a share of the profit if they buy something?" Guy asked.

Brittney cocked an eyebrow at him. "No."

"But it's commission."

"You don't work here. And it's my gallery."

"You're fond of saying that." He turned to Josh and Vanessa, pointing a thumb at Brittney. "She's fond of saying that."

Josh laughed. "You guys act like an old married couple."

Brittney's heart skipped a beat. "Shall we?" she said to Guy, indicating the models on their smartphones. If they didn't act fast, they'd lose them to the Wide World of Instagram.

"You have an idea?" Guy asked.

"That I do." Hopefully a workable one, too.

"Then we shall."

Brittney clapped to get the models' attention. "Okay, guys."

"Is the pizza here?" Dan asked.

"You're models." Brittney narrowed her eyes. "You don't eat pizza."

Tina shrugged. "It's our cheat day. And we asked for it with whole wheat crust."

"Well, I'm sure it's coming?" Brittney glanced at at Emily for confirmation, who nodded but noncommittedly. Meaning, she was on it now. Back to the models. "This time, for the next few photos, I want you guys to look at each other lovingly."

"Not at the camera?"

"No. At each other. Pretend we're not even here. It's just the two of you, and you're showing how much you love each other through your eyes. Cool?"

Dan shrugged. "Sure."

"Good."

Brittney stepped back. The models turned to each other. Some hint of smiles. Not bad from where Brittney stood. More connected. Guy snapped a few photos.

"And?" Brittney asked.

"It's worse."

"What?" She checked the display herself. Oh, God. It was worse. They just looked angry at each other. Or annoyed. They had a you-versus-me vibe, like how divorce couples must look at each other. Like the glare her mother would surely give to her father if he ever came back. The complete opposite of love. "What are we missing?"

"I'll get you some water," Emily said.

"Thanks." She sat down on a chair by the edge of the gallery, put her elbows to her knees, and blew air between her cheeks. Josh and Vanessa browsed through the paintings hung on the wall. They stopped at one. Josh made a joke, and Vanessa laughed, tossing her brunette curls back. Then they looked at each other and he put his arm around her waist and pulled her in. Their smiles grew larger. They were almost touching foreheads. They got lost in each other's eyes. Not lost, that wasn't the right word for it. It was like they'd found each other for the first time. Like it was love at first sight. The rest of them—Brittney, Guy, Emily, and the two numb nuts—might as well not exist. It was just the two of them. Josh and Vanessa. Vanessa and Josh.

It was freaking beautiful and left Brittney wanting the same thing for herself.

She snapped into gallery director mode. "Guy—"

But Guy was already on it. He had his camera up and snapped a photo.

"You saw it, right?" Brittney said, coming toward him. "Let's see." She studied the picture. "That's it! We got it!" She could hug Guy. Hug him and squeeze him for this incredible skill he had. More pictures like this, and they'd be set.

But Guy's face clouded over.

"What's wrong?"

He clenched his jaw and his eyes hardened. "I can't do this."

#

Brittney watched, mouth hanging open, as Guy grabbed his jacket, shrugged into it, and stormed out of the gallery like he'd done something illegal and the police were onto him.

Maybe not the police. But something had spooked him. He had seen the spark between Josh and Vanessa. Had seen it and taken the picture before Brittney needed to tell him to. He had done it of his own free will. As if that spark had compelled him.

That was the kind of photography he should be taking. It so obviously spoke to him on an instinctual level.

So then why was he running away?

"Wait!" Brittney called after him. "Guy, hold on."

Josh and Vanessa looked over, concern on their faces. Emily bit her lip. Only the models were indifferent, taking the opportunity to slip their phones out of their pockets. The building could fall apart over top of them, and they wouldn't even notice.

Brittney followed Guy. The bell at the front door sounded, meaning Guy had left the gallery. She ran after him and pulled the door open. She went to take a step forward, then caught her breath and backpedalled. She nearly crashed right into a guy dressed in a down jacket and holding a pizza box.

"Sorry," Brittney said. "Excuse me."

"Someone ordered a pizza?" the delivery boy said. Tattoos covered his neck and hands. He was probably around Emily's age. Nineteen or twenty.

"Yes, we did," Brittney said. She tried to step around him, but his down jacket was so bulky he blocked the doorway. The smell of pepperoni and cheese wafted up from the box. "But if you'll excuse me."

"I'll need to get paid."

"Emily!" Brittney said. "Pizza guy's here."

Emily showed up and stopped. Her body tensed, and her eyes went wide. Not only was she nervous around men, but when there was a guy with tattoos who was basically the perfect match for her, it was probably like how a deer felt when it saw a lion.

"She'll take care of you," Brittney said, smiling, inviting the delivery boy in and jumping outside.

Snow fell and cold air blew across her. She cursed, shivered, and rubbed her arms. She should've brought her jacket, but it was in the office, and she didn't want to lose Guy. She spotted him walking down Queen Street West. She took a step forward on the wet, slippery ground. The slush covering the sidewalks wasn't high-heel shoe approved. Her teeth chattered.

"Guy!" she said. She wouldn't catch up with him in these traitorous heels. She needed her boots. And her jacket. Her scarf and mittens would help, too. "Whoa!"

Her foot slipped on a patch of slush, and she tripped, falling hard on her tailbone. She yelped.

That got Guy's attention. "Oh shit." He returned to her—lucky for him he had his boots on—bent down, and helped her up. "Are you okay?"

She shivered. Wet, dirty snow soaked her hands and her legs. Her butt ached. She'd fallen hard, and the snow hadn't helped to soften the pavement. "Can we do this somewhere else?"

Guy put his arm around her and escorted her into a Starbucks. She went to the ladies' room and cleaned herself up. She stood under the hot air dryer, greeting whoever came in after her. She met their raised eyebrows with a half-smile, half-scowl.

When she was finished, she found Guy at a two seater. A cup of steaming tea waited for her. She sat down and wrapped her hands around the cup, warming herself.

"Better?" Guy asked.

"Much," she said. "You mind telling me what happened back there? You did a total one-eighty."

Guy scratched the back of his neck and stared into his tea. Then he sighed. "I can't do those photos you want. It's too much to handle. I don't want to see them. I know it's your gallery so… We just won't work together. I'll find another gallery."

Brittney leaned back in her seat and felt something drop in her chest. He'd tried so hard to work with her before, and now he was ready to give up after only one day. Whatever happened to being a team? "But you totally nailed that photo of Josh and Vanessa. It was perfect. And beautiful. It spoke to me. Spoke volumes. You could see the love between them. It was plain as day."

Guy shrugged. "Maybe."

"What do you mean, maybe?" He was trying to get out of this, but she wouldn't let him. Something more bothered him, and she intended to find it out. "You saw it yourself. That's why you took the photo without me telling you to."

"All I saw were two smiling people, holding hands, while the light was good."

"You know that's not true. You saw it, too. You wanted to take that picture for more than just good lighting."

"Maybe." He averted his eyes.

"Enough maybes. Tell me what's wrong." Brittney put a hand over his. "We're a team, remember?"

Guy glanced down at her hand, then up at her. She pulled her hand away slowly. Had she gone too far by touching him? His hands were softer than she expected, and the act of touching him came naturally to her.

"My parents," he said, "got divorced when I was sixteen years old. But their relationship was in shambles for as long as I can remember. It just took them sixteen years to figure out that divorce was best for them. Or best for my mother."

She knew a bit about this already from their conversation at Guy's apartment. Guy hadn't offered any details, and she hadn't asked. Seemed like she had to play therapist with him if he was going to continue working with her. "What about your dad?"

"He was stupidly in love with my mom. And mom thinks she was just a trophy wife. Biding her time until she was ready to cash in on dad's money."

Okay, so one hopelessly romantic father and one soulless mother. A recipe for divorce. Nothing uncommon about divorce, sadly. She knew a thing or two about it herself. "What does this have to do with the photos?"

"I tried to convince them they were in love. That whatever love they had was still there and that it had never gone away. We used to take family photos, and we'd all be smiling. You'd think, hey, now there's a happy family. But none of it was true."

"Lots of families are like that," Brittney said. "Mine included."

"Sure. Josh's, too. Except his mom and dad are still in a miserable relationship. The only difference was that I always believed I could change my parents. Like if I could show them the love they had for each other, which I knew deep down that they did have, all their problems would simply go away, and we'd be one big happy family."

"How'd you do it?"

Guy slung the camera off his neck and laid it on the table. "With the beauty of photography. I thought if I could capture their moments in love with my camera and showed it to them everything would be peachy. So I watched them. Every moment I could. When we were out to dinner. When we had guests over. When they read the Sunday paper out in the back porch. On birthdays, anniversaries, Christmases, Valentine's Days. I took so many photos. All of them looked like they were happy and in love. I saw a deep connection. Or so I thought."

He sipped his tea, stared out at the falling snow. It came down harder now. Clumps of snowflakes were falling in heaps on the roads. Getting back to the gallery was going to be a nightmare and a half.

Brittney waited for Guy to continue. She couldn't imagine what it was like for a boy to watch the love and marriage between his parents dwindle and fall apart. She'd been lucky in a way. Her father had just left. In some ways it was hard, but at least she didn't have to live through it day in and day out, wondering when it was going to happen or hoping that it would get better.

"Then," Guy said, "on their eighteenth anniversary, I gave them the photos. I went through each one, explaining how it showed how much they loved each other. I was like a scientist proving a new breakthrough in scientific theory to a board of skeptics."

Brittney smiled a small smile. That would've been a sweet present from a loving son. A chronicle of the love shared between two people. It was exactly what she wanted the gallery to be.

"But?" Brittney said.

"That day mom wanted a separation. She moved out of the house, leaving me and my father. Two months later she filed for divorce."

"I'm sorry, Guy." Sorry that all those years of work he had done, all that planning and watching his parents and taking photos, had all gone to nothing. It must have crushed him then. Still crushed him now.

"It's all fake," Guy said. "Whatever love you think you saw isn't real."

"It has to be real," Brittney said. "I saw it with my own eyes."

Guy shook his head. "You can't show someone love; it's intangible. It's not the same as showing someone an article of clothing. You can show someone a shirt, but you can't show them what love looks like."

"So then why did you agree to do it?"

"Because I wanted to work with you." Guy squirmed in his seat, and Brittney drilled him with a stare. There was more to it than that. "Okay, fine." He rolled his eyes. "Because I thought I had seen something."

"You did. It was exactly what we were looking for."

"But it hurt to see it. It just reminded me of all those years I had tried to save my parents' marriage. All for nothing. I don't want this to be for nothing."

"It won't be," Brittney said. "So that's why you stayed away from photographing people?"

Guy nodded.

"You still think it's fake?"

"I wish I didn't."

He still had that same hope he'd had when he was a child watching his parents. It hadn't died with his parents' divorce, only went into hiding. Again, she reached out to him, this time with both her hands, grabbed his fingers, and squeezed. He had to believe in the deep, genuine connections he showed in the photos, just as she believed in it. Believed in him. "You have this incredible gift to see the moment when love strikes between two people, and you capture it with your camera. Don't you want to show that to the world?"

"I don't want to lead people down a rabbit hole to disappointment and heartache. I don't want people to think that love lasts forever. It doesn't. It's just a moment. It could fade just as quickly as the camera flash."

"But those pictures you take will last forever." In print. In digital. Online.

"But in the grand scheme—"

"In the grand scheme, people break up, get divorced, leave each other, cheat, lie, whatever. All the time. Absolutely." There was no denying that. It had become a fact of life. Probably everyone in the Starbucks came from a family that was either highly dysfunctional or completely broken.

"Right. Your own father left your mother and you to pursue fame. You think that was love?"

Brittney shook her head. "I don't know if he ever loved me or my mother." Saying the words out loud hurt her chest. But it was true, and it had to be said.

"And you want to perpetuate that?"

"Guy, no one believes in love anymore. No one. They never say I love you. Why? Because, just like you, they're scared. They're scared of committing. They're scared of letting themselves go and surrendering." She herself feared it.

"You giving me a lecture on love now, Director?" Guy said, eyebrow arched. His tone had lightened a noticeable smidge. She had to keep encouraging him. She couldn't let one of her team members go. Her mother wouldn't, and neither would she.

"I don't know what love is," she said. "No one does. Not in this day and age. Maybe they did back in the day, but not anymore. People are selfish and only interested in themselves. I was like that."

"Me too."

"So is everyone else. That's why people don't care about love. It's too abstract. It's like all those photos you had taken before. All those photos with no message. It's just floundering around. But you have a real gift here. You can make it something concrete. Something people can grasp."

"And what?" Guy said. "Seeing is believing?"

"Yeah."

"Give me a break."

"I'm right, and you know it." She picked up the camera from the table. "You've been doing it ever since you got a camera. It's why you started taking photos in the first place."

"And why I want to stop."

"You can't stop. You owe it to yourself to keep going with this. You know you do. This is as much about proving love to everyone else as it is about proving it to yourself. Maybe even to your parents."

"I dunno."

"Work with me, Guy. Trust me on this. I believe it'll work."

"Really?" He took a deep breath.

"I saw those pictures. I saw the one you took today. It's all there. You saw it yourself. And others will, too. We have an opportunity here to change the way people think and view relationships. We, like, owe it to the world." She was making this sound bigger than it was for a small gallery, but she had to think big. Reach for the stars. Or star-crossed.

"Okay, Director." Guy smiled wryly. "Let's take it slow."

"Come back to the gallery. Let's work on this."

His jaw clenched. The boy in him was still scared. "Even if we do this, those models aren't going to work."

"I know…"

"And we can't have a gallery of just Josh and Vanessa."

"True." They were a good-looking couple and clearly in love, but they needed variety. Love from all walks of life, at all stages of life.

"We need real people," Guy said, sounding sure of himself, even a little passionate. "We need real couples. Who are really in love."

"How are we going to do that?"

"We have to go out and find them ourselves."

"Does this mean we're back in business?"

Guy sighed. "If someone gets hurt as a result of these photos…"

"The gallery has insurance," Brittney said. "I think."

"Yeah, but not for broken hearts."

Chapter Eight

On Monday, Brittney, Guy, and Emily sat in Brittney's office, a.k.a her mother's office. She'd begun to think of it as her own office, her own space. She'd even cleaned it a little and changed the background on the computer from a plain navy blue to a drawing of a heart with an arrow across it. If her first exhibit was going to be on love, she needed to absorb it fully. Take it all in. Become as much love as she could possibly be without sounding like a New Age priestess. The background on her smartphone was of a cheesy love quotation—an image of Tom Cruise from *Jerry Maguire* and his famous line to Renee Zellweger.

But now, spread out on the desk, sat a calendar for the month of January.

"I'm pretty wide open," Brittany said. Some of the dates had events and meetings written on them, but were now crossed out. Like on her first day, a lot of her mother's clients didn't want to work with someone as green as Brittney. It was either her mother or they'd wait until her mother was fine. Or—and this was the worst one—they'd go off to another gallery. Traitors.

"Me, too," Guy said. Of course, he was free. He had no other job than this. He had met with Brittney and Emily at the gallery every day since they decided to do the exhibit together. He was also part of the team, and Brittney slowly was getting used to having a photographer around her all the time.

"We could always do the exhibit next week," Brittany said. "Friday?"

"Not enough photos. We need more material. We haven't even advertised it."

"You're right." She should've thought of all that. This wasn't just a party she was planning where she could invite all her friends, most who were models and probably wouldn't come anyway. This was a business event. Marketing would play a huge role here. "End of January?"

Guy sucked in a breath. "Cutting it close."

"Why not make it something meaningful?" Emily said. She'd gotten more used to Guy over the course of the week. Her anxiety had been less severe around him, and she could now talk. Even played a song on the harmonica every once in a while.

"Does everything have to be meaningful?" Guy said. No doubt he was still miffed when Brittney had said his other photos—photos he'd spent years collecting—were meaningless.

"Meaningful is the wrong word," Emily said, frowning.

"Impactful?" Brittney ventured.

Emily snapped her fingers. "That works."

"Fine," Guy said. "Impactful. Momentous. Biblical. Whatever. Let's just pick a date."

Brittney turned the calendar page over to what she expected was February. Instead, the next page revealed all her mother's notes for January.

"Oh, Helene likes to have one booklet for each month of the year," Emily said when she must have seen the confusion on Brittney's face. "She keeps all her notes for each month that way. She thinks it's cleaner."

"Where's February?"

"Back where you found January."

Brittney stood up. "I'll go get it."

\#

Guy leaned back in his chair and sighed. It hadn't yet hit him all this was for him and his work. He felt caught in limbo. Between having a job, unemployment, and now organizing an exhibit, it all happened so fast. He hadn't had time to wrap his head around it.

Not to mention Brittney was an anomaly to him. He liked her. A lot. Not just because she put all her faith into him, but because he felt at ease when he was around her. She knew nothing about how to run a gallery, and this exhibit would be as much a first for her as it was for him, but she didn't seem nervous about it. She seemed to know what steps to follow and when. He couldn't believe she'd been a model. Scratch that, he could see it—she was gorgeous, after all—but he always thought models were fake and…and well, dumb.

"Hey," he said to Emily once he couldn't hear Brittney's heeled steps anymore, "let me ask you something."

"Sure."

Guy narrowed his eyes at her. "You're very comfortable with me now, I've noticed."

Emily shrugged. "I've gotten used to you. You're here practically every day."

"I like this place." And he'd stay for as long as he could, too. He'd dreamed of being part of a gallery.

"I do, too."

"Does Brittney?"

Emily frowned. "I think she does."

"Why is she doing this?" Guy asked. "I mean, she's doing it for her mother, I get that—but she could just make money doing something else, couldn't she?"

Emily's frown deepened. "Why don't you ask her?"

Guy shook his head. "Are you crazy? That'll cause World War Three."

Emily sighed. "She wants to prove that she's more than just a pretty face. She wants to show she's smart."

"She's not dumb." He truly believed that. She wasn't like those model friends of hers she'd brought in. Those models had been IQ-less.

"But most people think she is. She's doing this not only to help her mom out but to get some experience under her belt. She's applying for business school at UofT."

"She is?" That impressed him. University of Toronto was a top university. Einstein would have a hard time getting in.

"Yeah," Emily said. "She doesn't really talk about it, though."

"No?" Too humble maybe? Didn't want to jinx it?

"She doesn't think she can do it. She can't see it for herself."

"How do you know all this?" Emily hardly new Brittney. "Did she tell you?"

Emily leaned in close. "I watch, Guy." She wiggled her eyebrows. "And I see."

"Doesn't believe in herself," Guy said to himself, picking at his camera hanging off his neck.

Brittney's heeled steps sounded, coming loud and strong.

"Now, shhh." Emily sat erect in her chair. "She's coming back."

Guy winked. "I'll act naturally." When Brittney came back, carrying another calendar booklet, he said, "Hey there, Director, we were just talking about you."

#

"Talking about me?" Brittney said. She stalled, bringing the calendar up to her chest like a shield. There was a conspiratorial air to the room. "About what?"

"He's kidding. We were talking about the exhibit. Right, Guy?" Emily slapped him on the knee. Her face was red, not from shyness but from anger.

"I am kidding," Guy said, waving his hand dismissively. "We talked about the weather."

Brittney raised an eyebrow. "Oooookay."

"Did you find it?" Emily asked.

"Yep," Brittney said. She came around the desk and sat back down on her chair, the cushion having long since adapted to the shape of her bottom. The office felt more and more like her home every day. She laid the calendar on the desk. "Here's February. What do we all think?"

Guy and Emily leaned forward and gazed at the calendar with knitted brows. Brittney did the same, surveying the weeks and the special holidays.

"Why not Valentine's Day?" Emily said, eyes lit up.

Guy groaned. "God, no."

"Oh, come on," Emily said. "It's a perfect match. The exhibit is about couples and love. Valentine's Day is about couples and love."

"Uh-uh." Guy shook his head. "Too cliché."

Brittney nodded. "I agree. Not to mention couples will be out on dinner reservations instead of wanting to see an exhibit of an unknown artist."

Guy frowned. "Did you just agree with me while insulting me at the same time?"

"But how about the weekend before?" Brittney said. "Enough time to market the exhibit and we can still use the Valentine's Day angle."

Guy rubbed his chin, mulled it over, then nodded. "I'm game."

Brittney smiled to herself.

"And we can have a coloured theme," Emily said, the words

racing out of her mouth. Out of the three of them, she seemed to love the idea the most. "Like pink or—"

"Whoa." Guy raised his hands. "Pink?"

"Or red."

"I don't even think I own anything red."

"We could make it into a date night," Brittney said. Like Emily, the ideas were running through her mind, and she wanted to get as many of them out as possible. She took a pen, turned the page on the calendar booklet, and started scribbling. This stuff—this brainstorming session that the meeting had suddenly turned into—probably happened whenever her mother worked on a new exhibit, hence the notes page. "We'll put out Hersey kisses and cinnamon hearts."

"And rose petals on the floor," Emily said, clapping her hands together. "And couples who get their picture taken can have cards where the front is the picture, and on the back they can write love notes to each other."

Guy rolled his eyes. "Maybe we can invite Cupid to come, too."

"Maybe we can dress you up as Cupid," Brittney said.

Guy pointed a finger at her. "Do that, and I will shoot an arrow into my temple."

Emily clapped. "Oh, my God—how great would it be if we had arrow giveaways?"

"Arrow giveaways?" Guy said. Even Brittney had to admit they were getting a little carried away here. The point was to *avoid* cliché, not perpetuate it. But she liked the rise it was getting out of Guy.

"Yeah," Emily said, "like something they can take home with them. Arrows with hearts as the arrow heads and the name of the exhibition on the shaft."

"How are we going to pay for all this?" Guy asked.

Brittney shrugged. Her mother had a budget to spend on exhibits. She didn't think she could do all the marketing and promotional ideas, but she could do something to make this exhibit unique. "You gotta spend money to make money, baby."

Guy smiled. "Is that my new term of endearment? Because I like it."

Brittney shook her head. "Focus, Stumps."

"No, seriously," Guy said. "Call me baby any time you like. BB on text."

"Shut up or I'll put you in a Cupid costume."

"You wouldn't dare."

"My gallery, my rules."

#

The Eaton Centre was Toronto's primary shopping mall, one of the biggest malls in Canada and situated right in the middle of Toronto's downtown. It was easily accessible and people were literally *everywhere*, from men dressed in business suits working on the office floors above to whole families and groups of friends and tourists. The mall was crammed with people who sat on the benches, who milled about, who raced from store to store, who looked around for missing friends and family members in the throngs of mall rats. So many conversations happened at once that none of it was discernible—all white noise.

Pictures of models showing off clothing brands hung on huge posters. Brittney had been one of those models a couple of times in her career. She'd hated seeing herself blown up and hung like that for everyone to see. She usually steered clear of the mall whenever she knew one of her posters were being shown.

"All we have to do," Brittney said, loud enough so she could be heard, "is find people who are in relationships."

The five of them—Brittney, Guy, Emily, Josh, and Vanessa—stood bunched together.

"You really think this will work?" Guy asked.

Brittany shrugged. "Where else are you going to hang out during winter? The mall. And this place is packed!"

Eaton Centre was practically a zoo.

"There are a lot of couples here," Josh said, scanning the corridor they were in.

"And the light in here is pretty good, too," Guy said. Skylights above them let in natural light from the outside.

Hand-in-hand, couples walked by them. Some with smiles on their faces, and others who looked like they'd been together for so long and were waiting for the other to break it off. They definitely didn't want the latter couple for the exhibit.

"We gotta engage enough couples," Brittney said, "and schedule them in for the next two weeks to come by the gallery for a photoshoot."

"It'll help spread the word, too," Vanessa said.

"Exactly." Brittney had to admire Josh and Vanessa. They were good friends, taking time out of their weekend to come and help Guy. "It's the perfect plan."

"Are we all splitting up?" Guy asked.

"Yes. Cover more ground that way."

Guy smirked. "You're treating this like a CIA mission."

"Operation Find Couples."

Josh rubbed his hands together. "I'm game. Sounds like fun.

"Thanks for helping out, you guys," Guy said.

Vanessa put her hand on Guy's shoulder. "Of course. We're here for you."

Guy smiled, fiddling with his camera.

"Meet back here in an hour?" Josh asked.

Brittney nodded. "For a check-in. See how everyone's doing."

They left. Emily stood next to Brittney, biting her lip. "You know," Brittney said to her, "you don't have to do this if you don't want to."

Emily took a deep breath, her chest rising. She blew it out with a whoosh. "I have to take control over my anxiety at some point, right?"

"This is a big step."

"I want to help out. I'm so into the exhibit. I want to play my part."

"You could always come with me, and we could walk up to couples together? That way you're not alone."

Emily shook her head. She squared her shoulders and shot her chin out. "I'll be fine. I promise."

"Good luck."

Emily left, too, taking the escalator down to the lower floor. Brittney watched her the whole way. She hadn't expected Emily to come along for this one, but was grateful she did. No wonder her mother had hired her. She was hardworking and determined. If this process could help overcome her social anxieties, then all the more power to her.

"And then there were two," Guy said, and they both started walking down the crowded corridor. "Which area are you heading off to?"

"The food court. Couples must be hanging around there having lunch."

Guy nodded. "Good idea."

"And you?"

"I see one right now," Guy said, pointing at a couple leaning against a railing that overlooked the lower level. "Wish me luck."

He approached the couple and started talking. Brittney was too far to hear what he said, but now the pressure was on. First blood had been spilled. Her idea, Operation Find Couples, was happening. And now it was her turn.

She squeezed her hands into fists, took a deep breath, and gave herself a little shake. And here she thought she wouldn't be nervous. Maybe not in the same way Emily was, but nervous all the same. What if this idea of hers ended up a total bust? Maybe she could hire a couple of actors next? Sure, why not? She could fly in Zac Efron. No problem.

She spotted a couple walking leisurely toward her, both of them scooping up a shared frozen yogurt. She started toward them.

"Hi, Brittney."

She stopped. That voice. Cold ran down her back. She turned around, slowly, wishing all she had that it wasn't…

Oh, Heaven help her. It was.

Standing in front of her was Derrick.

In a city of nearly three million, Brittney never thought she'd ever run into Derrick. Once she'd caught him cheating on her and she had left everything behind—deleting his phone number, erasing his text messages and emails, throwing out everything that was his in her old apartment—she thought the ties between them had been severed and she'd never have to face him again.

But she'd been so wrong. Here he was, in a nice shirt that showed off his chest muscles and wearing that handsome smile that made her knees wobble. When she caught herself staring, she gazed down at her booted feet, down at her plain jeans and black coat. She tucked her blond hair—hair that was beginning to show its brunette roots since she'd had zero time and zero money to highlight it—behind her ear.

Did she look good? Not sexy or even beautiful. But at least *good*, decent. She swallowed and hoped her breath didn't stink.

This was so not the right time to bump into Derrick of all people.

"How have you been?" he asked in his smooth voice.

"Me? Good, good." She nodded and then kept nodding. She

couldn't stop nodding. "Great, actually. Fantastic." Anymore nodding, and she'd turn herself into a bobble head. "Ten out of ten."

"That's good to hear. I haven't seen you since you quit the biz. Been busy?"

You haven't seen me since you cheated on me, Brittney wanted to say but held back. No use unleashing her fury in the middle of the Eaton Centre and causing a scene. She cleared her throat. "I'm working at my mother's art gallery. I'm running it for her."

"Wow." The bastard arched his eyebrows. She found it demeaning. "Do you know how to do that?"

"It's not that hard," she lied.

"You're a smart girl."

That gave her pause. He'd never said that to her before. Had never even implied it. The only thing he cared about had been her appearance. She was pretty. No, she was *very* pretty. His exact words. Now he had half the mind to tell her she was smart, too? Was this some kind of trick?

Trick of not, hearing him saying it made her lower her defenses. He thought she was more than just pretty. That meant a lot to her.

"And you?" Brittney asked. She found she'd gotten a little bit closer to him. Close enough to smell his cologne.

"Same old."

She wanted him to hug her and forget everything that had happened before and go back to the way things had been. Back to when she had a career and a boyfriend and hundreds of likes and comments a day. Back to when she wasn't alone and unsure anymore.

She opened her arms to him and stepped forward—

"Baby!"

Brittney jumped back. A blond-haired girl wearing the skimpiest outfit possible in January tackled Derrick and held him tightly. In her hand swung a Sephora bag.

Derrick smiled, hugging the girl back, then leaving his arm around her waist. "Hi, babykins! Did you find that perfume you were looking for?"

The girl seemed familiar.

"Who's this?" she asked, giving Brittney the elevator stare, from root-showing hair to slush-covered boots.

"This is Brittney. She used to model. Like you."

Now Brittney remembered. This was the girl Derrick had cheated on her with. Worst, Brittney had even worked with her in previous modelling gigs. She'd even *liked* her. The home-wrecking bitch.

"Brittney this is—"

"Gina," Brittney said. "Hi. I remember you."

Derrick narrowed his eyes. "You know each other?" Then realization struck, and his eyes bugged out. "Oh, right. Yeah."

"Did we model together?" Gina asked Derrick.

"Sorta, babykins."

Babykins. Did Derrick call all his sex toys that term of endearment? It grossed her out now, whereas before it used to make her heart do a little dance. What a stupid name. What did babykins mean, anyway?

But, by God, Gina was pretty. And young. And with freshly-highlighted hair.

"Well, that was a complete bust," said a voice behind her. Guy. He came to stand next to Brittney, scratching the back of his head. "Turns out the couple was actually a mother and her son. Should've seen this mom, though. Totally hot. Nightmares for the kid, though." He shivered.

Without thinking it through, Brittney put her arms around Guy's neck and leaned into him, tilting her head to the side and showing off the same satisfied smile she used to give Derrick during their pillow talk. "I missed you, baby."

Guy blinked, then furrowed his brow. "Missed me? Baby?"

She snuck a sideways glance at Derrick. His confident, handsome smile had dropped from his face. Now for the kicker.

She leaned in, closed her eyes, and kissed him.

She only wanted the kiss to last a second or two. A quick peck to show her and Guy were an item. Nothing more, nothing less. But when her lips met his, it was as if they belonged there. Not only did she like the feel of his soft lips on hers, but she wanted more. She kissed him again, and he did the same, this time putting his hands around her waist and pulling her toward him. That hadn't been part of this script she'd made up on the fly, but that was okay; she liked that, too.

When she pulled back, her cheeks flushed. Her heart didn't just dance in her chest; it did the Macarena.

Someone cleared his throat.

Not someone—Derrick! She'd completely forgotten about him and Gina. She pulled her hair back from her face, smoothed out her coat, and hooked her arm around Guy's. "Derrick, this is my boyfriend, Guy."

Derrick's mouth dropped, and Brittney had never smiled so hard or so big in her life.

"It's nice to meet you," Derrick said, extending his hand out to Guy. "Name's Derrick. I used to photograph Brittney once upon a time."

"Nice to meet you too?" Guy said it in a question and took Derrick's hand in his, but it was obvious he was still wondering what the hell was going on.

Brittney didn't quite know herself. She'd panicked when she saw Gina with Derrick. She had no one. She had no time to find anyone else. She hadn't even had time to grieve losing Derrick. So much had happened too fast. Not more than two weeks had passed since she caught Derrick cheating, and it was clear he had moved on. She'd wanted to show the same, even if it meant faking it.

That was where Guy had come in. Poor, confused, eyebrows-cocked Guy. He searched her face for answers. She gave him a look, willing him to play along. She squeezed his bicep for added effect.

"You a photographer?" Derrick asked, his eyes indicating the camera hanging off Guy's neck.

"I dabble," Guy said, still facing Brittney.

"Dabble?" Brittney said, playfully slapping Guy on the chest. "Come on, honey. You have your own exhibit."

"*First* exhibit."

"First exhibit *this year*," Brittney was quick to fill in. "He's had many before. Tons."

"Oh, really?" Derrick asked, frowning. "I don't recognize your name."

"Oh, he's big," Brittney said. "Really big. Tell him, baby."

Guy's expression tensed, like he tried to figure out the last piece of a puzzle and just couldn't. "I'm big?" His small tone belied any declaration of bigness.

"That's pretty cool, man." Derrick said. "I'm a photographer for a big studio. I mainly do fashion."

"Oh, you poor bastard," Guy muttered, his hatred for fashion photography bolstering his words. Brittney should've started with that. Would've gotten Guy real riled up.

"Excuse me?" Derrick said.

"I said, you must not be poor."

Derrick laughed. "It's pretty lucrative. I DJ on the side, too."

Guy made a face. Half smile and half as if he'd smelled bad cheese. "Of course you do."

"He's fantastic," Gina said. "He deejayed with Yongelove."

"Yongelove?" Guy asked. He glanced to Brittney for help, but she shrugged her shoulders. She also didn't know who Yongelove was. "Is that a band?"

"He's a Toronto-based DJ."

"Naturally," Guy said. He slapped his forehead. "Duh!"

"So you're dating Brittney?" Derrick said to Guy, then turned to Brittney. "You must have a thing for photographers, eh?"

"You guys used to date?" Guy asked. At long last—the missing piece of the puzzle had been discovered.

"Used to," Derrick said. "Broke up recently."

The words still stung. Brittney dug her nails into Guy's bicep. Guy flinched, and Brittney eased her grip.

"Oh," Guy said. "You're *that* Derrick." His tone had shifted, becoming stronger, more confident, cuttingly sarcastic. Sadly, the tone he sometimes used with her. "The one with the bad case of venereal disease."

Derrick eyes widened, and his jaw clenched tightly. Gina pursed her glossy lips. "What's venereal disease?"

Guy shook his head. "God bless your platinum blonde hair."

"So, Guy," Derrick said, and his tone had changed, too, sounding more like a growl, "what kind of exhibit do you have?"

"Interesting you should ask. It's kind of like what you're doing. I photograph people. Couples to be exact. Couples who are in love."

"In love?"

"Yep. Two people come into my studio and I capture the moments they're in complete connection with each other. Think of it like a love spark."

"Love spark?"

"Industry term. It's not important. But what is important," Guy said, turning his attention to Gina instead of Derrick, "is that through my pictures I can show the couple their undying, unconditional love for each other. I can actually prove the existence of real love."

Gina put her hands to her heart. "Oh, my God. That is so sweet."

"No shit, right?" Guy said, grinning. "Maybe I can take a photo of you two?"

Gina's eyes lit up. "Oh, my God, can you?"

"Oh, my God, I can!" And right then, Brittney could kiss Guy again.

"Let's do it, baby!" Gina said to Derrick, pulling on his sleeve. The sudden movement made a cloud of fruity perfume puff in the air.

Derrick shook his head, glare clear on his face. "Maybe another time."

"Sure. Stop by the gallery. Anytime."

"Good seeing you," Derrick said to Brittney.

"Likewise," she said.

Derrick gave Guy, who waved bye to him like a child, one last glare before the two of them walked away.

"Thank you," she said to Guy when the pair was out of sight but not quite out of mind.

"You dated that guy?" Guy puffed out a breath. "Talk about poor judgement. So that's why you hate photographers. Let me guess? He cheated on you."

"With her."

"Really?" Guy made a face as though he did smell bad cheese. "That girl is pure plastic."

Yes, she was. But Brittney couldn't help but think she'd been the exact same way. Deep down, she still was that girl. She had acted that same way once. Said those same things. Dressed and smelled that same way. Tears stung her eyes. Try as she might, she couldn't will them back. And in the middle of Eaton Centre of all places.

"Oh, no, no," Guy said. "No tears. Come here." He wrapped his arms around her, pulled her in tightly. He rocked her side to side, rubbing her back. Even though it made her feel like she was being treated like a child, it still felt kind of nice. And safe. And like she had someone who had her back. At least someone to rub her back. She began to feel a little bit better, and the tears, miraculously, stopped.

"You want me to kill him?"

Brittney pulled back. "What? No!"

"You sure?" Guy asked, his arms still around her.

"Yes! What's wrong with you?" She reconsidered. "Maybe you could make it look like an accident?"

"Okay," he said, and his hand caressed the contours of her back. "I'll run him over with my truck."

"You don't have a truck."

"So homicide and auto theft. Could be my next calling."

She laughed into his chest. "You're an idiot." She wrapped her arms around him, breathed in his scent. "But thank you, Stumps."

"No, thank you. That kiss was phenomenal."

It sorta kinda was.

#

"What about Love Framed?" Josh said around the table.

Guy shook his head. "That's a terrible name."

"What?" Josh said, genuinely surprised. He waved a hand. "Come on."

"Not feeling it," Brittney said.

"Baby?" Josh asked Vanessa.

Vanessa shook her head, too.

"What about usie?" Emily asked.

"Usie?" Brittney raised an eyebrow. She couldn't see the connection.

"Yeah. It's like a selfie but with us in it. Get it?"

"How do you spell it?" Guy asked.

Emily spelled it out on a scrap piece of paper from the blue bin.

"You-see?" Josh said.

"No. *Us*-ee."

"Looks like you-see."

"Fine." She crumpled up the paper and tossed it back into the blue bin. "You guys wouldn't see talent if it hit you over the head with a tablet."

"It has to do with couples and pictures," Guy said.

Silence. Brittney thought about it. Associations with love and couples raced through her mind.

Then she knew.

"Why not Pictures of Me and You?"

Everyone let the title sink in. "How about pics instead of pictures?" Vanessa said.

"And spell it with an *x*," Josh offered.

"Sounds pretty good," Emily said, arms crossed. "But not better than usie."

"I like it," Guy said. "Pix of Me and You. What do you think, Director?"

Brittney smiled. "I don't think we're stumped anymore, Stumps."

Chapter Nine

At this rate, Guy's camera was only good enough for collecting dust.

He sighed, putting his arms on the table and leaning his head down. He waited. And waited.

Emily walked by. "Don't worry. Someone will come."

Guy managed a weak smile. "Thanks." He hadn't taken a photo in nearly a week. Not any for the exhibit and not any for himself, either. As nice as the gallery was, he'd rather be taking photos than sitting around all day waiting for a couple in love to stroll in. After the failure of Operation Find Couples, Brittney had a new idea, and with a few well-placed ads online, Operation Are You in Love? was born.

And still very much in its infancy.

Now all they had to do was wait. And wait. And wait.

To garner attention, Brittney had advertised the gallery and the exhibit as a challenge. A call to all couples to come to Collar Gallery and take a special photo that would prove, beyond the shadow of a doubt, that love existed between them. Who wouldn't want that photo taken and framed?

Apparently, not too many. None at all, actually. Either people weren't spurred by the challenge or there weren't, as Guy had always feared, any couples in love.

The door to Brittney's office was open, and Brittney was talking on the phone. Talking fast with one hand laced in her hair. "She okay?" Guy asked Emily.

Emily peeked into the office. "Just talking to her mom. Helene came home this week from the hospital. Can't really do much so Brittney hired a nurse for her."

Managing the gallery and now managing her mother's care. Brittney fit the role well. Hopefully she knew that, too. A nurse, though, probably cost her a ton. "Where'd she get the money?"

"Helene had some money saved up. And Brittney has some of her own, I think. From modelling."

"Right. Dipping into the savings, huh?" His stomach knotted. The silence of the empty gallery weighed heavily. Someone better come and come now. "This idea of hers better hit it off."

"It will. You gotta trust her."

He didn't really have a choice. He wanted to trust her, but so far the only pictures they had were of Josh and Vanessa. They needed couples and fast. How could Emily be so calm about it? Brittney didn't seem quite as calm, though. There were bags under her eyes as if she hadn't been sleeping that well. Guy himself was part of Club Insomnia, too. He looked and felt like shit. His stomach grumbled because he hadn't eaten much. Every day he expected an eviction notice from his apartment.

The chimes from the door in the main entrance clinked.

Guy perked up like a dog after hearing the word *treat.* "Company?"

Emily shrugged, and she started over to the front.

"I'll go," Guy said, jumping up from his seat. Anything to feel useful. At the front, a man and a woman, probably no older than thirty, came in. The man had his hands in his pockets, while the woman scanned the artwork on the walls.

"Hi," Guy said, smiling, "is there something I can help you with?"

The man pulled out a piece of paper from his pocket. He unfolded it and showed it to Guy. It was a printout of Brittney's ad challenge.

"Is it for engagement photos?" the woman asked. That was when Guy noticed the shiny rock on her ring finger.

"Not quite," Guy said, honestly. Maybe the ad wasn't clear enough? "It's for an exhibit I'm working on."

"You're the photographer?" she asked.

"That's me. Name's Guy Moraine." He shook each of their hands. "You guys getting married?"

The woman nodded. "And we're looking to get some engagement photos done, but my fiancé isn't too crazy about the idea."

Her fiancé shrugged. "I don't really like to get my picture taken. The flashing lights, the posing. Not really my thing, you know?"

"Trust me," Guy said, hand over his heart, "I get it." He couldn't help but agree with him either.

"But this isn't for engagements, is it?"

"It could be," Guy said, shrugging. Why not? Engagement photos were all about the couple, right? He'd never taken them before, but if he knew how to capture love, then he was the right man for the job.

"What is your exhibit, exactly?" the woman asked.

"I take photos of couples in love. I look for the exact moment when the essence of your love for each other shows on your faces and in your eyes, and I capture it in a picture." That sounded like something Brittney would say to sell the idea. Judging by the interest on the woman's face, it worked.

"How do you do that?"

The million-dollar question. He wiggled his eyebrows. "Why not try it and find out?"

"How much?" the man asked.

The woman elbowed him, and he made an audible *oof!*

"It's free," Guy said. "So long as we can use your photos in the exhibit."

"Do we still get to use them for our wedding?"

"Absolutely."

They introduced themselves as Carly and Peter. They were a young couple with probably not a whole lot in their bank account to spend on a wedding. Photos alone could cost several hundred, if not thousands, of dollars. "Let's try it."

They went to the back room and set up. Emily picked up what was going on and brought water bottles out for them, tried to make them comfortable. Guy thought it made them desperate, which they kinda were, given that Carly and Peter were their first customers. Emily shot him two thumbs up with a big grin on her face.

"So, how do you want us?" Carly asked. She picked at the shirt she wore. "Is what we're wearing okay? Shouldn't we be dressed up for this?"

"Not at all," Guy said, checking the settings on his camera. "What you're wearing is great. It won't be your clothing people will be looking at."

"Man's got a point, babe," Peter said. "This isn't for fashion."

Guy snapped a finger at Peter. "Bingo." He was starting to like Peter. "It's for love. So show me your guys' love."

Clary frowned. "How do we do that?"

Now that was the billion-dollar question.

"Oh, we have clients." Brittney strolled out of her office, tucking her hair behind her ears.

"Peter, Carly, let me introduce you to Brittney. She runs the gallery."

Brittney shook their hands. "It's so good of you to come in. Married?"

"Engaged," Carly said, showing off the ring.

"Congratulations. When's the wedding?"

"July."

"Best time to have a wedding. You're in good hands with our photographer. How'd you find us?"

"The ad," Guy said.

Brittney turned to him. "The ad." She smiled as if she could barely contain the urge to hop up and down and scream at the top of her lungs. "Here to take up the challenge, then?"

"Actually," Peter said, "we thought it was for engagement photos."

"You can use them for that, too," Brittney said. She sneaked a glance over at Guy to confirm. "I'll let our genius do his thing."

Genius? *Put on the pressure, why don't you?* He only ever took a photo of a couple's deep connection because the moment presented itself of its own accord. He'd never actually had to manufacture the moment himself. Brittney stood behind him, arms crossed.

"So…" He had no clue where to begin. "Just…act normally." Smooth. Maybe he ought to get them a newspaper to read. Have them discuss filing their taxes for the year. "How would you guys be, like, if you were in, say, your living room together?" That sounded dumb. "Or at a restaurant?" Even dumber.

Carly and Peter shared a glance. Carly took a sip of her water. And Peter reached out and held her hand, caressing it with his thumb. Guy snapped a few photos.

"Okay," he said, checking the camera's screen.

"Any good?" Brittney asked.

Guy showed her the display. The photos were, for lack of a better term, meh. They looked candid, which was what Guy wanted, but there was something missing. No spark, the key ingredient, and without the spark, these photos were just that—candid.

They were still faking it. Just because they didn't face the camera didn't mean they weren't still posing. Doing whatever Guy told them to do wasn't working. They had to be free, uninhibited, willing to let go and just do whatever they felt or wanted to do. They could bark like dogs or stick their tongues out, so long as it was natural. That was the only way to get to the truth of how they felt about each other. The truth within the candid. Guy wasn't only looking for the spark. He was searching for how the truth in people's lives manifested on their expressions, in their actions, with one another. He happened to choose love because he'd wanted to prove his parents had love for each other. He'd failed at that.

But he wouldn't fail now. Couldn't fail now.

It was the way that Peter took Carly's hand in his and stroked it with his thumb that made him realize this was love. Couples who were just going through the motions of being a couple didn't do those sorts of things. They did at the start, but it died quickly. Couples who were in love wanted to be closer to each other, connected, whole. They always touched whether by holding hands, sitting thigh to thigh or playing footsie. And it wasn't like Guy had asked him to do it, either. They were acting "normally." That was Peter's instinct, and it was a good one.

But not good enough.

The spark was still missing in action. Guy rubbed his chin. How many couples had he seen in love? Josh and Vanessa were a given. Their love was almost too much love. A few others, too. Friends from university or random couples around Toronto, people he didn't know but caught displaying public affection in a beautiful, genuine way.

Huh. This train of thought begged a question: when was the last time he was in love?

Never.

"Maybe try something else?" Brittney whispered to him, her face tense. She was nervous about this. Anxious. She wanted it to succeed. She, out of all people, had a lot riding on this.

An image of their kiss back at the Eaton Centre came unbidden to his mind. Of course, he had no clue what it had looked like since he'd had his eyes closed and his lips firmly on hers, but he pictured it from an outsider's perspective. Imagining it now brought with it other sensations: the fruity smell of her shampoo; the delicate touch of her mouth like the softest pillow; the smack of their lips when the kiss, regrettably, ended.

It had come as a pleasant surprise. He'd thought about it a dozen times since then, wondering if she'd liked it as much as he had. She seemed to at the time, but maybe she'd only acted as if she had to make Derrick jealous.

He wanted to kiss her again. Kiss her and hold her and tell her how great she was for making all this happen for him.

"Why don't you two kiss?" he told Carly and Peter.

Again, another shared look. This was the other thing that told Guy they were in love. Lovers that spoke with their eyes were true lovers indeed. They leaned into each other, and kissed. Not a peck either. The kiss lingered. Something about that kiss…

Flash. Guy took the photo. He checked the display and smiled. Brittney stared at him while biting her lower lip. Guy winked at her, then turned back to Carly and Peter. "Awesome. Now just look at each other."

"Look at each other?" Peter asked.

"Yup. Into each other's eyes. Let's see what happens."

The two of them turned toward each other. Guy paced around them, waiting for the perfect opportunity.

Silence. A full minute passed. It felt like an hour.

Carly giggled. "This is kind of silly."

Guy snapped a photo. "That's the point. Keep it up. You guys are doing great." He wasn't quite sure himself what it was they were doing. Whatever it was, it seemed to work. Whenever he had taken a photo of a couple, it was because the two of them stared at each other and there was something that passed between them that no one else could know. Something private and intimate. That was what he was waiting for. For them to say *I love you* with a gleam in their eyes, an expression, a sound.

The corners of their eyes crinkled ever so slightly as their lips moved, starting as a small smile, then getting larger, reaching to their eyes, spreading out into a toothy grin, and then finally climaxing in shameless, almost childlike, laughter.

It was beautiful. And Guy captured the whole thing.

"That's it," Guy said. "Get your inner child out." Because that was what it meant to be truly in love. To be childlike and not care what anyone else thought about you. To lose yourself in the comfort and warmth of your loving partner. "Let it all go. Seriously. Go freaking nuts!"

They laughed even more. They stepped closer and wrapped their arms around each other. Peter moved a strand of Carly's hair behind her ear. They were nose to nose. She giggled, he kissed her, then kissed her through another giggle. It was cute, imperfect, and yet perfect.

Guy's camera flashed like a lightning storm. The camera hadn't seen this much action in weeks. And he even enjoyed taking the photos, enjoyed seeing that candid connection between two people. These two really were in love.

"You guys okay?" Guy asked as the two of them sobered up.

"I forgot you were even there," Carly said.

"Me, too," said Peter.

"What were you guys thinking about?" Brittney asked. Good

thinking, Director. Any information to help them replicate this moment would be sheer gold.

Peter smiled. "I was remembering," he said, "the first time I said I love you."

Carly reached over and grabbed his hand. "I was thinking the same thing."

"Huh," Guy said. That hadn't occurred to him at all, but now they mentioned it, it all made sense. "I guess that's why you're getting married."

"How did you say it?" Brittney asked. She had her hands clasped over her chest. She seemed genuinely interested in their story. As if she could learn something from them that she could use.

Maybe Guy could use it, too.

Peter snickered. "It's kind of embarrassing actually."

"He couldn't say it to me," Carly said. "He would look me in the eyes, say my name, and then pause. And when I asked him what he wanted, he'd just mumble a big fat nothing."

"So I practiced it," Peter said, holding Carly's hand. "I practiced saying I love you to everyone except Carly. I said to it to my friends. My co-workers. Even my boss."

"And then when he became a pro, he said it to me."

"Must've been perfect pronunciation," Brittney said, smiling.

"He did okay." Carly had said it in such a way that suggested Peter did way better than just okay.

Guy shut the camera. "You both did great. Thanks for being part of the exhibit."

"When is it?" Carly said, gathering her purse.

"Uh…" Guy said. They hadn't confirmed the date yet. With the lack of clients and photos, they'd have to push the exhibit to March.

"We haven't really decided on that yet," Brittney said. "To be honest, you guys were our first clients."

"No way," Carly said.

Guy shrugged. "You guys said yourselves you thought this was for engagement photos."

"We're going to tell all our friends," Carly said.

"That would be appreciated," Brittney said. "Who knows? Maybe if we get enough clients, we can have the exhibit in February."

"We'll make it happen," Carly said. "Right, honey?"

"Absolutely," Peter said, all smiles. The man had changed. He'd come into the gallery a non-believer and now left as a poster child.

The next three days saw more couples pouring in, including friends and family of Carly and Peter. Once Guy had snapped their photos, they told their friends and family, and so the exhibit grew larger. People were even coming from out of town. Guy's camera no longer collected dust. Instead, it needed extra batteries.

So many people were coming that Emily had to take appointments. No longer would she only sweep the floors or play on her harmonica. She had work to do. As did Brittney. And Guy was going nuts.

"Are we ready for this?" Guy asked Brittney before the gallery closed for the night.

Brittney counted off on her fingers. "I got framed photos. Print outs. A whole host of giveaways. Food. Beverages. I even know how I'm going to set the gallery up."

Her phone quacked. An email from Emily. The subject line read *OMG LOOK AT THIS*. The body included a link, which brought Brittney to TDotEvents.

"Oh, my God," Brittney breathed.

"What's up?" Guy stood over her shoulder.

The front page featured Collar Gallery.

Featured the Are You in Love? Challenge

Featured the Pix of Me and You Exhibit.

"I think," Brittney said, "we're going to need more food."

Chapter Ten

"Cheers!" Josh said, raising his glass of red wine in the air. Everyone else, Brittney, Guy, Vanessa, and Emily clinked glasses. They sat at a long table in the middle of one of those loungey-bar places that served food as well as drinks. Plates of food, some empty, others with scraps left, were laid out on the table. They were on their third bottle of Merlot.

Brittney sipped, and the wine went down smoothly. A little too smoothly. She had to pace herself. She'd be no use to anyone tomorrow if she was hungover.

Tomorrow was the big day. The day of the Pix of Me and You Exhibition. All their hard work would be on display tomorrow, for better or for worse.

It better be for the better, or God help her and her mother.

Josh stood up on wobbly legs. He tapped his wine glass with a spoon. "Just a few words," he slurred. He must have had at least a bottle and a half of the wine himself. Lips purple, teeth stained, red in the face. "I've known Guy since we were in diapers. We went to school together, university together, we even worked together, and I can honestly say I never thought I'd see the day where Guy would actually *do* something."

Guy picked up a piece of lettuce and tossed it at Josh. "Sounds like there's a new opening to apply as my new best friend. Any takers? Emily?"

Emily shook her head. "Uh-uh."

"But in all seriousness," Josh forged ahead. He hiccupped. "I'm proud of you, Guy. You really did something great here. You both did." He swung the glass over to Brittney who sat next to Guy. Wine whooshed up the glass and spilled over and onto the table. "If it hadn't been for you, Brittney, Guy would've never gotten a successful exhibit."

"We won't know how successful it'll be till tomorrow," Brittney said.

"No contest," Josh said, waving his free hand. "People will eat it up. Like these tapas. You guys were featured in TdotEvents for Godsakes! It's going to be huge!" He made a sobbing face. "I'm just so happy."

"All right, Sobs McGee," Guy said, "sit down."

"Really, honey," Vanessa said, her hand on Josh's forearm and pulling him down gently. "Is this how you're going to be with our vows?"

"I watched this man go from delivery boy to genius photographer!" Josh yelled. People at other tables looked over.

"Enough," Guy said. "You're drunk."

"Everyone!" Josh said to the restaurant. "Everyone! An announcement."

"Oh, God," Brittney said, lowering her head, hand on her forehead.

"My friend here is an amazing photographer," Josh said, ignoring Vanessa's pleas to leave these nice people to their dinners. "Come to his show tomorrow. Pix of Me and You. That's what it's called. It's pictures of you and your lover. How amazing is that? Wouldn't you want to go?" He pointed to a couple. "You guys want to go. I can see it."

"Seriously, honey," Vanessa said, pulling on his sleeve harder. "You're scaring everyone."

"I love you, Guy," Josh said, lifting his glass high as he was dragged back down to his seat by his loving, if embarrassed, fiancé.

"Love you, too," Guy said.

"It's like he's a proud father," Brittney said to Guy.

"Yeah. I wonder how my folks are doing."

"Aren't they coming tomorrow?"

Guy shrugged. "I dunno."

"You didn't invite them?" Brittney said.

"Wasn't thinking of it. I haven't spoken to them in weeks."

"Invite them!"

"Nah." Guy shook his head. "They're not really into this kind of stuff."

Brittney gave Guy a flat stare. "Stumps."

Guy returned the look. "Brittney."

"Go call your parents."

Guy shook his head. "Uh-uh."

"Let's take a vote," Brittney said, turning to the others. "Show of hands. Who here thinks Guy should invite his parents to tomorrow's exhibit?"

Everyone put their hands up. Josh put both hands up.

"You haven't invited your parents?" Vanessa asked, eyes wide.

"I haven't spoken to them since New Year's. And that was just a text."

"Go call your parents," Emily said.

Guy shrugged. "I'm good. Seriously."

"Go call!" Josh screamed, adding his two corks into this.

"See what you did?" Guy whispered to Brittney. "This is all your fault."

"Majority rules here," Brittney said, smiling. She knew Guy's relationship with his parents was rocky, but surely his parents could play nice with each other to come tomorrow.

"This isn't a democracy, guys."

"I bet they'll want to hear about this," Brittney said. "What kind of parents wouldn't want to see their son's exhibit?"

"Mine," Guy said, a finality to his tone.

Josh slammed the table with the palm of his hand. "Call your parents." He pounded the table again in time with his words. "Call. Your. Parents. Call. Your. Parents. Call. Your. Parents."

Everyone else picked up the chant. Any second now the restaurant manager would barge in and kick them out.

"Okay! Okay!" Guy said, waving them to stop.

"So you'll call them?" Brittney asked.

"I'm going to the washroom. Is that okay with everyone?"

"And then you'll call them?" Brittney said. She wasn't going to let up on this. His parents were the reason this exhibit existed, the reason Guy took the photos he did. They'd trained him for tomorrow's big day.

"You're really harping on this," Guy said. "You harp. You're a harpy."

Brittney smiled, confident she'd win this round. "Call your parents, and I'll stop."

Guy groaned, getting up from his seat. "I'm going to the washroom." He pointed a finger at her. "Don't follow me, harpy."

#

As much as he hated to admit it, Brittney did have a point. When was the last time Guy had spoken to his folks? Not by text message, but spoke to them with words that could be heard instead of read? He hit a blank wall. Probably last Christmas, but even that was foggy. Mom had been on one of her vacations, dad had been working at the hospital, and he had spent Christmas with Josh's family.

After his trip to the washroom, he stood out in the hallway, took out his phone, and dialled.

He started with the more difficult of the two parents.

The phone rang. Once, twice, three times before it was answered.

Loud music blared out of the speaker. Guy yanked the phone from his ear. "Hello?" he said, bringing the phone back up to his ear. "Mom?"

A whoop sounded. Loud and shrill. Again, he pulled the phone away from him and cursed.

"Mom? It's me, Guy." *You know, your one and only son. That Guy.*

"Guy?" Mom said. "Everyone, it's my son calling me. Calling his mommy. Everyone, shhh, shhh." She was at a party somewhere. If the loud music didn't give it away, then her slurring voice certainly did. "Hi, my baby boy."

"Yeah, hi," Guy said. "Where are you?"

"Vegas!" She screamed another *whoooo!* She sounded like a twenty-two-year-old on spring break instead of a mother in her late forties.

"Of course you are." Guy shook his head. This was a bad idea. A very bad idea. If only Brittney could hear this torture. "So you're not home. I guess that means you can't come to my exhibit."

"What exhibit?"

"I'm having a photography exhibit at a gallery in Toronto."

"You should do an exhibit here in Vegas."

Guy rolled his eyes. "Maybe next time."

"I'll come to that one, okay, sweetheart?"

"Sure." She probably wouldn't either. Even if all the stars aligned, she'd find something else better to do. Some party she could get drunk and lose herself in. "Are you drinking?"

"Only a glass." She giggled.

"Right." Maybe only a bottle and working on her second.

Guy heard a man's voice through the phone. Something about how she should hang up. His mom giggled again, this one a little huskier, something Guy did *not* want to hear. "Listen, honey, I've got to go, okay? Talk soon, okay?"

"When are you coming home?" His voice sounded weak, small. Like the plea of a twelve-year-old calling for his mom.

"Oh, I don't know. Listen, can't talk right now. Later, okay? Mommy loves you very, very much." She made kissing noises.

"Just be care"—the line went dead—"ful."

Well, that happened and with no surprises either. When was the last time his mother went to anything of his? Missed graduation, forgot his birthdays. At least she sent him a card on Christmas, even if she didn't sign it. The only way he knew it was from her was the return address.

Round two: his dad. He might not even pick up.

He dialled the number. His father picked up on the second ring.

"Hey, Dad."

"Guy?"

"Yeah, it's me. Long time, no talk. How you doing?"

"Just finished with the hospital. Everything okay?"

"Lost my job." He might as well bring his father up to speed on everything that had happened and led him to this phone call.

"What?" His father coughed, probably choking on cigarette smoke. "When?"

"Over a month ago."

"Jesus Christ. What have you been doing then?"

"That's what I wanted to talk to you about," Guy said. "I have an exhibit tomorrow. For my photos. It's at this gallery. I'd like you to come."

"Tomorrow?" His father paused, and Guy knew he was only

pretending like he could find a way to come. "I'd love to, son, but I'm at the hospital all night. You know how things are."

Guy nodded, even though his father couldn't see it. Yeah, he did know. Dad had to work like a resident to make ends meet and pay for the alimony for his divorced wife. It hadn't always been that way, but the divorce killed his wallet.

"I just thought…" Guy trailed off. What was the use?

"That's great, though. I'm glad you finally got an exhibit. My son, the famous photographer."

"Not sure about fame." After all, it wasn't an exhibit in Vegas.

"Either way, I'm proud of you."

Now that was nice to hear. Guy took in a breath, feeling warmth swell in his chest. His father had never said that to him before. He figured he'd always been a disappointment to both his parents. "Thanks, Dad."

Dad yawned into the phone. "Listen, I've got an early day tomorrow."

"Sure, Dad. Can I just talk to you about something before you go?"

"I dunno, can you?"

Guy rolled his eyes. Some things never change. "*May* I talk to you about something?"

"Shoot."

"It's about a girl. I met someone."

"You didn't get her pregnant, did you?"

"No!" Guy said. "Jesus. We've never even kissed. Okay, not true. We kissed. Once. But it wasn't a real kiss. We were pretending to be boyfriend and girlfriend."

Dad sighed. "Isn't this something you and Josh can talk about?"

"He's inebriated at the moment."

"What about this girl?"

"I like her, Dad. Like I really like her. She's smart and creative and passionate. She makes me laugh. I get along with her so easily. She's the owner of the gallery. We've been working on this exhibit together. All this is because of her."

"She pretty?" Dad asked. Of course, his number one vice: pretty objects. Hence his mother.

But Brittney was pretty. Of course, she was. She'd been a freaking model. But that hadn't even occurred to him. That wasn't the reason why he liked her. "Yeah, Dad, she is. She's gorgeous." Her beauty was a bonus, the icing on the cake, the digestive after a delicious gourmet meal. "A real looker. Used to be a model."

"Not bad, son. Ask her out."

"You think?"

"What do you have to lose? Do it after the exhibit."

Not a bad idea. With the exhibit over tomorrow he could ask her out and not worry about making things awkward if she said no. "I'll do that. Thanks, Dad."

"Is that what you needed? Some positive reinforcement?"

"Something like that."

"Well, you have my brains and your mother's beauty. You're the perfect catch."

"Not sure about either of those things," Guy said. He was technically unemployed, definitely unemployable. His scratched at his scraggly beard and picked at his teeth.

"You want me to send you some money?"

"No, no. I'm okay." Dad had enough on his plate. He didn't need to add his son to his expense column.

"You sure?"

"Positive."

"You can always move back in with me. Could use the company."

"I live in a better apartment than you," Guy said, and that was saying a lot, given how shitty his apartment was.

"True," Dad said. "Move back in the old house with your mother?"

"I'm good."

#

Brittney searched for Guy. She craned her neck to get a better look. He was nowhere in sight and had been gone awhile. Their table had been cleared of the plates and the waiter had left the bill without them asking for it. A sure sign that their behaviour—and by "their" she meant "Josh"—had taken its toll.

"You okay?" Emily said.

"Huh?" Brittney leaned farther, lifting off her chair slightly. He must be calling his parents. Hopefully it was going well. "Guy's just been gone a long time."

"You're worried about him."

"Was that a question?" It hadn't sounded like one.

Emily shrugged, sipping a glass of water. She didn't drink like the rest of them. Said the alcohol worsened her anxieties. Josh drank more than enough for the both. "Just an interesting observation."

Guy came into view. She couldn't tell by his expression if he was happy or not. He had one hand holding the phone the other cupping his ear. "Good." She sighed, sitting back down. "He's on the phone. Probably talking to his parents."

"You like him."

Brittney blinked. "What?" She shook her head. "Of course, I like him. I wouldn't be in business with him if I didn't like him."

"No, no. You like him in an I-want-to-have-his-babies kind of way."

"Are you crazy?" She glanced over at the other side of the table at Vanessa and Josh. Vanessa was busy taking care of her drunk fiancé, who had spilled wine on his shirt. Thank God for that because she didn't want them hearing what Emily had insinuated. "No way. Uh-uh."

"Admit it." A smile spread across Emily's face. "You're attracted to him."

"He's not that good looking," Brittney said, but her tone betrayed her. Guy did have a certain charm to him. Boyish, but not childish. Not exactly rugged. He always seemed like he had just gotten out of bed, and it was kind of cute. "Okay, he's kind of good looking."

"Are you kidding me? He's cute."

"Maybe if he got some new clothes and shaved that ratty beard." If only he put in ten minutes on his appearance. But he didn't. He hated that sort of thing.

"Gorgeous eyes. Perfect lips."

Brittney gave Emily a cocked eyebrow. "I think *you* like him."

"Nooooo." She leaned closer to Brittney. "What I think is that he likes you back."

"You think so?"

"You care that much?"

Emily had her. Maybe Brittney really did like Guy. He was a damn good kisser and very talented, even if he didn't want to be talented in the thing he was talented in. Stubborn, okay. Maybe a little bit of an underachiever. But he was working on that with this exhibit.

He paced back and forth from the hallway, coming into view, going out of view. He ran a hand over his hair. "He looks upset."

"He does," Emily said. "Maybe it's not going too well with his family."

"His parents are divorced. And he's never really talked about them." Great—

she may have just sent him on a suicide mission. One-stop ticket to heartbreak, and just a day before his exhibit.

"I think we just sent him to the electric chair," Emily said.

"It's all my fault." He caught her staring at him and their eyes locked for a second before he looked away. "I'm going to go see that everything's okay."

Emily smiled. "Like a good girlfriend would do."

"Stop that."

She reached him as he got off the phone, his back to her. She tapped his shoulder. He jumped and turned around. When he saw it was her, he breathed relief.

"Everything all right?" Brittney asked.

"Yeah," he said, stuffing the phone back in his pocket. "Just talking to my folks." He sounded exhausted.

"Are they coming tomorrow?" Brittney asked, almost too afraid to ask. She bit her lip.

Guy shook his head, lips pursed.

"I'm sorry."

"It's all right," he said, stuffing his hands in his pockets. "Listen…"

"Yeah?" Brittney's heart fluttered. She didn't know why. Something in the way he said listen.

"I just wanted to thank you for everything you've done for me. With the exhibit and opening the doors of your gallery to a no-name like me."

She smiled, put her hand on his shoulder. "I should be thanking you. I wasn't getting much traction myself. You're my first client."

"You would've done fine. You're pretty capable."

"Thanks." Her voice caught in her throat. If you asked anyone else, being called capable wouldn't likely be on their top five best compliments. But she melted. "You're not so bad yourself."

Guy sighed, leaned back against the wall and crossed his arms over his chest. "I'm pretty nervous about tomorrow, though."

She could see it on his face, the faint worry lines around his eyes and forehead. "Me, too," she said. "But it'll be great. Everything is set up. We've got amazing coverage. More coverage than we could have ever asked for."

"That's what scares me. What if all these people come, and nobody likes it?"

"They'll love it."

"How can you be so sure?"

"Because we're giving people what they want most." She truly believed it. It was the type of thing that just about anyone wanted to see. Young and old, male or female, married or single. Even if you claimed yourself a player, you'd still want to know if this whole love thing existed. The audience appeal was wide and vast.

"I don't know anything about love."

Was he referring to his parents and their lack of love? Or did he mean that he'd never loved anyone himself? He'd never spoken of a girlfriend, but he flirted with her all the time. She always took it as his boyish, playful manner, but maybe there was something more to it than that.

"That's not true," she said. "You don't know how to explain it or define it. No one does. That's why you're showing it. You can see it, Guy. It's an incredible… I dunno. Gift. Talent. Whatever you want to call it. You can see more than a couple holding hands or laughing at an inside joke. You see the love inside them, and you manage to bring it out and capture it with your camera. It's really something."

"And what if other people don't see it?"

"I see it," Brittney said. "In every picture you took and that we've displayed in the gallery, I see it."

Guy snickered. "Did it make you a believer in love?"

Brittney smiled. "Yes." His photos gave her hope, especially after she'd pretty much shunned love after what Derrick had done. She believed that love, true love, the kind of love Josh and Vanessa had, the kind of love that Guy photographed, still waited for her. It waited for her to grab hold and take it for herself.

Guy sighed dramatically. "Everyone's going to have a date tomorrow. I'll be the odd man out."

"How could you not get a date for your big day?" She could tell he was only kidding around, but he wasn't the only one who could have some fun. Funny—she knew him a lot better than she would have first thought. She'd gotten used to his mannerisms over the past month. She could guess what he'd say and do, and be right about it.

"I'm very picky," he said, and his mouth curved ever so slightly.

"Better find someone quick."

"I know, right? Time is running out."

"What are you looking for?" she asked.

"Well, she'd have to be super smart, super accomplished, and super amazing at what she does."

"Any idea who this superwoman might be?"

Guy shrugged. "Was kind of hoping it'd be you."

"Moi?"

"Yeah. Unless you have a date already."

She thought a moment, then the corner of her lip curled up in a smile. "I was going to bring Emily."

"Emily? No, come on."

Brittney put her hands up. "She's a sensitive one. Can't leave her alone."

"I concur. But you're going to have to cut the umbilical cord eventually."

She laughed, a real belly laugh. It'd been awhile since she'd laughed like that. It wasn't even that good of a joke. So what had made her laugh so hard? She felt comfortable around Guy, that was it. Comfortable and safe enough to let herself go and laugh like a little girl. When she sobered up, Guy said, "Brittany Director Collar."

It sounded like a wedding proposal, all formal. "Yes, Guy Stumps Moraine."

"Will you be my date to the exhibit?"

"Yes," she said, "I will."

She'd never been so sure of something in her life.

Chapter Eleven

Bowls of cinnamon hearts and chocolate hearts were strewn about on tables draped with pink and red cloths. On other tables stood champagne glasses with bubbly and fresh water for those who didn't drink. Rose petals drifted on the floor. Every wall was covered with Guy's photos encased in black frames. Still frames, on the back a vignette of how the photographed couple fell in love, rested in stacks on a table in the front.

If she hadn't done the set up herself, Brittney wouldn't have recognized the Collar Gallery. It had transformed for this very special day. Her mother had told her that the opening night of any exhibit meant the gallery changed, taking on the theme of the artwork. It had to be an immersive experience.

"You look great," Emily said.

"Thanks." Brittney had makeup on and a red and black dress she had worn for a shoot that she'd liked so much she hadn't given it up. It hugged her body, showing off enough cleavage and leg to be respectfully sexy but not garishly slutty. She took a breath and did one last scan of the gallery. "We got everything, right?"

"Everything from your list," Emily said.

Brittney had made a task list of everything they needed, and ticked off each task once completed. Her mother suggested it and gave her a copy from her files. Worked pretty damn well. It covered everything from tables, food, drinks, lighting, advertising. And Brittney loved checking the boxes off when a task was completed. Made her feel like she was doing something, making progress.

Still, something was missing. Probably nothing, but it was one of those things that would bother her the whole night.

The front door chimed. Heeled shoes sounded. Brittney checked the time on her phone. It was almost game time. That better be Guy.

It wasn't. Josh and Vanessa came in, Josh dressed in a dark blue suit with a white collared shirt and pink tie, and Vanessa in a matching dark blue dress with sparkling silver heels that Brittney would steal if she had the chance to.

Vanessa surveyed the gallery with wide eyes. "Wow, guys. Everything looks fantastic."

Brittney's shoulders sagged, the tension fleeing her body. First person to see the gallery other than Emily and Guy, and it was a compliment. So what if Vanessa was a friend? Still counted. "Thanks."

"You ready for the big night?"

"No," Brittney said with a smile. Part of her wanted this and part of her wanted to hide under her desk and suck on her thumb like she used to do when she was a kid.

"You'll do great."

"Guy's not with you?"

Josh was on his phone. "I texted him before. He's coming."

Then the door opened again, and this time it was Guy.

But not a Guy Brittney recognized. This Guy was cleaned up. Sharp. Even, dare she say, professional. He wore a charcoal suit with a pink collared shirt and sleek black shoes. Polished? Probably. He'd even trimmed his beard. Granted, he still had his I-don't-care attitude. His hair stuck up in the back a little. But that was better than coming in sweatpants and a hoody.

"You look…" Brittney started.

"Halfway decent?" Guy said. He pulled the sleeves up on his jacket. Seemed like the jacket was a bit big for him.

"I would say three-fourths. What's that?"

"Got you a little something," he said, passing her an envelope. "Happy Week Before Valentine's Day."

She smiled, and her heart bounced in her chest. "You didn't have to."

He shrugged. "Just a little thank you."

"What is it?" Brittney asked.

"A diamond necklace."

"In an envelope?"

Guy rolled his eyes "Maybe a macaroni necklace."

"Thanks, Stumps," she said, kissing him on the cheek. When she pulled back, Emily gave her a raised eyebrow and snarky look that said *Tell him how you feel, dammit!* before she went to the gallery's foyer. "I didn't get you anything." She didn't know she was supposed to. Gifts weren't discussed. That wasn't on Mom's task list.

Guy opened his arms to the gallery. "You got me all this."

"It's starting," Emily called from the foyer. "People are already lining up to get in."

Guy clapped his hands, rubbing them together. "So it begins."

"Happy Week Before Valentine's Day, everyone," Brittney said, as she made her way to greet her customers while thinking to herself that this better be a freaking success.

Beautiful couples, shivering in the February cold, lined up outside the door. Brittney opened the proverbial floodgates to the gallery, and the couples flowed in, some of whom Brittney recognized from their work with Guy. But the majority were new.

Brittney stood by the door, welcoming everyone. "Hi, and welcome to the Pix of Me and You Exhibit where you'll see love in all its forms." Wow, that sounded cheesy. She'd have to think up something cleverer. "There's a coat check in the back as well."

"Are you the artist?" a girl asked.

"I wish," Brittney said. "I'm the gallery director. The artist, Guy Moraine, is here tonight, of course. You can see him inside." She wanted to describe him as looking better than most days but decided against it.

"Think we could get a picture taken?"

"You'd have to ask Guy, but I'm sure he wouldn't mind."

They went inside, and Brittney ushered in a few more.

A flash sounded from the corner of the room. Brittney jerked and let out a yelp louder and shriller than she'd care to admit. The all-too-familiar flash had been intended for her. She wanted no part of that tonight. She didn't want to be reminded of a time when she felt stupid and weak. Sure, she had dressed up nice enough to have a photo taken of her, but that didn't mean she wanted one.

The culprit was a man she had previously let in. He wore his jacket open and held a camera in his hands. A slimy smile donned his face. She had to hide her scowl.

"I'm with *416 Magazine*," he said. *416 Magazine* was an alternative weekly magazine mixing news, arts, and events all into one. "Just doing a piece on this gallery. It's pretty interesting."

"Thanks," Brittney said, with as little venom as she could muster. She wanted to tell him off but didn't want to jeopardize any publicity. *Play nice*, she told herself.

"You think you could spare a few words?"

"Uh…" She welcomed more couples in, waving them in as fast as she could. If she looked busy, she wouldn't have to spare any words, let alone a few.

Taking the hint, the photographer said, "Maybe a little later."

"Sure."

He turned around, took a few steps, then turned back. He frowned, rubbing a hand over his chin. "Don't I know you from somewhere?"

"I don't think so." Her stomach knotted. He better not recognize her from her modelling days.

"You look so familiar." He checked her out, from the top of her head to heels. She pulled her skirt down, feeling exposed. "Like I've seen you wear that dress before."

The dress was a bad idea. She should've given it away and bought something new, something cheap. "I can't imagine where—"

The journalist snapped his fingers. "You're a model, right? Yeah. Brittney Collar. Duh. I'm so stupid. Wow. So this is what you're doing now?"

"Yup." The jig was up, caught red-dressed. "You found me."

"Found you is right." His smile broadened and grew slimier. It was like he sensed a new story. Forget the gallery, he had the model who'd disappeared off the grid with no warning. "You just deleted your whole brand. Your whole image. Disappeared like Houdini."

She'd sure like to disappear now.

"You are even hotter in person." That made her cringe. For her, the worst compliment from a man was being called "hot." Scratch that, it was the second worst; the absolute worst thing was to be called "hawt." "Think you'll ever go back to modelling?"

"Uh…" Brittney searched for a way out, but the journalist had her cornered. She didn't want to offend him, but she also didn't want to answer any of his questions either. She craned her neck back hoping for Guy to come. Or Emily. Or even Vanessa or Josh. Someone or something. She'd welcome a falling meteor.

"She's fine where she is, wouldn't you say so, Brandon?"

Brittney whipped back around. Her mother—her sweet, loving, superheroine of a mother—stood at the doorway dressed in an elegant black gown. She looked stunning, her neck brace off and her bruises and scars fully healed. The only thing that marred her appearance was the glare she openly gave to the photographer, Brandon.

"Who are you?" Brandon asked, eyebrow cocked.

"I own this gallery," Helene said.

Brandon swallowed, taking a step back. "How do you know me?"

"I know all the journalists and photographers at the event magazines." Helene stepped into her gallery, a place she hadn't been back into since the accident. "They run my ad campaigns for new exhibits."

"Right. Collar. Helene." He pieced it together, and the more he pieced together, the more the colour drained from his cheeks. "Of course. I remember you, too."

"Here for the exhibit or to harass my daughter for an exclusive on her modelling exodus?"

Now Brandon was cornered. He shrugged. "A little bit of both?" His voice was small, its confidence and assurance gone, his slimy face replaced with a look like he'd been punched in the stomach.

Helene shook her head slowly. "Try again, my boy."

"I'll go do what I came here for," Brandon said, pointing to the back.

Helene smiled, her expression transforming from she-devil to she-angel. "Enjoy your stay."

Brandon walked off down the hall. He didn't glance back at them.

"Thanks, Mom," Brittney said, her nerves settling. "But what are you doing here?"

She waved her hand. "Like I'd miss my daughter's first exhibit?"

"You sure you're up to it? How are you feeling?"

She looked great, that was for sure.

"As full of energy as a twelve-year-old girl," Helene said. "Okay, a twelve-year-old girl on pain meds."

Brittney's eyes widened. "You didn't drive here, did you?"

"A taxi driver was nice enough to bring me. Besides, I wanted to see what you've done with the place."

"It's spic and span."

"Where's Emily?" Helene's tone turned all business.

"Coat check."

"Who's doing the orders when someone wants to buy?"

"Uh…"

Helene's nostrils flared. "You didn't hire extra help?"

Brittney shrugged. Now she felt like she was the one at the mercy of her mother's hellish glare. "Was that on the task list?"

Helene put her hand on Brittney's arm, guiding her away from the entrance and toward the exhibit. "Tell me something, sweetheart." She had on a deceptively sweet tone. "How good are you with numbers?"

#

With eyes wide and shoulders tensed, Guy watched people pour into the gallery. He gripped the slender champagne glass like it somehow gave him superhuman confidence the tighter he held onto it. At the moment, however, it wasn't working. He was cramped up, closed in, boxed shut. There were a lot more people here than he'd expected. Even when he imagined the best-case scenario, he forgot to imagine not just the sheer number of people, but the smiling, laughing, loving faces of couples dressed up in suits and dresses and Windsor knotted ties and dazzling high heels. Who knew this many people cared about art?

These people hadn't come just for the art, though. They'd come to see love. Guy had to admit, he would never have gotten this many people if Brittney had agreed to use his other photos.

Brittney had been right about this whole thing. She had orchestrated it from small beginning to flourishing end. She'd been right about the exhibit's theme, his talent, the setup, the promotion.

She was an incredible woman.

"You should go mingle," Emily said, nudging him with her elbow. She was at the far back of the gallery behind the coat check counter. Guy stood near to her, leaning on the counter.

"I'm good." He drained the rest of the champagne and left it on the countertop, then stuffed his hands in his pockets. Mingle? That was a fancy term for networking, wasn't it? Sounded like something Josh did, not Guy. He had no clue what to say to so many people.

"But you're the artist. The star. This is part of your job. Go and market your work."

Guy shook his head, balled his hands into fists. "The work speaks for itself." That sounded like a cop out even to his own ears.

Emily blew out a breath. "But you got all dolled up."

Now it was his turn to exhale the breath he'd been holding. "I look the same." If anyone, Emily was dolled up. As in, she really did resemble a doll. Hair, makeup, getup. Granted, with all the tattoos, she was more of a gothic doll, but still a doll.

"Oh, please. You're wearing a suit. A new one, too."

"Not new. One of Josh's old ones." Which explained why the sleeves were a tad bit too long. Still, way better than wearing his dad's old suit.

"You shaved," Emily said.

"I trimmed. Big difference." He even liked it trimmed.

"Big difference is right," she said, her eyes sparkling. "You're a changed man."

"Haven't changed a bit," he said. The only thing he'd change was the topic, adding, "Brittney, on the other hand…"

Emily nodded. "She looks like her modelling pictures."

"Really?" Guy said, eyebrows raised. He couldn't deny how beautiful she was tonight. She usually dressed more professional and businesslike. Not so much makeup either. But tonight she looked ready for the Miss America pageant.

"Haven't you seen her photos before?"

"Yeah, right. Have you met me?" Even when he'd found out she was a model, he had zero interest in Googling her model photos. He gained nothing by seeing a fake Brittney. Sure, she looked good tonight. Spectacular even. But he liked her without all the fancy getup just the same.

Though that dress of hers hugged parts of her body that her business-wear hid. And the red went with her blond hair and unblemished skin. She looked like… Well, she looked like a model.

Emily rolled her eyes. "For someone who hates portrait photography, you sure got a lot of people photographed in your exhibit."

Guy narrowed his eyes at her. "I liked you better when you wouldn't talk to me."

"Heard that one before." She pushed him gently. "Now go mingle. Let me do my work, and you do yours."

Guy groaned and his shoulders sagged. "*Fiiiiine.*"

He left Emily with the coats. He put a smile on his face and approached the people he knew, couples he had photographed and were in the exhibit. He'd photographed couples from all walks of life. Young couples, old couples, interracial couples, gay and lesbian couples, a couple where the husband had a disability, couples from different religions, like the Sikh couple whose husband had worn a turban and a bushy beard. Love came in all shapes, sizes, and forms. On the surface the photos looked different, some having a level of seriousness to them while others were straight out whacky fun, but deep down they all shared the same thing, had the same message, showed the love the couple had for each other.

Guy warmed up his social muscles enough to stretch out and talk to the new people he didn't recognize, asking them how they found out about the place. Most had heard about it online at the TDotEvents blog. Others had heard from friends and friends of friends. Everyone told them how much they loved his work. New couples seeing the photos for the first time asked if they could get a photo done. Guy hadn't thought that would happen, but they offered to pay him, and who was he to deny them such a loving request? He was, after all, the love photographer.

Huh—he'd even begun to believe it himself.

"Excuse me, are you the artist?"

Guy turned around. A man in a dark purple suit, crisp white shirt, and black tie stood in front of him. The man was all sharp and clean edges. Nothing rumpled or wrinkled. His face was smooth, too, like a sculpture of Apollo. "Yes. I'm Guy Moraine."

The sculptured man put his manicured hand out. "Tyler Fawkes."

Guy took the man's hand—soft as a pillow—and shook it. Then kept shaking it. The man's name echoed in his mind. Guy frowned. "Fawkes. Fawkes. I know that name. Where do I know that name?"

Tyler Fawkes smiled wryly, reached into his suit jacket pocket, and pulled out a card. "Maybe this will jog your memory?"

Guy took the card. Fawkes Photography Studio was printed on the front. Now that was a name he knew. The biggest photography studio in Canada.

Guy looked up at Tyler, back down at the card, back up at Tyler. This was the president of Fawkes Photography. This was *the guy* every photographer wanted to meet. And here he was, standing in front of Guy, at Guy's exhibit, talking to Guy.

"Holy shit."

#

With her mother in tow, Brittney couldn't help but see mistakes in the exhibit's setup. Photos that should've been placed a little higher or lower on the walls, others that should've been grouped together for a stronger impact. Offering a variety of drinks instead of water and champagne, the latter having taken a toll on the budget. Having the servers come by with food platters instead of leaving the food out on tables like a buffet.

Yet no one was complaining about the food or drinks. Instead, people laughed and chatted and generally seemed happy to be here, enjoying the exhibit, the couples, and crowds around them. Even Guy was mingling, talking to someone in a dark purple suit.

Helene's eyes widened. "This is the busiest the gallery's ever been."

"You're kidding."

Helene shook her head, then smiled at Brittney, taking her hand and squeezing. "This was a brilliant idea, sweetheart. Exhibit openings are never this busy. You picked the right topic. Chose the perfect time. And have a very talented photographer."

"It all kind of… fell into my lap," Brittney said, heat rising in her cheeks.

"That's not true, and you know it."

Deep down she did, and pride swelled in her chest at what she'd managed to accomplish here. She sighed heavily—one of those oh-my-God-I-can't-believe-I-made-it-this-far kind of sighs. All the tension from tonight, tension she'd kept bottled up since the first day she walked into the gallery as its director, eased out of her. But she hadn't made this night happen alone. Guy had been the one who found her and who had the talent. Brittney had put the moving pieces together, seeing the puzzle for what it was. That was what businesspeople did, right? People with brains? Project managers? They managed expectations and put two and two together for maximum results. They made things work.

But it had been a team effort. She couldn't have done it without Guy.

"I'm pleasantly surprised," Helene said.

"You didn't think I could do it?" A sinking feeling grew in the pit of her stomach.

"No, I knew you could do it. I just didn't think you'd believe in yourself enough to pull it off." She kissed Brittney on the cheek. "I am one proud mother."

Brittney's mouth hung agape. It wasn't the first time her mother had said that she was proud of Brittney, but it had always seemed like it was just something mothers said to their daughters. This time, though, Brittney had made something happen with what her mother had given her—which wasn't that much—and she had made a success of the gallery and of herself. She stood up tall, pulling her shoulders back. Yeah, she felt proud of herself, too.

"Hi, stranger," Emily said, coming up to Helene and Brittney.

"Emily!" Helene gave Emily a gentle hug, a smile spreading across her face. Emily had worked at the gallery for nearly a year before the accident, and given how close Brittney and Emily had become over the period of a month, it was only natural that Helene and Emily would be as thread to fabric.

"You feeling better?"

"Much better, my love. I see Brittney's kept you busy."

"You might have to start paying me," Emily said, wiggling her eyebrows.

"You signed up for a free internship, and a free internship you shall have."

Emily's shoulders sagged. "You know they abolished slavery."

"But think about all the experience you're getting," Brittney added.

"Just from this night alone," Helene said. "This is gold for resumes."

"But I want to work for you," Emily whined. She clasped

Helene's hands together and brought them closer to her, a glimmer in her smoky, gothic eyes. "You're the only one for me."

"Finish your degree first."

It was almost as if Emily was Helene's other daughter, which made sense. For the past month, Emily had felt like the little sister Brittney never had.

"I'm going to look at the displays," Helene said.

"I'll come with you," Brittney said. Helene was still recovering, and the last thing Brittney wanted was for her to fall.

"No, no. I'll manage."

Brittney and Emily stood together, watching the gallery packed with couples. It felt so strange. Usually the place was so empty and quiet. Usually it was only Brittney, Emily, and Guy.

Emily said something, but she said it in a whisper.

"I missed that." Brittney said, leaning closer to Emily. The chatter had grown louder. Music! She missed music. Even some slow background music would've done wonders. Then again, where would she find the funds for speakers?

Emily had her head down, her hands behind her back. She swayed on her feet. "I said you inspired me."

Emily must have meant the dress, the makeup. "Does this mean you're going to stop dressing less like a punk rocker?"

She laughed, raising her head. She had a cute smile under all that gothic makeup. Whoever snatched her up would be one lucky guy. "No. You see this?"

"Your harmonica?"

"I booked the upstairs at Sneaky Dees. They have events up there some nights. I'm going to play live. Do a performance in front of all these people I don't know. I want to tackle my social anxiety by doing something completely out of my comfort zone. Just like you did."

Brittney blinked. "I did?"

Emily waved her hand to the gallery. "This is far from modelling on Instagram."

True. After all, none of these photos had been of her. And whereas modelling left her feeling superficial, the exhibit left her feeling fulfilled for the first time in her life.

"I want you to come to the performance. You will, right?"

Brittney winked. "Save me a front row seat."

"Oh, no." The colour drained from Emily's face, making her cheeks paler than they already were. "You'll have to sit in the back. I can't perform if you're sitting right at the front with your eyes on me. Hell no."

"I thought you said you wanted to tackle your social anxiety?"

Emily nodded. "Baby steps."

Brittney sighed. "I'll be right outside then. Watching from the window."

"Perfect." She leaned into Brittney conspiratorially. "Who are Josh and Vanessa talking to? The dude with the camera?"

"Some journalist. He's doing a piece on this exhibit." And he was a piece of work himself.

"That's amazing."

"What would be more amazing is if we sold some pieces."

"I'll set up the cash if you send them over to me."

"Deal."

#

Tyler Fawkes laughed. *The* Tyler Fawkes had laughed at something Guy said. Was there a better sound than hearing Tyler Fawkes laugh? Not right now there wasn't. Tyler's ha-ha-ha was music to Guy's ears. A choir of joy.

"Sorry," Guy said, scratching the back of his neck, "I didn't mean 'holy shit' in a bad way. I meant it in the best way imaginable. "

"I'll take it as a compliment."

"I just can't believe you're here. You're like… a god in the world of photography. My hero." Guy laid it on a little too thick. *Ease back or you'll scare him off.* "How did you find out about the exhibit?"

"Same as everyone else in here. Blogs, social media. You guys must have one hell of a publicist."

Yes, they did. The publicist was called a great idea and word of mouth.

"This is good work," Fawkes said, indicating the displays on the wall.

Guy's heartbeat quickened. His legs turned to jelly. He swallowed, trying to keep calm, and wiggled his toes to stay present. He didn't want to miss a thing. "Thank you. That means a lot to me coming from you."

"What made you do this kind of work?"

"The gallery director got it out of me."

Fawkes frowned. "You don't usually take these kinds of photos?"

"I used to, but hadn't in a long time. Until now, actually. She saw my old ones and loved them and wanted to do more. Looks like she was right." He hesitated. What if Fawkes thought Guy only did this type of photography? Then he'd be pigeon-holed. As much a success as the exhibit was, his passion in photography was diverse. He wanted to be truthful with Fawkes so he added, "But it's not my real passion."

"What is?"

"Anything but this."

Fawkes laughed again. A jolly laugh, the kind where you throw your head back and your shoulders shake. If he wasn't so slender, he'd make a great Santa Claus for the kids at Eaton Centre. "I must say, though…" He pointed to one of the photos, a young newlywed couple that Guy had to admit was one of his favourites, too. "You have a real talent for it."

"I appreciate that. But if I could photograph something else, that would be great. I've got a bunch of photos in my portfolio. Fine art pieces, landscapes, architecture, animals. I'm a pretty good photo editor, too."

That sounded like something he'd say in an interview. Was Fawkes interviewing him now? Some kind of impromptu interview? Careers were made this way, right? Networking and mingling. Schmoozing, Josh called it. And to think he'd thought he was going to sit by the coat check all night with his hands in his pockets. Ludicrous! If only he could wish his resume to magically appear in his hand, he'd be set.

"My team does get a lot of different contracts," Fawkes said. "And from all over the world."

"Don't I know it," Guy said. "I'll admit I've creeped you a bit. Only through Google, though, I swear."

That earned him another chuckle from Fawkes. It was like a point system. He had to keep Fawkes laughing. Charm the pants off him. Funny people were considered charming people, and charming people were considered good people to work with, and good people to work with were hired and given contracts all over the world. That was how Josh climbed the corporate ladder, charming up and down the office hallways.

"Do you have an agent?"

"None."

"Studio?"

"You're standing in it."

Fawkes eyes widened. "You did all this by yourself?"

"I had help. Brittney. Her team here."

"That's the modelesque lady over there?" Fawkes asked. "The gallery director?"

"That's her."

Tyler studied her with a photographer's eyes, a world-famous photographer's eyes. "She's stunning."

"And smart," Guy added.

"Where do you see yourself going next?"

"Ah, that's a good question." A good question to which he had no good answer. After tonight, he'd probably start looking for jobs at different studios. Maybe take on some freelance work. Already he'd gotten a few business cards from people tonight to take photos.

"Why'd you do this exhibit?"

"Money and fame?"

Fawkes laughed. "No, really."

"I wanted to prove to myself that I could do it. And get noticed for it. I didn't think it would get this big, though. Definitely didn't think it'd catch your attention. Don't you have assistants who come to these things?"

"Usually, but this one struck a chord. Did you always want to be a photographer?"

Guy put his hand at waist level. "Ever since I was about this tall. My dad bought me a camera when I was little, and as you can see"—even now the camera hung off his neck—"I've never let it go."

"You definitely have an eye for beauty," Fawkes said. "I'm divorced, and yet these pictures could persuade me to believe in love again. "

"Got to see it to believe it, right?"

Fawkes smiled at him. Just smiled and stared at Guy, like he silently tried to figure out what to make of Guy. Guy stared back, willing good vibrations from himself to Fawkes. This was the moment. Their little interview had come to an end. Guy could feel it in his bones. It'd been seconds that Fawkes stared at him—literally no more than three or four seconds—yet it felt like an eternity.

Finally, Fawkes said, "How would you"—Guy watched his lips

move, and they seemed to do so in slow motion, each word echoing in Guy's mind—"like to work for me?"

"Are you serious?" Guy blurted out, then pressed his lips together. People like Tyler Fawkes didn't offer jobs as a gag.

"Even more serious now that I know you did this all on your lonesome. Look around you, Guy. All these people are here for you. You even have the media here. That's uncommon for an exhibit. You've got a gift. I'd be happy to have you on my team."

"Holy shit."

Fawkes laughed. "Holy shit is right. You have my card. Call me, and we'll talk about your future."

"My future? With Fawkes Photography?"

Fawkes cocked an eyebrow. "You going to say holy shit again?"

#

Money exchanged hands. Credit cards were swiped. Red dots were added to the photos to delineate which were sold and which were still on sale. Once Emily set up the cash register, the art enthusiasts broke off from the throng and got down to business. And business was good. Some of the photos sold in the hundreds.

It was odd, though. A small part of Brittney believed no one would want to buy a photo of a couple they didn't know but were clearly in love. She knew the exhibit would be interesting enough for people to come in and see the photography, but to purchase? It was like buying a picture frame but keeping the stock photo in the frame instead of replacing it with one of your own.

But, wait—that wasn't it at all. Those stock photos were the kinds of photos that Guy hated, fake and disingenuous. Brittney herself didn't like them. The photos in the exhibit, on the other hand, were real, honest, and showed emotion. They told a story that was relatable, something everyone wanted. They made you feel. They were art.

"I hope you enjoy your artwork," Brittney said to the couple buying a piece Guy did outside instead of in the gallery. The wife hooked her arm around her husband's. They were older, and the way they looked at the photo they had purchased seemed to rekindle something inside of them. They'd be able to pick up their piece a few months after the exhibit was over.

Guy came up to her. He held a business card with both hands up to his chest. The smile he wore lit up his face, his eyes big and bright. Doubtless, she must've had the same expression. She was making money, running a business.

She was so excited her hands shook. "I need a break," she said to Guy.

"Me, too," he said through his toothy smile. If happiness was a drug, he was on it. "Meet you in the basement?"

"Definitely."

He started off first. Brittney told Emily to take over the fort if need be. She nodded vigorously. She probably wouldn't really talk to any of the customers because of her social anxiety, but Helene would help.

Less than ten minutes later, Brittney went to the back where the washrooms were, then down a flight of stairs to the basement where storage was kept. Pieces of artwork from past exhibits, sold and waiting for pickup in paper and plastic, leaned against the walls.

Guy paced, kicking up dust with his feet. He looked handsome, happy, and like he'd burst if he didn't tell her what he wanted to tell her. He grabbed both her hands. "Thank you so much for everything you've done."

"No, no, thank you," Brittney said. It warmed her heart to know she'd done something right outside of putting on a skimpy dress and snapping a few photos.

"Even more amazing—I think I got a job out of this."

And the night's boons kept booming. "Congratulations!"

"With like a big photography studio. Like big. Like dream come true big."

"I'm happy for you, Guy. Really, I am."

"I feel like a million bucks. Like a success finally. You have no idea what this means to me. It's all thanks to you."

He pulled her in and wrapped his arms around her, squeezing her. Seconds rolled by, and neither of them had made the move to separate. She nestled into the nape of his neck, her hands along his back. She breathed him in, smelling the laundry detergent he used. It smelled nice, like home. She couldn't help but think how lovely it would be to cuddle with Guy on a couch watching TV or in a bed taking a nap. She smiled, breathed a silent chuckle through her nose. Why was she having these thoughts right now? And why did the image of her with Guy seem so…picturesque?

She relaxed, leaning her body weight into him. Weeks of hard work poured out of her. He held her tightly, didn't let go or step back even though she'd let herself practically free fall into him. He kept her up with no protest. He was solid. She closed her eyes and the curl of his longish hair tickled her cheek. He caressed her back. Slow, long strokes. It sent a tingling sensation down her spine—not unpleasant at all, but comforting. She felt safe.

She felt right, too. None of this seemed out of place. Not that they touched all the time. Actually, the last time had been at the Eaton Centre where she'd had her unfortunate run-in with Derrick. But Guy had been there for her, backed her up. The two of them had been a team then, too. Relying on each other. Supporting each other.

Gently, she pulled back and met some resistance. It seemed like he didn't want to let her go, but when he realized what she was doing, his hold on her eased. In her heels, they were eye to eye. So close she felt his breath on her mouth. He looked at her eyes for a moment, then his gaze shifted to her lips, then back up to her eyes.

His heart beat fast. She could feel it. So was hers.

He tilted his head ever so slightly. She closed her eyes. His lips brushed against hers. A feathery touch, a very light kiss. It was almost as if he was asking for permission.

Yes, you can kiss me.

She leaned toward him and kissed him fully. Their lips mashed together, overlapping.

Their kissing came more powerfully. Like a dam had been broken. His hand cupped her cheek, while the other hand was on her hip.

And while they were kissing, people upstairs, dozens of couples, were looking at love captured in a single moment.

In this moment, they themselves would've made one of those pictures.

Did she really just think that? Guy's pictures were of love, but this was just… kissing. Right?

His hand lowered from her hip to her ass. More than just kissing, then.

And she wanted more. He pulled her into him, kissing her as he had that day at the Eaton Centre, only this time with more purpose, powerful and stronger. Full of passion and truth. All the qualities of his photos.

Yes, this was definitely more than just kissing.

"You're so beautiful," he whispered to her.

She stiffened.

"Gorgeous."

Her eyes opened.

"Hot."

She stopped kissing him back. The comments from her Instagram account popped up in her mind. Hot. Gorgeous. Beautiful.

"I've never met anyone as beautiful as you."

She pushed him while he was in mid-kiss. He stumbled back. "What's wrong?"

"I can't believe you just said that."

He blinked. "That you're beautiful?"

"Is that why you like me? Is that why you kissed me now?"

"What? No, of course not. That's not why I like you."

"Then why did you say those things?"

"Did you think I wouldn't notice that you happen to be pretty, too?"

She stepped back. *Pretty*. Guy had never called her pretty. Plenty of other men had called her that before, men who had used her for her looks, who only wanted her for her appearance. That hadn't been Guy, until now. He was just like the rest of them, only liking her for who she was on the surface.

Would he have even kissed her if she hadn't been wearing this dress? All he saw was her appearance. It was all she had; everything that made her…her.

She thought Guy was different, thought he was the one guy who could see below the surface. She'd been wrong. "We shouldn't have done this," she said, wiping her lips.

"I thought—"

"You thought wrong," she said.

"Hold on," he said. "I like you, Brittney. Really I do."

She shook her head. "No, you don't. You like me now because of this dress and the way I look."

He shook his head, chuckling. The jerk actually chuckled. "That's not it at all. You're seeing this all wrong."

"I know what I heard."

"I got caught in the moment." He looked her up and down. "And for Chrissake, you *are* pretty."

"I wished I hadn't worn this stupid dress or put on this stupid makeup," she said, more to herself than to Guy. She should've never gotten done up for this occasion. It had ruined everything with Guy. *She* had ruined everything with Guy. He probably wouldn't have kissed her if she'd been plain jane.

Guy took a tentative step toward her. "Let's just start again, okay?"

It was too late for that. "I can't. I'm sorry." She spun on her heel and went back upstairs, Guy trailing behind her.

"Come on, Brit."

People still milled about, checking out the photos, talking to Helene. "Now's not the time," she said to him.

"Then when's a good time?"

"Guy. Stop." She brushed past him, toward Emily at the cash.

"You okay?" Emily asked.

"I'm fine," Brittney said. Tears stung her eyes, but she willed them back.

Luckily, someone dressed in a dark purple suit intercepted Guy before he could follow after her. That must have been the job offer Guy had mentioned before.

"I'll be seeing you?" the purple suit said, hand outstretched to Guy.

Guy's eyes were on her still. He blinked, then swallowed. He smiled at the purple suit then took his hand, shaking it. "Yes, of course."

With purple suit gone, he went up to her. "Brittney—"

"Sorry, Guy." She raised a hand up to his face. "But I have customers to serve for your exhibit. Congratulations for tonight."

Emily gave them each a puzzled look.

"Yeah," Guy said, eyes on the floor. "Congratulations to you, too."

Chapter Twelve

The morning after was cleanup duty. Brittney cleared the tables of drinks and food while Emily swept the crumbs off the gallery floors with a broom. Together they collapsed the foldout tables and moved them to the basement. With the room cleared of tables, Emily mopped, washing off champagne spills. Though last night wasn't a party, there were more than enough people that some degree of mess was bound to happen.

These kinds of messes could be washed up, cleaned, and made fresh and new again. Disinfectant smells replaced champagne smells. The same wasn't true about the mess Guy and Brittney left on each other. No magic broom for that.

Not like she'd see him again anyway. The exhibit was over, their partnership *finito*.

"Last night was amazing," Emily said.

Brittney smiled as she started taking stock of all the photos that had been purchased and which ones were left. They'd made more sales than previously thought, exceeding her expectations. Most couples who had taken photos with Guy to be part of the exhibit ended up buying their own photo, even though they had a copy of it; they wanted the enlarged and framed version. Others, though, bought photos with no connection whatsoever. Those were the better sales.

"Went a lot better than I thought," Brittney said. Perfect night with a not so perfect ending with Guy. "We have to wrap up the photos for the people who bought them."

Emily nodded. "I'll do that once the exhibit's over." Right—last night was only the exhibit's opening night. Now the photos would stay up in the gallery for at least a month. People could come in and peruse the exhibit without all the hustle and bustle of an opening night. "Someone might even come in and buy."

That meant she might still have a run-in with Guy. Would he come in today? He used to come in around this time every morning. But with that new job of his, maybe not.

Her smartphone quacked. A new text message, and it was from Guy. *Hey, we need to talk.*

She texted back *About what?* but then regretted pressing send. That sounded a little harsh. Still, she didn't want to talk to him. There was nothing to talk about. Whatever photos she didn't sell when the month was over would go back to Guy. She'd make sure all communications with him would go through to Emily.

"Is that Guy?" Emily asked, twisting the mop in the bucket's wringer before lathering it up again and slapping it on the floor.

Brittney shook her head. "Junk mail." She switched her phone on silent, but before she could stuff the phone in her pocket another message popped up.

Talk about me and you, Guy texted with a little smiley emoticon at the end. Brittney got the joke, and she suppressed the little tug at the corner of her lips. What was this now? Texts of Me and You? She thumbed away with righteous fury. *There's nothing to talk about.* Then stuffed the phone in her pocket before he had a chance to send another one.

"What did happen with Guy?" Emily asked. "He left before even some of the guests left."

"Dunno." Brittney shrugged. She was too embarrassed to tell Emily what had happened in the basement with Guy. With their kiss and the fact that the only reason he kissed her was because of how she looked last night. He probably wouldn't want to kiss her now; she had little makeup on and wore the most conservative business suit she could find in her mother's closet. She looked like an office nun. "Maybe the night had tired him out a lot more than he at first thought."

"Have you talked to him today?"

Brittney shook her head, too ashamed to lie with her tongue. Things had seemed so great with Guy, too. She liked the way he held her. Liked the way he kissed her. She even liked his eyes and the love they saw in all those couples he photographed. But those eyes hadn't been for the real her.

"Bet you can't wait for that article to come out," Emily said. "There must've been a few reporters last night."

Brittney swallowed. "Trust me, I can wait." Last thing she wanted was to read a review. What if they didn't like it? What if they didn't get it?

The door chimed. Brittney and Emily glanced at each other. They weren't expecting company. It was a quarter past eight on a Sunday. Didn't people sleep in anymore?

Emily started mopping faster. As if that would help.

Brittney went to play interference, meeting the person at the hallway. "Mom? What are you doing here?"

"Since I'm much better," Helene said, "I thought I'd come back to work."

Emily dropped the mop on the floor, raced to Helene and hugged her. "Good to have you back."

Helene smiled. "It's good to *be* back."

Brittney frowned. "You sure you're up to this? You shouldn't push yourself too hard. Last night you were here pretty late. You need rest." According to the doctors, her mother still needed a few more weeks of at-home rest before she was fit for duty. Still, Helene looked every bit like the businesswoman Brittney remembered. Tall in her heels, shoulders back to show off the lapels of her suit jacket.

Helene waved the comment aside. "I've gotten plenty of rest. I'm so rested I'm restless. It's time to get to work." She slapped her hands, rubbing them together. "You don't want me here?"

"I do," Brittney said. "I just worry about you, that's all."

"No need to worry."

"I guess you could sit in your office. Check your email. Emily and I are just cleaning up. With the opening of the exhibit finished, there's really not a whole lot on the horizon." Which brought with it a whole new set of problems. Like, how was Brittney supposed to bring in new business? Maybe it was good that her mother was here now. The coaching would be appreciated.

"Not to worry," Helene said, "I already have an appointment with an artist."

Brittney blinked. "You do?"

"Yes. And he's new. Well, new to the gallery. He's not a new artist. He's also a photographer, and a damn good one. He's from Montreal. Hugely successful there, so I'm happy we'll be hosting him."

"We?"

"Yes, me and you. You're the photography expert now, sweetheart."

"I am?"

Helene laughed. "Would you stop asking questions? I want you to take this client on."

Did it get suddenly hot in here, or was it just her?

A new client? So soon? And another photographer? Brittney got along with Guy, but it had taken a lot of work to get to that point of comfortable disharmony. Who knew what this photographer would bring? And she definitely wouldn't categorize herself as a photography expert. "When's he coming?"

"Today."

Brittney gaped. "*Today?* On a Sunday? When?"

Helene checked her watch. "He's supposed to be here nine o'clock sharp."

"In other words," Brittney said, "in a half an hour."

So much for prep.

#

I want to apologize for last night, Guy had texted to Brittney as he walked Spadina Avenue. He shifted his gaze from trying to find the building that housed Fawkes Photography Studios to his phone to see if Brittney had texted him back.

He'd walked up four blocks before she'd sent, *For what?*

Her texts were cold, if a text message could ever be conceived as such. So she was still pissed at him for last night.

As he walked he texted, *For kissing you.* He cocked his head to the side, then shook his head, deleting the message. That was a dumb message. Then again, wasn't that what he was apologizing for?

Okay, okay—in truth, he had no clue what he was apologizing for. He retyped it, then added *I guess???* to the end of the message. He pressed send then swore under his breath. He had no idea what he was doing. Maybe he should call instead? Hah—like she'd pick up.

He checked the addresses, then spun on his heel and back-pedaled a few doors down. Of course, he'd missed it.

At the front door of the studio, he paused, took a breath, and walked in.

"Hi," he said to the secretary in the front. "I'm Guy—"

169

"Guy!" Fawkes appeared from the back. "So glad you could make it." He checked his watch. "You're early."

"I'm a big time morning person," Guy said, slapping a smile on his face even though the last thing he felt like was smiling. What he really wanted to do was yawn. What he really *really* wanted to do was figure out what was going on with him and Brittney.

And what he really really *really* wanted was a him and Brittney.

"How was the rest of the opening?" Fawkes said, putting an arm around Guy's shoulders and leading him to the studio, where the smell of coffee and pastries waited. "Make a lot of sales?"

"I think so. I'd have to ask the gallery director." Maybe that was his in to see her. He peeked at his phone from his pocket. Nothing.

"I'm sure you did great," Fawkes said. "Let me introduce you to everyone."

Guy met five people, including the secretary at the front desk. One of them was a digital editor, another one was a marketer, another a makeup and costume and set designer, while the last two were photographers that worked under Fawkes on different contracts.

The first thing Guy noticed was how well dressed they all were. Suits. Even the digital editor guy who probably sat by his computer all day had on a pair of slacks and a tie. None of them wore jeans. All polished shoes and ironed shirts. Fawkes himself had put on a different suit—this one a light blue. Guy, on the other hand, wore a plain white shirt with jeans. At least he had the foresight to check for any holes in his clothes. Seemed he'd be in the market for buttoned down shirts and some chinos—whatever the hell chinos were. He'd have to go shopping with Josh.

"Everyone, this is Guy Moraine," Fawkes said. "He was the one I was telling you all about this morning." To Guy he added, "We usually start here at eight sharp. But on the weekends, you can come in a bit later."

Eight sharp? Oh, Heaven preserve him.

"You should've all seen his work last night," Fawkes said. "I've never seen an exhibit so packed with people. It was wonderful to see. I couldn't stop chatting about you at our morning meeting check-in and how excited I was to have you here."

Guy had never had anyone speak so highly of him, especially from an employer. Usually he never got along with his bosses, but right now Guy felt like he could do no wrong. Last night's exhibit had given him immunity in Fawkes's eyes.

The two photographers, a guy and a girl, who could've passed as brother and sister, shared a small smile. Something passed between them, some kind of inside joke that Guy wouldn't know and, apparently, Fawkes didn't know either.

"Hi, everyone," Guy said, sweeping his hand in a crescent.

His greeting was met with silence. He distinctly sensed that no one liked him. Did it really matter? He was Fawkes's rising star. Besides, Guy would be out on assignment most of the day anyway so he didn't need to be liked by the other photographers. All he had to do was keep to himself, do his work, and not be too much of a bother. This wasn't like the office he worked in with Josh. This was the real thing, his dream come true. This was one job he cared about.

"Sorry, I'm late," a man swooped in, grabbing a Danish from the table in the front. He had a Starbucks coffee in his hand.

Guy's chest seized.

"Guy," Fawkes said, "I want you to meet Derrick. Derrick, this is the photographer I was telling you about."

Derrick took a bite of the Danish then placed his coffee on the tabletop and stuck his hand out to Guy. "Heard you had quite the show last night."

This was the same Derrick that had dated Brittney and had broken her heart. "Yeah, it was… really good."

Derrick narrowed his eyes. "Do I know you from somewhere?"

"Don't think so," Guy said. Derrick was probably so full of himself he couldn't even remember the time he and Guy had met. He had no clue Derrick had worked here. Brittney hadn't said anything. But of course, why would she?

"You sure? I swear you look familiar. Like we've met before."

"We're both photographers?" Guy shrugged. *We're both photographers* was a much better answer than *We both know the same Brittney*. As much as he didn't like Derrick for what he'd done to Brittney, he still wanted this job, and he hadn't been the most cordial to Derrick the last time they'd met.

Derrick shook his head slowly. "No, that's not it. I definitely know you."

Oh boy, he was on to him. Whatever Guy did, he would not tell Brittney that he was working with her ex-boyfriend.

Fawkes slapped Guy's shoulder and Guy jumped. "He's quite the photographer. Very talented. Good eye."

"I bet," Derrick said. "You don't get hired in one of the best photography studios in North America just from one exhibit. Is that your work there?"

Derrick pointed at the folder Guy gripped in his hand. "Yeah," he said. "Not just the ones from the exhibit, but other photos, too. I like a lot of different types of photography."

"Don't we all," Derrick said. He gave the brother-sister duo a knowing look. Was there some new-guy-in-the-office-thing going on here? "I was supposed to go to the exhibit too, but missed it. Sorry about that."

"No worries," Guy said, and thanked God and all His Magnificent Glory that Derrick hadn't shown up. Guy had disappointed Brittney enough last night. If Derrick had shown up, she probably would've clawed his eyes out, ripped his heart out, and eaten it in front of everyone.

Guy's phone went off. His cheeks heated up. "I'm so sorry." He scrambled for the phone in his pocket.

Fawkes chuckled. "Not a problem."

"I'll turn it off," he said, but first glanced at the screen. A new text message from Brittney. It said, *I liked the kiss too.*

Now that was a good sign, right?

"Judging by that smile," Derrick said, "that must be from your girlfriend?"

Guy's smile widened, then he fired another text.

#

"Brittney," Helene said, "I'd like you to meet Anthony Barros. Anthony, this is my daughter, Brittney."

Brittney shook Anthony's hand. Firm, strong grip, he nearly crushed her hand. He was older than her, probably early forties. Silver hair, tall, with a bronze tan in the middle of winter. He reminded her of some of the clothing designers she'd worked with in the past.

"It's nice to meet you," Anthony said with a slight French accent.

"Same here," Brittney said. She tried to keep her expression calm and professional while on the inside her heart jumped, her stomach knotted, and every thought in her mind screamed at her that she was way out of her league. She cleared her throat. "Please have a seat. Can I get you some coffee? Or water?"

"Water would be nice," Anthony said as he sat down in Helene's office.

"Great. Mom, could you come with me, please?"

"I'm sure Emily can get it."

"She can, but I need to speak to you about something. It'll be quick." She flashed a polite smile over at Anthony.

"Excuse us," Helene said to Anthony.

Brittney brought Helene to the kitchenette in the back and took a bottle of water from the fridge.

"What's wrong?" Helene asked.

"I don't know if I can do this. I'm not ready." Brittney broke the seal on the water bottle and drank it herself. Then she opened the fridge again and took out a fresh bottle for Anthony.

"Of course you can do this. You did it yesterday. With great success."

"But that was with Guy. Things with Guy were easy." She thought about that for a second. "Actually, they weren't easy. It took a lot of work."

"Welcome to the world of the artist." Helene rolled her eyes. "They're all little divas."

"But Guy was different." She could be bossy with Guy. They would fight and argue, but at the end of the day they both needed each other. This Anthony Barros guy had no allegiance to her. "I don't feel very confident about this."

"Oh, honey." Helene tucked a stray strand of hair behind Brittney's ear. "You'll do fine. You've learned a lot here in just a short time. Besides," she added, her hand cupping Brittney's cheek, "you'll have me by your side."

"Did you even tell him he'd be working with me?" What if Anthony wanted to only work with her mother like the other artists had? None of them wanted to work with Brittney because she was too green. A baby in the industry. She'd only recently left her diapers but still rode a bike with training wheels. "Maybe he just wants to work with you."

"I haven't told him, yet. We'll tell him together."

"Why didn't you tell him? Did you think he wouldn't come?"

Helene chuckled. "Do you hear yourself?" She shook her head. "Everything is going to be fine. I promise. Now let's go back and have a meeting. You sit behind the desk and I'll sit next to Anthony, okay?"

"Okay," Brittney said. She smoothed out her skirt, threw her hair back. She'd had one successful opening under her belt. No reason she couldn't be a success two times in a row. "This is what I wanted. This is what it means to run a business. I can do this."

"Yes, you can. Now let's go back."

Before they left, her phone quacked and she checked her messages. Another one from Guy. It read, *I did too. I want to do it again.*

She moaned. Could this day get any more stressful?

"Who is it?" Helene asked.

"Guy," Brittney said. She texted him back, *I don't think that's such a good idea*, then switched her phone on silent.

Back in the office, Brittney and Helene took their places as planned, Brittney the head honcho behind the desk and Helene beside Anthony. He had his portfolio in a sleek, black leather case laid out on the desk. Also on the desk was the gift Guy had given her last night. A pink envelope with her name scrawled across it. She snatched it off the desk and stuffed it in her purse.

"Thanks so much for taking the time to meet with us," Helene said.

"Us?" Anthony asked, eye brow cocked.

"Yes." Helene gestured to Brittney. "My daughter will be handling your exhibit here at the gallery. She just finished one, actually. The one you see out in the gallery now."

"I see," Anthony said, adjusting in his seat.

"Is there a problem?" Helene asked.

Brittney bit her lip. She knew exactly what the problem was. Anthony had been told about this gallery and its owner, Helene Collar. Nothing had been said about Brittney, certainly nothing about how Brittney would be handling the exhibit. After all, who was this Brittney girl with one exhibit under her belt?

Yes, there was a problem, and Brittney was it.

She kept her back straight, refusing to slump in her chair. She summoned an expression she hoped read, *Yeah, I'm a pretty big deal, and you'd be lucky to work with me.*

"I was told I would be working with you," Anthony said. "I didn't know you had other people working for you."

Helene smiled, her professionalism not wavering in the slightest. "I assure you, my daughter is quite capable. The exhibit last night was the busiest it's ever been. My assistant is still cleaning up from last night." To drive her point home, they could hear the wet slap of the mop on the floors.

Anthony looked at Helene, then gave a sideways glance at Brittney. Helene nodded her head toward Anthony, urging Brittney to say something.

Brittney coughed in her fist, breaking the silence. "Why don't you tell me what it is you'd like to show in the gallery, Mr. Barros?" Helene smiled. Good question to start off the meeting. Brittney had been the boss of this place for over a month. Today was no different.

"I have travelled all over the world for many years gathering different photos," Anthony said, but he spoke to Helene, not to Brittney, as if Helene had asked the question. "I want to do a show on the exploration theme." He unzipped his portfolio, and opened it up. "I've travelled to Europe, Africa, Australia…"

Helene raised a hand, stopping him. "Sounds interesting, Mr. Barros. But you should be speaking with Brittney on this. She's the one who you'll be working with as you decide which photos to include in the gallery."

Anthony paused. A scowl flashed across his face. When it was clear that Helene wouldn't budge on this, he leaned back in his seat and crossed his legs. "I will be working with her only? Not with you?"

Helene nodded. "That's correct. If she needs my help, I'll be here, but she'll be holding the reins on this."

Anthony took a breath, and for the first time since the meeting began, he turned his gaze to Brittney. She felt his eyes studying her, measuring her worth, and wanted to hide under the desk.

"Tell me about yourself," he asked. "What makes you qualified?"

"Uh…" Brittney stalled. She sneaked a glance at Helene, who sent her an encouraging smile. "Well, like my mother said, last night's gallery was a great"—she swallowed a lump in her throat—"success."

"Is that the only exhibit you've done?"

Brittney stalled again. She wanted to lie and say she'd been working for her mother in the gallery for years, but she had no way of backing that up if he probed further, and she had no doubts that he would. "Pix of Me and You is the only one I've done."

"Pix of Me and You? That's what it was called?" Anthony made a face as though he'd smelled something funky. He donned no wedding band. Probably had never been married or, worse, had been divorced. "Have you ever travelled?"

"Only to the United States," she said, her palms sweaty. She'd gone down to California on a few occasions to take photos, but she wouldn't consider herself a world-traveller.

"What did you do before this?"

Brittney gulped. "I was a model."

Anthony's eyebrows arched. "A model?"

Brittney nodded. "Yes, for Instagram."

Anthony snorted. "You're kidding? Tell me, what do you know about art?"

"Mr. Barros," Helene intervened. So Brittney wasn't the only one hearing the venom in Anthony's tone.

"Apologies," Anthony said to Helene but not to Brittney. "I'm just confused. You want me to work with someone who has no experience with this kind of photography and who knows nothing about art." Back to Brittney, he asked, "Did you even take art in school?"

"Uh…" This probably wasn't the best time to tell him she'd never been to university.

#

Guy sat at what would be his work station—a plain desk with cabinets on either side full of paper clips, staples, and pens. He didn't have a computer and was told that most of the photographers brought in their own laptops. The only one who did have a computer was the digital editor.

Fawkes got called away for a phone call in his private office before he could tell Guy what his next steps ought to be. So Guy waited. He sat and watched the others do their thing. The brother-sister combo whispered to each other and made jokes. Derrick was on his laptop with headphones in his ears.

Guy took this opportunity to check his phone and sent Brittney another message. *I want to see you and talk to you. I've got gallery withdrawal.*

He wanted to clear the air with Brittney. But more than that, he wanted to sit down with her somewhere—a coffee shop or the gallery—and tell her about his day and listen to her tell him about her day. They'd never had that sort of conversation before, but that was because they were each other's days. Now that he wasn't with her anymore, he missed spending time with her, missed having her around. He wanted to tell her about his new job, to share it with her, invite her to be a part of it. He'd tell her he'd royally screwed up the dress code. She'd get a kick out of that one and probably roll her eyes at him. He wanted Brittney to be a part of his life. Wanted to make her laugh. He'd dress in sweatpants to work every day if he knew it'd make her laugh.

He wouldn't tell her about Derrick, though. Maybe after Guy surpassed him in this job he would, and they'd laugh about it later.

Wow, was he already thinking of them as an us?

The secretary's heels clicked on the floor. She escorted a man dressed in a suit to the back where the boardroom was located. Then she knocked on Fawkes's door, opened it, and said something to him. Afterward, Fawkes came out of his office and caught Guy's eye.

Guy shoved his phone back into his pocket. Fawkes was coming right for him. Guy tried to look busy so he fiddled with his camera's settings.

"I've got an assignment for you."

"For me?" Guy said. Things moved fast in the Fawkes Photography Studio.

Fawkes nodded. "The client is waiting in the boardroom. Come sit in, and we'll go over the assignment."

"Okay," Guy said. "Do I need to bring anything?"

"Just your portfolio and your brilliant eyes."

That Guy could do. He gathered his portfolio, and the two of them went into the boardroom and sat down with the client.

"Good to see you again," Fawkes said, shaking hands with the client. "Guy, this is Tom Phillips."

"Nice to meet you," Guy said.

"Likewise," Tom said, scanning Guy from head to toe. Guy stuck out in his casual choice of style.

"Guy just joined us recently. Today, actually. He's a fantastic addition to our team."

Tom nodded, but said nothing.

"So, what can we do for you?"

Tom Phillips was an interior decorator, and he wanted a website with photographs showing the homes and offices he had decorated for his clientele. The contract was to go around to all the places Tom had decorated and take pictures. When Fawkes told Tom that Guy would be handling the contract, Tom wasn't too thrilled about the idea.

"You're kidding?" Nope, not thrilled at all.

Fawkes's brow crinkled. "I don't think so."

Tom pointed to Guy. "No offense, but he's going to take pictures of my work?"

Guy felt a stab of pain in his chest.

"He's quite capable, I assure you."

"What about Derrick?"

Another stab. This time with a proverbial spear. Did that comment also come with a "no

offense" attached to it?

Fawkes shook his head. "I have him on too many assignments. He's overworked."

"How long will he be? I can wait."

"Mr. Phillips, I'm sure you'll be happy with Guy's work. He's got talent. On par with Derrick."

On par? More like surpassed.

"He doesn't look like it," Tom said.

Fawkes laughed that laugh of his. "We haven't exactly gone through the dress code for the office."

Unbelievable. Who gave a crap about appearances? They didn't matter. What a person wore measured nothing, showed nothing. You could look like the best photographer in the world and still be an idiot. Derrick was a case in point.

"Guy, you brought your portfolio, why don't you show Mr. Phillips your work?"

"Sure," he said. He'd be delighted. His talent would speak for him. Talent you couldn't fake, unlike looks. The only image that mattered was the image in his photos.

He opened the portfolio and went through his work. He included some of the photos he'd done from the Pix of Me and You exhibit but showed most of the ones he already had done before since that was what he wanted to do. He focused on the photos of various rooms he'd taken. Phillips took them all in silently, but with each photo Guy showed, his face grew more and more crestfallen.

In the middle of a pitch, Fawkes put his hand on Guy's forearm, and Guy stopped talking.

"Is there a problem?" Fawkes asked.

"I want photos that tell a story." Tom picked up a photo, one of Josh's cubicle with Josh typing away on the computer. "These don't tell me anything. My four-year-old daughter could've taken this photo. What's the story behind these?"

"Story?" Guy asked.

"Yeah, like the visual story. I want to tell my clients that this is a space that they can share movie moments with their families or the spot where all their hard work comes alive. But these photos are very… dull."

Guy's cheeks flushed. Fawkes spread the photos out and studied them.

"I get it," Tom said. "You're new. But I can't take the risk."

Fawkes sifted through the photos. "I see your point."

Now Guy's heart pounded.

Fawkes stood up and got Derrick's attention, waving him in.

No, not Derrick.

Derrick waltzed in all suited up and with a big smile on his face. "Everything all right in here? Mr. Phillips, I didn't know you had an appointment with us today."

They shook hands. "Seems like you're a busy guy," Tom said.

"Never too busy to talk to you."

"Good," Fawkes said, "because Mr. Phillips has an assignment for his interior decorating company. He's specifically requested you. Think you got time?"

"Of course."

"Think you could also teach Guy here a thing or two?"

"Yeah," Tom said, "the newbie needs help."

That wasn't a stab of pain. That was Guy's heart being thrown into the meat grinder. Guy, a newbie? Derrick teaching Guy?

This was the first day of a new job in Hell.

Derrick slapped Guy on the shoulder. "I'd be happy to. It's just me and you, tiger."

Guy winced. Tiger?

"I'll leave you guys to it, then," Fawkes said. "Don't worry, Mr. Phillips. You're in good hands."

#

Anthony flipped his leather case shut, the sound so sharp it made Brittney flinch. "I see no point in continuing this meeting further."

"Mr. Barros—" Helene began.

"My apologies, but I hoped to work with someone who knows this business. Not someone who knows how to put on a dress and look beautiful for the camera. You are beautiful, there is no doubt about it, but I need more than that."

Brittney was losing the client because she wasn't good enough. Because she lacked smarts, experience, depth. But that wasn't her any more. She'd learned something these past several weeks with Guy.

She looked at her mother's expressionless face, then back at Anthony, whose cheeks had flared red. She swallowed. "You're right, Mr. Barros," she said, making sure her tone was like steel. "When I started working for my mother, I didn't know what I was doing or what I was getting myself into. I lost a lot of clients. People who, like you, trusted my mother and wanted to work with her instead of me. But then I took a chance on an unknown photographer, and he took a chance on an inexperienced gallery director. Even though neither of us had a clue what we were doing, last night's gallery was something I'm proud of. Sure, we made mistakes. Lots of them. But I learned and I adapted, and I assure you I can help your exhibit reach the same success."

Helene nodded at her daughter, her face beaming.

But Anthony still had a grimace on his face. "I came all this way with an expectation in mind." His voice rose. "I wanted to show my work here. I've heard nothing but good things about this place. It has a reputation even in Montreal." Anthony only spoke to her mother now, not sparing a glance at Brittney. "But I can't put my career in a model's hands. One exhibit doesn't make her an expert."

Helene nodded slowly, her lips sealed. The glow had vanished from her face.

"I came here for you, Ms. Collar. To work with you. I'm sure your daughter," and again he said this without even looking at Brittney, "is a very nice person, but she is not capable of this work."

The air fled Brittney's lungs as if she'd been kicked in the stomach. She'd given it her all, and it still wasn't enough. She felt stupid all over again. Inadequate. He made her feel like last night's success was just a fluke.

"Mr. Barros," Helene began calmly. Why couldn't Brittney have been more like her mother? Strong and unyielding. Instead, she was every bit like her father. A failure. Shallow. A surface with no depth. "Brittney works as a director at this gallery. Last night, she had the best opening night this gallery has ever seen, and she did it all by herself. I wasn't there to guide her at all. It was all her doing. Not only did it attract a lot of customers, but it also brought the media.

That simply doesn't happen with exhibits, and you know that. She didn't have the benefit of my buyers' list to help her out either. She built it all herself. And she did it all in a month's time. On top of it all, she's my daughter and if you can't work with her, then you can't work with me."

Brittney couldn't believe her ears. Anthony couldn't either, judging by his bug-eyed look and red face.

"So what's it going to be, Mr. Barros?"

Anthony snorted and shook his head. "I have never been so insulted in my life."

Helene shrugged. "You know where the exit is."

Anthony shot up from his seat, gathered his portfolio, and stormed out of the office.

Emily rushed into the office. "Whoa. What happened?"

"I lost the client," Brittney said in a small voice, her head lowered.

"You didn't lose anyone," Helene said. "He was a self-righteous jerk."

"I'm sorry, Mom."

"Don't apologize. It's fine." But there was a sharpness in her tone.

Emily coughed, fanning her face. "He wore a lot of cologne."

Helene stood up, flattened her skirt. "Brittney, do you mind? I'd like to check my email."

"Yeah, of course." Brittney got up off the desk chair. "I'm going to grab a coffee."

"Sure," Helene said, but she was already getting lost in email. "Can you close the door behind you?"

Brittney and Emily left. "Everything okay?" Emily asked.

"Yeah, I just need some fresh air," Brittney said. She trembled, her nerves shot. She shrugged into her coat and stepped outside.

She'd lost the client and managed to make her mother's first day back at the gallery the worst day ever. She'd left her mother feeling disappointed in her. It was the one thing she wanted to avoid above all else.

She checked her phone. Another text from Guy.

Guy had never acted the way Anthony Barros had. Even in their worst fights, he had acknowledged her as a human being and listened to what she had to say. He knew Brittney's past, and yet he still relied on her, believed in her.

Anthony Barros had been the opposite, and she had the feeling that every other artist after him would act the same.

She had no idea how to deal with a client. Guy she could deal with because he had no one else to go to either. They had needed each other. She couldn't always rely on that with other artists.

Maybe it'd be good to see Guy. He always had a way of cheering her up. Who knew? He probably had an amazing first day at his new job. Maybe hearing about it would give her some much-needed confidence in herself.

She texted him back.

#

The meeting finished, Guy went back to Fawkes's office.

"You look like you've just gotten the lesson of a lifetime," Fawkes said.

That wasn't how Guy would put it. He felt drained, standing at the doorway, his shoulders heavy, his head like a brick. The meeting had gone longer than he thought it should. If he never heard about furniture again it would be too soon. If someone so much as said the word "chair" to him he'd snap.

"Isn't Derrick a genius? Bet you learned a lot."

A genius? The man waxed poetic about how amazing his photography skills were. An Adonis of the camera. If Guy had any worries that Derrick remembered him, he didn't anymore; clearly

Derrick had eyes only for himself. Worse, he had Tom Phillips totally captivated, hanging off every bullshit word he said. How could Brittney ever be interested in a guy like Derrick? The man was a tool. He represented everything Guy hated.

"It was a great learning experience," Guy lied. He'd have to suck it up until he proved his worth. He'd already done so last night. He could do it again, this time with different types of photography. Maybe he could learn a thing or two from Derrick, and then use it against him. "Sorry about what happened."

Fawkes waved a hand. "It's okay. I've got another assignment for you." He passed him a sheet. "Something more up your alley."

Guy took it, and read the front page. The client was a company named LosIce. "What's this?"

"They're a clothing company. Independent. They're looking for a photographer to take pictures of models wearing their clothes. Thought it'd be perfect for you."

Fashion photography? That was far from Guy's perfect. "Why me?"

"You seem to have a knack for people photography. Fashion and portraits."

"I don't think so." The words were out before he knew it. He wanted to slam his head on the door frame.

"That was your whole exhibit last night. That was why I hired you." Fawkes said that last bit like a warning.

"I'll take it," Guy said, reminding himself that he had to start somewhere.

"Good." Fawkes said, then turned back to his computer.

"It's just that…"

Fawkes blinked several times, as if he couldn't believe this conversation hadn't ended.

What Guy ought to do was shut up. Just stay quiet. Turn around and walk back to his empty desk suffering the quiet scrutiny and giggly whispers of the other employees. But he couldn't. An employee could talk to their employer, right? What was so bad about telling your boss what your expectations were?

"It's just that," Guy said, "I was hoping I would be doing other kinds of photography instead of fashion photography. I'm not really a fashion photographer."

Fawkes smiled, but this one was all show and no joy. He swivelled in his chair to face Guy. "I give assignments as they come depending on workloads and experience. Since you're new here and don't have a lot on your plate and just almost lost me a client, I think you should take this job."

"Right." The message was loud and clear. "Got you. Just wanted you to know my expectations."

Fawkes reared back. Whoops—had he said something wrong? Too demanding, maybe? Guy was screwing this up badly, and all because he didn't want to take fashion photography. It wasn't like he'd be taking photos of his mother and father. He'd be taking it to help an independent company. Sure, it was fake, but if it helped an indie clothing company be the next Guess, who was he to judge?

"Duly noted, Guy. Is there anything else?"

"No. Thank you, Mr. Fawkes."

Fawkes nodded, turning back to his computer.

Guy made for the door, scanning the assignment. "Oh, Mr. Fawkes, when and where's the assignment?"

"Ask one of the others, Guy. I can't be holding your hand through this."

"Right. Sorry, Mr. Fawkes." He retreated, closing the door behind him.

Bad first day at work? Check. Piss off your boss? Check. Next item on the list? Redemption. Guy had to redeem himself in Fawkes's eyes. This morning he'd been the rising the star, and by noon he was already falling. He could not lose this dream job.

So what if the assignment wasn't dreamy? He could get into it. He'd have to. Brittney had seen something in his ability to take photos of people. As did Josh. As did Emily. He had to get over it.

He checked his phone. New message from Brittney.

We can meet. But no kissing!

Guy smiled, sending back, *My lips are sealed.*

Chapter Thirteen

Guy had told her to meet him at the Dog and Bear, a pub close to the Collar Gallery. Brittney had been before on Friday and Saturday evenings when the pub, serving your standard pub fare, turned more into a nightclub with loud music and lineups out the door. Thankfully, tonight wouldn't be one of those nights, and when Brittney showed up, there were only a few tables occupied and older men watching the hockey game at the bar.

Brittney spotted Guy standing by a booth and waving her over. She took a deep breath and blew it out as she went to him.

She stopped in front of him, close enough that she could see the fine hairs of his beard, but far enough that she couldn't touch him. She had no idea how to greet him, and at that moment, it seemed like the biggest crisis facing her. Their relationship had changed over a single night. She had no idea how to treat him, how to behave around him. Should she hug him? Was a handshake appropriate? Finally, she gave him a nod and sat down, and he sat down across from her. Two glasses of water stood between them.

"Feels like it's been a long time," he said.

"The exhibit was last night," Brittney said, stating the obvious in an edgy tone. She took another breath, wrung her hands in her lap under the table. Maybe this wasn't the grand idea she thought it'd be. She was still upset by today's events. But none of it had been Guy's fault, she reminded herself.

"I know," Guy said. "Just so much has changed."

So he felt it, too. Things were different between them, there was no doubt about it. An awkwardness, which had never been there before, hung in the air.

"How's the new job?" she asked. He had changed, too. From unemployed to working in one of the best-known photography studios in North America.

"It's good," he said. "They have me on this great assignment. It's a one-day thing, so it'll be done by tomorrow. It's really great. A dream come true." His voice was tight. "Really, really great."

Brittney cocked an eyebrow. "So it's great?"

He nodded. "Yeah, yeah. Really great."

"What's the assignment?"

"Ah, you know," he said. He picked up the glass of water and brought it to his lips. "Photography for a clothing company." He drank.

"Fashion photography?" Brittney said. "That's not like you at all."

"I know, but it's a start. Everyone's gotta start somewhere. Anyway, how about you?"

"Great also." And that was about as far as she'd go on the day's events. She swiftly changed the subject. "Why'd you call me here?"

"I wanted to see you. I wanted to talk about that kiss."

"I thought I said—"

"You said I couldn't kiss you, but you didn't say I couldn't talk about it."

Brittney leaned back in her chair, arms crossed. "So talk."

Guy put his elbows on the tabletop and leaned in. He looked at her like it was the first time he was seeing her. That was ridiculous, of course. But it was the way his eyes took everything in, seeing what no one else could see. He'd never looked at her like that before. No one had. And she, of all people, knew what it was like to be under the eye of a photographer. But those photographers she'd worked with never saw her. They focused on what she wore. At the lipstick and eyeliner on her face. At the skin she showed and skin she didn't show. But Guy looked inward. It made her self-conscious. She dropped her gaze, then peeked up at him again. His stare never wavered. The whole Dog and Bear could collapse on top of them, and yet she knew his eyes would still be on her. For the first time since she'd known him, he seemed more like a man and less like a boy.

Self-conscious for sure, but his close regard left her stomach warm and fluttery, like the feeling just before a laugh.

Finally, he spoke, a voice that was soft but clear. She heard every word. "I kissed you last night because I like you, Brittney."

Brittney blinked. "Like me?"

"Really like you. I felt I always liked you. Ever since we first met. But then I didn't really realize it until…"

"Until when?" she asked, uncrossing arms.

"Until a couple of nights before the exhibit."

"Why then?"

"Did you see the gift I gave you last night?" he asked.

"No."

He winced. With the exhibit's opening night and today's disaster with Anthony Barros, she had no time to open his gift.

"Oh, I see," he said.

She waited to see if he'd tell her what it was, but he didn't. Quite frankly, she was in no mood for opening gifts from anyone, let alone Guy.

He cleared his throat and pressed onward. "And then when I saw you last night," he said, "I couldn't take my eyes off you."

Ah, there was the rub. How many times had she heard that from a guy? "Because I was all dressed up? I looked like I did when I was a model?"

"I don't know what you looked like when you were a model. I didn't know you then, and it's not like I paid much attention to fashion magazines. But you were beautiful. The most beautiful girl I'd ever seen. And I know what those fashion magazine photos are like. I've done photo editing. I know how to make someone far prettier than they are. But when I saw you last night, I saw you in your best light, in your best pose. I saw in you what I always hated about fashion photography because I could never capture it in a photo. I saw a real, genuine beauty."

"So you only like me for my looks? That was the reason you kissed me?"

"Not at all." He scratched the back of his neck. "I'm not explaining myself very well here."

"No, you're not."

He reached out and held her hand with both of his. Her hand felt small in his, and his palms were warm. Not sweaty, just warm. "You're a pretty girl, there's no denying that. But there's more to it. I never knew what it was like to be a success. You made that happen."

"So you used me?" Brittney said, slipping her hand away from his grip. "You used me to be a success, and you think I can make you more of a success? That's why you like me?"

Her heartbeat raced. Why couldn't she get a normal guy to like her for her? Why did it always have to be about them? They liked Brittney because she was pretty, and she made them look good. Now it was because Brittney helped him be a success. It was all about him. Why couldn't it be about who *she* was?

"I like you because you make me into a better person." He chuckled softly. "You literally *made* me a better person. A better photographer. I have a job now because of you. A job I actually like in a field I've struggled to break into for a long time."

Brittney shook her head. "I'm happy for you, and I'd be lying if I didn't say I liked that kiss—"

"Or that you like me?"

She stared at him, into his hopeful face. "But I can't be with you."

"Why? Because I'm a photographer?" His voice rose a pitch. "You think I'm like Derrick who cheated on you? I'm nothing like Derrick."

"I know that." The two were complete opposites. The only thing they had in common was photography.

"Then why?"

"You kissed me last night because I was beautiful," she said, her gaze down on the table at his hands, hands that held a camera that took pictures of dozens of couples who had real love for each other, something neither of them had. "That's why. You even said it while we were kissing. I don't want to be someone's eye candy."

"You're getting this all wrong." He had a pained expression on his face.

"It's true, isn't it? Otherwise you would've kissed me before last night. You would've told me you liked me."

"I didn't know you felt the same way," Guy said. "We were working together on this exhibit. I thought if I told you, it might ruin our working relationship. Ruin the exhibit."

"Right. The exhibit was more important to you than me. And I was just a means to that end."

Guy shook his head. "That's—"

"And then you saw me last night all gussied up like a trophy wife."

Guy reared back, his eyes wide. "Trophy wife?"

"That's all guys want from me. All they want is some eye candy they can show off with. I'm sick of it. Why can't I just find a guy who likes me for more than what's on the surface?"

"I do," Guy said softly, his head lowered.

"You're just like your father. He liked your mother because she was pretty, right? And look how far that got him. Careful, Guy, I may just do the same to you."

"You're nothing like my mother, and I'm nothing like my father."

"Didn't seem like it last night."

"You know who's obsessed with your looks?" He pointed at her. "You. Only you. That's all you think you have. You're so focused on that. You're so caught up with it that you don't even know what qualities you have underneath. You have no freaking idea. You're blind to it, but I'm not. I know what you have underneath, and let me tell you, it has nothing to do with how you look. But you have such a chip on your shoulder that there's no way a guy can win."

She smirked, covering up how much his words rang true. But only a little. She couldn't control how guys perceived and treated her. Her history lent itself to guys who only cared about her appearance. She knew she had something more to give and share. But what? This whole time she'd been trying to figure it out and it had all fallen apart, taking her back to square one.

"Why don't you ask me?" He beckoned her with a hand gesture. "Go ahead—ask me what qualities I see in you."

She glared at him, arms crossed over her chest. Her mouth wouldn't open, the words refused to come. Her throat closed in on her.

"You see," he said, "you're too afraid to ask me. You're too afraid of what I might say, because the only one who has a problem with how they see you is you."

"You think you have me all figured out?" she said. Who was he to tell her what she was afraid of, who she was, and who she wasn't? Didn't matter that they spent every day for weeks together—that had been strictly business. He knew nothing of who she was. "Maybe you ought to focus on yourself instead of thinking you know so much about me."

"What does that mean?"

"Look at you, Guy. Is that how you went to work? To your new dream job? You hide who you are in baggy clothes and raggedy hair and a bushy beard, and you think it's cool. You think you're being a rebel. You think you're an artist who doesn't care what people think about you. But you do care. That's why you hide. And you don't just hide what you look like, you hide everything. You hide your talent. You even hid your feelings from me until last night. And most of all, you hide from the truth."

"Truth about what?"

"That despite what happened with your parents, love does exist."

"I believe in love," Guy said.

Brittney snorted. Obviously, he was lying. "No, you don't."

"I have to."

"Why? Because of the exhibit?"

"No, because of how I feel about you."

"You love me?"

He slammed the table and water spilled from the glass. "Of course, I do! That's what I've been trying to tell you!"

He loved her. He hadn't said it exactly, but she was the reason he believed in love again. Not the photos he took of all those couples, but the way he felt about her.

But that wasn't possible. And if it was, he loved her for the wrong reasons. She couldn't love him back; she wouldn't dare. This wasn't how she wanted it to be. Not at all.

She wasn't afraid of what Guy would say about who he thought she was. She was afraid she wouldn't be able to see it herself, afraid that whatever Guy had seen had only been a façade she put on to make herself dress the part of gallery director. She was afraid that wasn't truly her. How could he claim to know her when she didn't even know herself?

"I have to go," she said. sliding out of the booth. She practically ran out of the Dog and Bear, her coat hanging off her arm. Guy called after her.

The cold wind hit her hard. She shouldered on her coat and zipped up as she sped down the sidewalk. Guy followed after her, asking her to stop. She ignored him.

Love her? How could he possible love her?

He ran past her and turned around, stopping in front of her. He'd left his jacket back at the Dog and Bear. His breath came out in wisps of fog. He shook from the cold. Yet he seemed like he barely noticed. "What's going on with you?" He rubbed her arms up and down, as if she was the one without a coat on and shivering. "Tell me what's bothering you."

"I've let people use me all my life."

"No, you haven't. Don't be silly."

"Yes, I have. It's why I became a model. When my dad left, I just wanted him back. I thought if I became famous, maybe he'd come back. Fame was what he always wanted for himself, but maybe if I'd gotten to that place, he'd come back to me. And I used my face and body to get there because it was all I had. I let people use me. My agent. Derrick. All those clothing brands I modelled for. But he never came back. It was all for nothing. And now you want to use me, too."

"It's not like that."

"Please, Guy," she said, stepping away from him and hailing a cab. "Just let this go. Nothing will ever happen between us."

#

Brittney had spent the cab ride back to the gallery dabbing her eyes with a tissue and redoing her eyeliner. She was still red in the face.

The cab driver did what cab drivers did best, ignored the crying girl in the backseat and got her as quickly to sanctuary as possible.

Back at the gallery, Emily sat in the front foyer, playing a simple melody on her harmonica.

"Where've you been?" Emily said.

"Out," Brittney said. She'd been gone since the event with Anthony Barros. "Had to clear my head." She went to the office in the back, Emily following behind her, but the room was empty, the computer screen off. "Where's Mom?"

"Home," Emily said. "She wasn't feeling well. A little lightheaded. Probably too much for one day. I was waiting for you to get back."

Lightheaded? The events of this morning must have thrown her off edge. Brittney let it go with a sigh and sat down at the desk. A pile of mail waited for her. She sifted through it, one envelope catching her attention. "Oh, my God."

"What?"

The envelope was from the University of Toronto. On her application form, she had put her mailing address as the gallery instead of the house since she was at the gallery more often than not.

"It's from the university. My application."

"Well?" Emily said, excited. "Open it."

She took the letter opener her mother had and ripped open the envelope. She unfolded the letter and read it. Then read it again. And a third time. Each time she willed the words to change, but they didn't.

"What's it say?" Emily said.

"The Admissions Committee has carefully reviewed your application to the University of Toronto. After much consideration, I regret to inform you that we are unable to offer you a place in the Rotman School of Management program." Her voice lowered. "We appreciate the interest you have shown in the University of Toronto. Best wishes as you pursue your educational goals."

She dropped the paper down.

"This is the worst day of my life."

"It's okay," Emily said, in a soothing tone. "They get a ton of applications. You're not the only one. You don't need them anyway. You have this job. You're already running a business. Who needs a university to tell you how to do that?"

She did. She needed the validation. She needed it now more than ever.

"I don't want this job. I never wanted to be a gallery director." It'd been her mother's idea from the start as a way to bolster her resume and show her as a serious candidate to the admissions committee. So much for that plan. "I'm no good at this anyway. I embarrassed myself with Barros."

"He was an asshole. Helene wouldn't have worked with him anyway."

"He thought I was stupid. He thought I shouldn't be in this business."

"He's one artist, Brittney."

"But he was right." And deep down she knew it, too. She wasn't the right fit for the gallery. She didn't have the skills, the knowhow, the experience. Something else waited for her, but what? She couldn't go back to modelling, no way. But she couldn't stay here either. "In that meeting I had no idea what I was doing. What to say or how to think. I wasn't even smart enough to know I had to have a cash register for last night." She laughed at herself, a bitter laugh. "I'm so stupid."

"You had a lot on your mind," Emily said. "These things happen."

"Not to my mother. And she has a degree in both art *and* business. What do I have? Nothing. A high school diploma. Big deal. I barely passed."

"None of that matters."

"Stop saying that! Of course, it matters!" She pulled her hair back. "I disappointed my mother. I let her down. I couldn't even get a client who had come all way here from Montreal to work specifically with this gallery. It was practically a done deal, and I scared him away. He wouldn't even look at me. I've got no right being here."

Emily crossed her arms over her chest. "So what? What are you going to do? Go back to modelling?"

"It's something." But one she was hesitant to jump on. "I was stupid to leave it altogether."

"You're stupid if you go back," Emily said, her tone sharp.

Brittney lifted up the rejection letter. "I don't have any more options."

"Fine then. Give up. Go back to modelling. Because you were so happy there."

"Maybe I will." Maybe she could model on the side while she applied to other schools. University of Toronto wasn't the only school with a business program. Maybe she could start as an administrative assistant somewhere. Work her way up. This couldn't be it for her. If that meant doing a few modelling gigs on the side to make ends meet, so be it.

"If they'll even take you back," Emily said.

"I had an agent. He'll take me back."

Emily laughed. "You burned that bridge."

"Fine, then I'll get someone else. There are plenty of agents who would want to work with me." Back when she was a model, she'd get calls all the time from other agents trying to steal her away from Ackerman.

"You deleted your whole account. You gave up on your fans. You think they'll want you back after pulling a stunt like that?"

"I don't have to listen to this." She pointed to the exit. "You should go home. You don't have to stay so late at my mom's gallery all the time."

"This could be your gallery, but no, you've given up on this, too." Emily made for the door. "You're so worried about letting your mother down. You know something? The only person you're letting down is yourself." Emily waited for Brittney to say something, but Brittney kept silent, her gaze on the rejection letter, reading it over and over. "I can't believe I admired you."

Emily left, leaving Brittney all alone in the gallery. After wiping her tears and cleaning up her face for the second time that day, she locked up the gallery and took the subway and then a bus ride home.

She dreaded the conversation she was about to have with her mother. Telling her she hadn't gotten into university and was thinking about going back to modelling would be the toughest thing she'd had to do all day. She kept reminding herself this wasn't giving up, despite what Emily said. There was a place for her somewhere. She just needed to find it. She had to try on different careers, just like she tried on different clothes until she found the one with the right fit.

She wasn't ready to raise the white flag yet. Maybe Guy was right—maybe she was afraid of who she was or who she could become. She'd have to face those fears and overcome them.

But now—now she might as well be the star in her own scary movie, because that was exactly what she was—scared.

"Mom?" she called in the house, but got no answer. The house was quiet.

She went into the kitchen and found nothing, not even dinner cooking. The living room, nothing. She went upstairs and into her mother's room.

"Mom?" Silence. She walked in and around the bed, and there lying on the floor was her mother, a pool of blood around her. "Mom!"

She took her phone out and dialled 911.

Chapter Fourteen

No mistakes, human or otherwise. No mistakes, human or otherwise.

That was Guy's mantra the next morning as he got ready for his first assignment with Fawkes Photography Studio. Yesterday he'd made all the mistakes allotted to him as the new guy in the studio, and it had cost him Tyler Fawkes's praise. But no more. With today's assignment, he'd be back in the light of Fawkes's eyes, a laurel on his head.

And he'd do it with fashion photography. Sure, he'd had his hang-ups about it before, but he had to start somewhere, and right now that starting point was to get the job done and done well. He had to swallow his pride and pay his dues. Tyler-freaking-Fawkes, photography legend, counted on him.

His pride wasn't the only thing he swallowed. He swallowed yawns, too. God, was he tired. Anxieties kept him tossing and turning all night. Not only anxiety over work either, but about Brittney. He couldn't get her out of his mind. That heartbroken look on her face. The tears in her eyes. The hopeless tone in her voice.

He'd told her he loved her yesterday. Was he crazy? She thought he was, but he didn't. So what if he'd never said it to another girl before? He'd never felt it for any of the girls in his past relationships, all ending in less than a month. Brittney was right—he had ignored love. Ignored it and shunned it. But she made him believer; had given him a come-to-Cupid moment.

He loved her because she strove to be a better person. She wanted more for herself than her beauty. And in his eyes, she'd done just that. She'd done it by making him a better man, by believing in his work as a photographer, and supporting him and working with him to see that the Pix of Me and You Exhibit was a success, and that exhibit had been a work of art unto itself.

She'd made him a better man and he'd made her a better woman. They grew together, made the perfect team. That was what he'd tried to tell her yesterday. He hadn't used her as a means to an end. No, instead he had relied on her, trusted her, and she'd done the same for him. Together they'd grown to be different people.

If only he'd said this to her yesterday instead of the blubbering idiocy he came up with last night.

He had to forget about it. Today was a new day.

No mistakes, human or otherwise.

He'd get his new job on track first—a job he considered a gift from Brittney—and then he'd figure out a way to get her back.

The assignment would be shot on-site. The clothing store, LosIce, was in the fashion district and catered to women. The second Guy walked in, he wrinkled his nose and frowned. The place reeked like a tanning salon. Rows of clothes hung on racks with a private section for shoes, all high heels. Judging by the dressed mannequins, the clothing looked uncomfortable and so revealing that it was unsexy.

Guy sighed, wiped the frown off his face. He had to put on an enthusiastic smile and make the best out of it. No mistakes, human or otherwise.

"Can I help you?" a woman asked him.

"Hi—Oh, my God." The woman wore a bra for a shirt. Guy caught sight of it—how could he not?—and shot his gaze up at the ceiling, then at the clothes on the racks, then at the black wood floors, anything but her D cups pointed in his direction. "I'm the photographer," he added, lifting the bag he kept all his equipment in.

"The photographer?"

"From Fawkes Studio."

He focused on her face and not what lay below her neckline. She had a confused look on her face. He was at the right place. A wooden sign above the cash register read LosIce.

He was about to ask for the store manager when he heard girls giggling in the back room and the familiar sound of a camera flash going off.

Guy tilted his head to the side. Now that was odd. Unless LosIce had hired two photographers, the only camera flash that should be going off was his own.

Guy moved past the bra-girl and started for the back room.

"Sir, you can't go back there."

"Sure, sure," Guy said, entranced. He grabbed a random shirt and passed it to her. "Here, cover yourself up."

As he got closer to the back room, he heard more giggling, then a familiar voice. "Okay, now turn around and arch your back. Stick your butt out and let's see what those short shorts are made of."

It couldn't be—

It was.

When Derrick glanced up from his camera lens, his eye caught Guy standing in the doorway. "*Heeeeeey!*" he said, grinning, a little too happy to see Guy. He put five fingers up to the models, five drop dead gorgeous girls wearing the everyday lingerie-styled shirts and pants of LosIce. "Let's take five, okay?" The girls giggled, biting a nail, swaying their hips back and forth, pouting like they'd miss him.

Guy stood stunned. "What are you doing here?"

"I'm taking photos," Derrick said, as if Guy had asked the stupidest question known to humankind. A backdrop stood, the girls standing in front of it, and lights flashed down on them. "What's it look like I'm doing here?"

"But Tyler gave me this assignment." He had the contract in his back pocket as proof.

"He re-assigned. Tyler's fickle like that."

"I don't believe you."

Derrick shrugged, sparing a glance to the girls and then back at Guy with a villainous glimmer in his eye. "Give him a call."

As a matter of fact, he would. He took out his cellphone.

Shit—he had no minutes left on it.

"Here, use mine." Derrick pulled his own out. "I'll even dial him for you."

The phone rang a few times before Tyler picked up.

"Hi, Mr. Fawkes," Guy said. "It's Guy."

"Oh, hi Guy. You with Derrick?"

"I'm at LosIce for that assignment you gave me yesterday," Guy said, emphasizing the word *me*. "Derrick's here. He says I've been… um… re-assigned?" The word left a bitter taste in his mouth.

"Not quite." Fawkes sighed. "Look, Guy. I was doing some thinking with Derrick, and we don't think you're the right fit for Fawkes Studio."

Losing feeling in his legs, Guy leaned against the doorframe. "You had this conversation with Derrick?"

"He was concerned after your performance with Mr. Phillips yesterday."

"It was one client." Guy glared at Derrick who had the smallest but smuggest smile on his face. "I can do better next time. I was just, you know… first day nerves."

"I get that. Really I do." Didn't sound like he did. It sounded like he'd already made up his mind and didn't give a crap about what Guy had to say. He was probably filing his nails or getting a pedicure. "But we reviewed your portfolio last night and, to be honest, Guy, it really wasn't up to our standard."

Our standard? Since when did Fawkes Studio become Fawkes and…whatever Derrick's last name was. Dickhead, probably. Fawkes and Dickhead Studio.

Derrick had Tyler Fawkes eating out of his hand like he had these models eating out of his hand. The man was a monster.

"I thought I was up to your standard at my exhibit."

"It wasn't like your stuff at the exhibit. It was so bland. Boring."

It would have been better if Fawkes had punched him in the face rather than say those words.

"I can go back to doing the other photos. Fashion photography. Portraits. I'm good at that."

"But you don't like it. You said so yourself. And if you're not passionate about it, how can I trust you'll get the job done?"

"Because I—"

No mistakes, human or otherwise.

"I'm sorry, Guy. You're just not what we're looking for at this time."

"So that's it? I'm fired."

"Not fired," Fawkes said. "You never really worked for me, per se."

Guy pinched the bridge of his nose. He could forget about being paid for his time yesterday.

"Listen, I've got to go to a meeting. I'll mail you your portfolio, okay? No need to come back to the studio. Oh, and ask Derrick if he wants to go for lunch today."

Guy hung up the phone and tossed it back to Derrick who caught it deftly.

"What'd he say?" Derrick asked, with an expression that said he knew exactly what Tyler Fawkes had said, as if he'd written the script for him, word for word.

"See you around, Derrick," Guy said, as he turned around and started his way out of LosIce.

"Oh, buddy. I'm sorry." Derrick walked with him, arm over Guy's shoulder. "I wish there was something I could do. Tyler can be a real dick sometimes."

Strangely, he sounded sincere. Maybe he hadn't expected Guy to be fired. Maybe that had been Fawkes's idea. Maybe Derrick really did feel sorry, and whatever Guy saw was in his head. "It's all right. Nothing much you can do."

Derrick patted Guy on the chest. "If you ever need anything, just give me a call."

"I don't have your number."

"You don't?" Derrick stopped, moving his hand from Guy's shoulder to his back. "Ask Brittney." He slapped Guy on the back. "She'll give it to you."

Derrick's smile curled up so broadly, and with such malice, that this time he really did look like a crazed villain. He'd known who Guy was all along, probably since the moment he walked into the studio yesterday and saw Guy with Tyler Fawkes. He'd orchestrated this entire downfall. Guy had fallen right into his plan.

"Give her my regards."

#

It was easier seeing your mother on a hospital bed for the second time… said no one ever. Brittney sat by her mother's side, legs crossed, chewing on her thumb nail. She watched the heart monitor, listened to the beeping sounds. She had dozed off here and there throughout the night but wanted to stay awake to see her mother when she opened her eyes. She wasn't even tired anymore. She'd gone beyond it, adrenaline keeping her up. The nurses had given her a pillow and a blanket, but both items rested untouched on a countertop next to her chair.

It was mid-morning when her mother breathed in deeply and her eyes fluttered open.

Brittney squeezed her hand, gave her mother a moment to take in her surroundings. When Helene's focus fell on Brittney, Brittney smiled. "Hi, Mom."

"Brittney?" She had a pained expression on her face. "Where am I? What happened?"

"You're at the hospital. You fainted. At the house. Do you remember?"

Helene squeezed her eyes shut, sucked air in her nose, and then breathed out through her mouth. She was probably fighting a massive headache. "I remember feeling a little lightheaded at the gallery, so I left. When I got home, I was so dizzy I just wanted to get to bed and lie down for a bit."

"Didn't quite make it to the bed."

Helene put her hands under her and tried to get up, then plopped back down.

"Easy, Mom. You banged your head pretty badly."

Helene touched the bandages around her head. "Stitches?"

Brittney nodded. "Seven stitches." She put the bed covers over her mother. "It was pretty bad."

"So everything is okay?"

"Yeah. The doctor should be in again to check up on you."

"Good." She laid her head back on the pillow. "You must've been so worried."

"Never mind worried. I was terrified." Her mother was her pillar, her strength. Her eyes watered. More crying? She was turning into a water park.

"I'm sorry, honey."

Brittney smiled, a tactic she used to stave off the tears. So far so good. "You're okay now. That's what matters." There must've been something on Brittney's face, because her mother's eyes narrowed. "What?" Brittney asked.

"There's something you're not telling me."

"Nothing. I'm fine. Honest."

"I know when my baby girl is not fine."

"I'm not a baby anymore. You should rest."

"Spit it!"

Brittney mashed her lips together. The last thing she wanted to do was pile more stress on her mother. She licked her lips, pulled a strand of rebellious hair behind her ear. "I got a letter from the university yesterday."

"And?"

Brittney swallowed the lump in her throat. "Didn't get in."

Helene put her hand over Brittney's, rubbing her thumb over Brittney's knuckles. "There's always next year."

Brittney looked down at her mother's hand over her own. As difficult as this next part would be, she knew her mother would support her and love her whatever she decided to do. "I've been thinking about going back to modelling. Only temporarily, though. You know, only until I get into a university or get another job somewhere."

Helene stopped rubbing Brittney's hand. Seconds trudged on and not a peep from Helene. Brittney chanced a glance up at her. Helene's eyes were wide open. So much for post-surgery tiredness.

"What about the exhibit? All that time you spent in the gallery? You learned so much."

"It wasn't good enough. I wasn't good enough. I'm good at modelling. I'm sure there's something more, I just haven't found it yet. But I will."

Helene nodded. "I didn't raise a mannequin."

"Then why do I feel like one?" Her gaze lowered, her voice softened. "Maybe I'm just one of those girls that go through life as a shiny object. A trophy wife."

"Don't say that." Helene tapped Brittney's hand. "Look at me." Brittney couldn't face her mother. "I said, look at me." Brittney sucked her lips in and raised her head. Instead of anger or pity or disappointment on Helene's face, Brittney saw confidence and calm. "There's more to you than what's on the outside. A lot more. I know there is."

"Why? Because of the exhibit?"

Helene laughed. "Heavens no."

"Then what, Mom?"

"You think a degree in business will give you wells of depth?"

"It shows I'm smart. That I can carry a conversation outside of what the world of Instagram has to offer."

Helene laughed again.

"Stop laughing, Mom!"

When Helene sobered up, she had that same soft, warm smile on her face that she'd had when Brittney had gone to her after she quit modelling and felt like her life was falling apart. "Honey, I've met businesspeople who are so incredibly boring you'd think they had no depth outside of sales. You're a smart girl. You were smart and clever enough to make your very first exhibit a glowing success."

Brittney rolled her eyes. "We haven't read the reviews yet."

Helene blew air between her lips. "I don't need to read the reviews. I saw it with my own eyes. But you're not trying to prove you're smart."

"Then what am I looking for?" If Brittney had gone off on the wrong foot, then where was the right one?

"To be a part of someone's life. To care for them and do good things for them and love them. To do more for someone other than put on skinny jeans and snap a photo. You want to be something more to the people you care about."

"I was more. I used to give up my modelling clothes to Goodwill all the time."

Helene cocked an eyebrow. "Did you ever actually deliver them there yourself?"

She'd gotten the bag of clothes together and sent it down to the concierge in the condominium building she lived in, but never took the clothes to Goodwill herself. She'd been too embarrassed about it, had never told any of her model friends or Ackerman. She'd been surrounded by self-interested people, and she hadn't wanted to threaten that social bubble she was part of. One time she'd even given a top away that the clothing designer wanted back, and she had to come up with a lie for why she didn't have it and ended up paying for the shirt instead of telling the truth. She had wanted to do a good thing for someone, and believed she was, but she'd only ever gone halfway in doing it. "I did love someone."

"Who? Derrick? That jerk-face you now hate more than ever?"

"Just because he didn't love me, doesn't mean I didn't love him."

"Think about it, sweetheart. Did you really love him?"

Her mother had caught her again. No, she didn't love Derrick, and that wasn't her anger at him talking either. Even in their best of times, she couldn't see herself with Derrick in one of Guy's love spark photos. "So then how do I get this thing that I so obviously lack?"

"You already have it," Helene said. "You have it with Emily. You know how much that girl adores you? She thinks the world of you. She didn't think that when you first met. She thought you were a stuck-up pretty girl."

"She said that?"

"Yes. I defended you, of course, but she didn't believe me. Not until you and her worked together on the exhibit. Speaking of which—honey, you helped people realize what love is. You brought it out of them."

"Guy did that."

"But you were there with him. Helping him. Supporting him. He couldn't have done that without you."

Brittney rolled her eyes. "More like he *wouldn't* have done it without me."

"You have everything you've been searching for. You may have been blinded to it all those years modelling on Instagram, but taking over the gallery helped you realize it. Helped me see the daughter I always knew you could be."

That was what Guy and Emily had tried to tell her yesterday, that she didn't need to get into a university business program or be a 24/7 success to prove that she was more than her looks. She was more because she supported and helped the people around her, the people she cared for and loved. She wasn't just a means to an end. Guy hadn't used her to get his dream job, to be a success. She'd helped him become that; she'd been part of his life. There was beauty in that kind of relationship—and love, real genuine love, the kind of love she had spent the last month and a half discovering for herself.

"Mom, I really screwed up. Really, really screwed up. I yelled at Guy. I even yelled at Emily." Poor, little social anxiety Emily.

Thinking about Guy, she remembered his gift. It was in her purse. She took out the envelope with her name scribbled across it.

"What's that?" Helene asked.

"Something Guy gave me as a thank you."

She opened the envelope and spilled the contents on the hospital bed. Brittney snickered. Photographs, of course. She browsed through them and caught her breath.

Each photograph was of her, a candid picture of her working at the gallery. Her with Emily. Her at her desk typing on the computer. Her on the phone. Her with the couples he'd photographed. Her setting up the gallery for the exhibit. Her the night of the exhibit.

Guy had seen Brittney be more than she believed herself to be. He had seen her true self and had taken these photos to prove it to her, to make her a believer in herself.

Helene spread the photos out on the bed. "Seems like he saw it before I did. Now there's a boy who loves you. The question is, do you love him?"

She did. But was it too late?

"I see you're up." A man in green scrubs swept into the room, a hospital chart in his hand.

"You must be the doctor who put these in my head," Helene said, pointing to her bandage.

"That's me all right." The doctor checked the heart monitor. Brittney caught a glimpse of the name tag hanging off his scrub shirt. Dr. Moraine.

Guy's father.

She saw the similarities. The same hazel eyes, the same dark unruly hair. The same slender build.

Seeing him now and remembering what Guy had told her about his parents' relationship, Brittney knew she couldn't give up on Guy. Guy's parents had been obsessed with outward appearances, and it had gotten them as far as a divorce, a lost love, and an abandoned son. That wasn't a life she wanted for herself. She couldn't let her obsession with her own looks take away the one person who really saw her.

She had to tell him she was sorry, tell him she loved him.

"Nice photos you got there," Dr. Moraine said as he snuck a peek at the photos on Helene's bed. "My son happens to be a photographer."

"Is he now?" Helene said, giving Brittney a knowing glance.

Brittney stood up from the chair. "Mom, I gotta go. Is that okay?"

"Of course, honey."

"Thanks." She kissed her mother on the cheek and started her leave, then stopped and turned around. "Oh, and Dr. Moraine?"

"Yes?" He looked up from her mother's chart.

"I'm sure your son is a fantastic photographer. You should be proud of him."

He tilted his head to the side. He couldn't piece the puzzle together as well as Helene had. Even so, the corner of his mouth curved up. "I am," he said. "Every day."

Chapter Fifteen

Taped to the door of Guy's apartment was a yellow sheet of paper. In all bolded caps, the sheet read EVICTION NOTICE. Guy tore the notice down and read the contents. He'd have to be out of the apartment by the end of the week if he didn't pay his rent.

Well, that hardly sounded fair.

But of course—why not add more to the shit pile that was Guy's day? Wasn't like he had a job to pay for the apartment anyway.

He crumbled up the notice, tossed it in the hallway, and went into his apartment.

He peeled off his coat and threw it on the futon bed. His hands shook. No, his whole body trembled. Not from the cold either. Everything in his life was falling apart, and he couldn't pick up the pieces and put them together again. In one day, he'd lost his dream job, the only girl he ever loved, and now his shitty apartment.

And now what? Maybe he ought to move back in with his dad. His father had offered, after all. His other option was moving in with his mother, a fate worse than death. She probably wouldn't want him back at the house, anyway. He could hear her snide remarks in his mind. She'd say, "You're twenty-five and you want to move back home?" and then sip from a bottle of Grey Goose.

School—maybe he should go back to school. Guy shook his head.

And study what, exactly? He only cared for photography. Not like he had a slew of vocations he could pick from.

Thankfully, he still had the job application for Taco House.

He looked over at the collage of photos on the wall. Years of photos. His daily practice, his ten thousand hours, up for all to see, and it had proven to be all for nothing. His rapid heartbeat knocked against his ribcage, and his hands clenched into fists. The collage had been his pride and joy. It showed all his hard work and held the promise of future success. But when he saw those photos now, he hated them. All he saw was failure.

He swept his hands over the photos, tearing them down. Not carefully either, not one by one, but ripping them down, letting them pile up on the floor. Hand after hand clawing the wall.

He'd been so lost in his rage he almost missed the knock on his door. Would've missed it altogether if the knock hadn't been so loud and urgent.

Guy stopped clawing and fell into the wall, leaning against it, his cheek on the cool surface. The tips of his fingers tingled.

More rapping on the door.

He groaned. It was probably the superintendent telling him to get his shit together and move out. Probably already had a new tenant lined up. Someone with a decent job and a girlfriend, no doubt.

Knock-knock-knock.

"I'm coming, I'm coming." He opened the door. "Vanessa? What are you doing here? Shouldn't you be—"

The wedding. Josh's wedding was tomorrow. Shit—with everything going on lately it had slipped his mind completely until now. Panic swept through him and would've killed him if he hadn't picked up his rented suit with Josh a week ago. Josh's idea, and thank God for that man's foresight.

That begged the question then: what was Vanessa doing here on the day before her wedding? With a face like she'd been crying, all red cheeks and puffy eyes.

"Can I come in?" she said.

"Sure." Guy stepped aside, opening the door wider. She strode in, and he closed the door behind her.

Vanessa plopped down on the futon bed. A first for her. Usually when she came into the apartment—a rare occurrence—she treaded carefully. She hated this place. Thought it was dirty and messy. A jungle of clutter. She'd tried cleaning it a few times but could never quite get rid of all the grime or change the funky smell that clung to the walls and furniture. She called it a boy's zone, where no woman was allowed entry.

"Everything okay? Is Josh okay?"

Vanessa nodded, then shook her head no. Her face crinkled up like she was about to burst out in tears.

"Something is definitely not okay."

"I don't think I can go through with the wedding."

"That's ridiculous." He sat down next to her. "You and Josh were made to marry each other." Seriously, if they didn't marry, it would be like disobeying one of the laws of physics.

"I can't do it. I'm so…" She trailed off.

"Everyone gets cold feet the day before their wedding." No way of knowing if that was true, but he'd heard it often enough on TV and movies that it had to hold a kernel of truth.

The truth here was that Guy had no idea what he was talking about, and Vanessa should've picked any other person other than Guy to go to about this.

"I'm scared, Guy." The tears spilled from her eyes and streamed down.

Guy put an arm around her and hugged her, rocking her back and forth. "You know, I expected I'd have this conversation with Josh, not with you."

She sniffed. "He hasn't come to you?"

"I don't think Josh has ever had a problem in his life." In their past as roommates, Guy was the one with the problems, and Josh was the one with the solutions. "You're marrying a solid man. A pillar of strength."

"Well, he's marrying a nervous wreck."

"It's okay." Guy went hunting for a box of tissue. Some old napkins from a pizza delivery lay on the kitchen counter. He picked them up, then noticed the grease. That was out. Next stop was the washroom where he found a towel. "Here."

As upset and tear-faced as she was, she still gave the towel a cocked stare.

"It was Josh's."

She took it and dabbed her eyes with it. "Thanks."

Guy sat back down. "Now tell Uncle Guy what's going on."

"It's going to sound silly."

"Try me," Guy said, smiling. In this scenario, Guy would play the pillar of strength. He'd pretend to be Josh. Think like Josh, act like him. If he screwed it up, Josh would never forgive him.

"I guess…" She sniffed, tucking her hair behind her ears. "I guess I've been with Josh for so long I'm worried I haven't really lived."

"You're right." Guy snorted. "That does sound silly."

Vanessa slapped him with the towel. "Not helping!"

"Okay, okay, I'm sorry." He pursed his lips, thinking. There was something else she wasn't telling him, something more that she kept hidden. "You guys have done more living than most people I know. What about all those trips you guys went on together? And no one parties harder than Josh. The man can get drunk on a weeknight and still crush it at work. Trust me, I lived with the man—he never stopped."

"We have done a lot together. Seen a lot. Gone to a lot of places." She smiled a bit. "He's so much fun."

"So then?"

The smile disappeared. "What if we end up like my parents? What if I get, I dunno, bored with him?"

Ah, so that was it. Guy had met Vanessa's parents once before. Miserable people. Fun killers. Frowny faces and bitchy stares. They were people lost in what ifs and dwelled too much on the decisions they could've made instead of dealing with the decisions they had made.

"You guys are nothing like your parents. Josh isn't like your dad."

For one, Josh had a highly paid and professional job. And two, Josh had his life planned, and no matter how drunk he got, he never did anything to jeopardize that plan.

"But maybe I'm like my mother."

"Your parents got married because your mother got pregnant with your sister." This was a fact Vanessa had shared with him and Josh back in university when they were becoming a trio of best friends. "They felt like they had no choice. And maybe they would've gotten married anyway if they'd had a normal relationship, but that's not on you guys. You and Josh are choosing to get married because you love each other."

"Does he love me?"

Guy chuckled. "All he talks about is how much he loves you. It's like the man has no hobby. Don't you love him back?"

She smiled, took a moment. Memories passed over her eyes. Then her smile faded. "But what if I'm not good enough for him?"

"You're perfect for each other."

"How do you know that?"

"Seen it with my own eyes. I was there when you first started dating."

But she still wasn't convinced. Words could only say so much. He had to show her.

Again, he went on a hunt in the jungle, like Indiana Jones on a quest for buried treasure. Guy lifted up garbage left on the floor only to be disappointed.

"What are you looking for?" Vanessa asked.

Photos, the same photos Josh had shown him to prove where his talent truly lay in photography. He hadn't believed it then. But those photos had convinced Brittney to work with him.

Now where the hell were they?

"Aha!" Guy found the box under Josh's bed. He brought them back to Vanessa. She opened the box and looked through the photos.

"When did you take these?"

"Here and there." Guy shrugged. "When the shot was right." He'd never shown these photos to Vanessa before.

"I wondered why you didn't want to take photos of us for your exhibit."

"You guys are the reason the exhibit exists. Watching you guys fall in love was the first time I saw real love and captured it with my photography."

They made him believe in love again after his own parents' divorce. He'd been there from the start of their relationship, watching their love story unfold chapter after chapter. If only it hadn't taken this long to figure that out.

"Do you still believe you and Josh will end up like your parents?"

She shook her head. Fresh tears came to her eyes, but she was smiling this time. "Thank you."

He smiled back at her. "Now, if you don't mind, I'm sure you've got to get ready for tomorrow's big day. And as for me"—he stood up—"I've got to pack my things and move out."

"Move out? To where?"

"My dad's place probably. Call me Mr. Evicted."

"Can't you make the rent with the sales you made?"

"Yeah, I just haven't picked up the money yet." Even if he did pay for this month's rent, so what? He'd have to think about next month and the month after that, and that'd be difficult when he was minus gainful employment. Moving back with his dad—while not ideal—was better than the streets. He needed time to figure out his next step.

"Stay with Josh at our apartment."

"With you guys? On the night before your wedding? No thanks."

"No, silly. I'm going to stay at my mom's tonight and get ready there. You can stay with him. He'd appreciate your company. What do you say?"

"I'll get my tux."

#

After leaving the hospital, Brittney hopped in a cab and went straight to Guy's apartment—only to find he wasn't there. He'd left, and good riddance for that, or so the superintendent would have her believe. He'd be back to pick up the rest of his crap. She went upstairs to see for herself. She bumped into one of Guy's neighbours who told her he had left with some girl, and the two of them had mentioned something about a wedding.

Right, the wedding. Josh and Vanessa were getting married tomorrow. She hadn't been invited herself—naturally, she barely knew Josh and Vanessa—and she had no idea where the wedding would be held.

She tried calling him, but all she got was a message back saying Guy's phone was out of service. Should she leave a note with the neighbour? Slip it under his door?

Either way, she'd have to wait. But what if he read the note and then threw it out? What if he had so much junk in the apartment that he ignored the note altogether, then packed up his things and moved to someplace else entirely, and she'd miss her chance to see him, to talk to him? She couldn't take that risk. Her emotions ran circles around her heart, eager to get out. She had to tell him, and as soon as she could. He was going to his best friend's wedding thinking that the only woman he ever loved didn't love him back.

But in order to get to him, she needed help. She didn't know where Josh and Vanessa were getting married, but she knew someone who did.

She checked the time on her phone, seven at night. Again, she got in a cab and arrived at Sneaky Dees on College Street.

Sneaky Dees was loud, busy. People drinking craft beers and eating cheesy nachos. The hostess told Brittney the show was upstairs.

Upstairs was even louder, an indie rock band playing on a stage. The crowd, full of young hipsters in flannel shirts, skinny jeans, and boots, went nuts over the band. Probably some local group with a local, loyal following. The song finished, and the band thanked everyone and got off stage. A toque-wearing, bearded man standing beside Brittney lifted a fist in the air and screamed at the top of his lungs. Brittney stiffened, the sound—a little too high pitched for someone whose beard showed a great deal of testosterone—seared her eardrums.

Brittney looked around but couldn't find Emily. She better not have missed her performance.

An emcee got up on the mic. "And now for our next act, I'd like to welcome up to the stage, Miss Emily Twill."

Some applause followed but pitiful compared to what the last act had. Emily got up on the stage, standing under the spotlight. As usual, she wore all black, her makeup done to make her face whiter than it was, her lipstick a bright crimson. She had short sleeves on which showed off all her tattoos. She clutched her harmonica in her hand. She didn't tremble—at least not visibly—but her movements were so robotic, so purposeful, Brittney could tell Emily was trying hard not to screw anything up.

Brittney clenched her jaw, had her hands in tight fists. If she was this nervous for Emily, it was a miracle Emily hadn't fainted from her anxiety.

Emily cleared her throat and brought her lips to the microphone. "Hi, every—"

The microphone screeched. Brittney winced. The crowd moaned and groaned.

Emily pressed her lips together, closed her eyes. She took a moment and breathed deeply. She opened her eyes and tried again with the mic. "Hi, everyone." She smiled and Brittney did, too. "My name is Emily, and I'd like to play a song for you on my harmonica." She paused, as if waiting for a reaction. None came. "Okay, so… here goes."

She licked her lips and brought the harmonica up to her mouth.

She trembled. Trembled so much Brittney could see it. The spotlights were like a beacon showing her anxiety like a giant zit on her nose.

She'd won the battle with the microphone but hadn't won the war.

"Excuse me," Brittney said, weaving through the crowd to get to the front of the stage. Even though Emily had told her she'd be more nervous if she saw Brittney at the front, the truth was Emily needed her. Needed her to help give her the confidence to send her social anxiety packing.

More than anything, Brittney needed to show Emily she wasn't alone in this. She had friends, supporters.

She got nearly to the front, but the crowd was shoulder to shoulder, and she couldn't push through. Emily looked over to her left. Brittney followed her gaze to someone about Emily's age and was vaguely familiar.

A boy. Scruff on his face. Tattoos all over his arms. It was the pizza boy who had delivered the pizza for the models for Guy's photo shoot. Were they dating? They must be—and he was here showing his support like any good boyfriend would do.

Then Emily looked to the centre of the crowd, and Brittney caught her gaze. Brittney gave her an encouraging nod, letting her know she could do this, and that she was here to watch her succeed.

Emily smiled, then brought the harmonica up to her mouth, closed her eyes, and began to play.

The music sounded beautiful, soothing. The crowd swayed to the melody. Emily continued to play with her eyes closed. She played like no one else was there, like how she would at the gallery.

Finished, she lowered the harmonica. An air of calm surrounded her. She commanded the crowd's attention. She stood like a conqueror—not only of the crowd but of her own anxiety. "Thank you," she said into the mic.

The crowd exploded in applause and cheers as Emily exited the stage.

Amidst pats on the shoulder and congratulations from those around her, the pizza boy went to her, gave her a hug, and kissed her on the mouth. Emily basked in the fanfare. She probably hadn't been surrounded by so many crowds in her life before. She handled it well, thanking everyone who congratulated her. If she had any anxieties over it, she didn't show it.

Emily excused herself and approached the bar where Brittney waited. Though her cheeks were redder from all the excitement, Emily stood taller, her chin up.

"Wasn't that the pizza boy?" Brittney said, eyebrow cocked.

"It's been going on for a while. Probably wouldn't have happened if it wasn't for Guy's exhibit."

Brittney smiled. She, too, wouldn't have gotten to where she was if it hadn't been for the exhibit. "You did great up there."

"Thanks."

"I'm proud of you."

Emily beamed, puffing out her chest. "Thanks for coming. I didn't think you'd show up."

Neither did Brittney, and she would have missed it, too, if it hadn't been for her mother. Missing this would've ruined her friendship with Emily, a friendship she hoped to make lifelong. "I'm sorry, Emily. I didn't mean those things I said. I was being…"

"An idiot?" Emily ventured.

"A big idiot."

"What matters is that you're here now."

They shared a sisterly hug, and Brittney realized then just how much she missed Emily, how much she had wanted Emily to be part of her life.

"Look…" Brittney began.

"Oh, I see." Emily rolled her eyes. "Now the real reason you came here comes out."

Brittney felt the colour from her face drain away.

"I'm kidding," Emily said, slapping Brittney on the forearm. "What's up?"

"I screwed up with Guy, and I need your help to fix it."

Emily wiggled her eyebrows, a sparkle in her eyes. She'd seen Brittney's feelings for Guy before Brittney had made sense of those feelings. Without a doubt, she'd seen the same for Guy. She was probably the reason why Guy had started taking those photos of Brittney at the gallery in the first place.

It had all been because of Emily, her best friend, her little matchmaker.

Emily rubbed her hands together. "I'd love to help."

Chapter Sixteen

"The wedding is at the Liberty Grand," Emily said, "in the Exhibition Place."

They were in Emily's parents' Ford Escape. Brittney sat in the back, Emily in the front passenger seat, and her boyfriend, the tattooed pizza boy, whose name was Jeff, was driving.

"Never been there before," Brittney said. She'd been to the Ex as a kid once, but never any of the historic buildings.

"Me neither. Supposed to be really beautiful, though."

Emily's plan was to find out where the wedding was being held through the wedding planner, a.k.a. her mother, but it didn't quite work according to plan. Emily explained the situation between Guy and Brittney, and when her mother said no, Emily accused her mother of breaking up the love of two people, which was a direct violation of what she did for a living. Unsurprisingly, insults hadn't worked either, and thus Plan B was born: cracking into her mother's computer. Emily did it remotely, from her own laptop, and managed to find the file for Josh and Vanessa. When asked where she learned how to hack into computers, Emily said that when she suffered from social anxiety and hardly went out—and it was here she wiggled her eyebrows—she developed other certain skills.

Emily looked back at Brittney. "So what are you going to say to him?"

Brittney bit her lip. She made a list in her head. At the very least, Guy was owed an apology. Next she had to tell him how she felt. How she felt about herself and about him. The task was tantamount to climbing Mount Everest. She'd never said these things to a guy before. But she wasn't saying it to any ordinary guy. She was saying it to Guy Moraine. Her Guy.

"You look phenomenal, by the way."

"Thanks," Brittney said, smoothing out her dress. She'd put on a form-fitting blue dress with black heels., Hopefully the result was elegant, sophisticated, and beautiful.

"I don't think you need to say anything," Emily said. "Just go in looking like that, and you'll win him over."

"That's not the point, Emily."

Emily winked. "I know, I know."

She wanted to look good for the wedding. And she wanted to look good for Guy. She couldn't go traipsing in wearing jeans and a sweater.

She wanted him to have all the pieces of her.

The car screeched to a halt, and Jeff parked in front of a big, looming building, the parking lot cleared of all the snow. The Liberty Grand was like a castle, a lot bigger than what Brittney expected. Stairs led up to the main entrance of the, for lack of a better term, keep. Curtain walls spread out to either side of the keep, leading to towers.

If this was how big it was outside, who knew what it was like inside. A maze for sure. Some kind of labyrinth. Hopefully there'd be staff to direct them. Signage at the very least.

"Thanks, baby," Emily said. She snapped off her seat belt and gave Jeff a peck on the cheek. She and Brittney got out of the car.

Jeff rolled down the window, his tattooed hand hanging off the windowsill. "I'll find a parking spot and meet up with you guys later."

He drove off, and they climbed the stairs to the arched doors, modernized with glass.

They walked in. A sign showed the day's events. Four weddings. Emily scanned the sign. "Here. Josh and Vanessa. Patriarch Room." She frowned. "Now where's the Patriarch Room?"

The building had high ceilings and an expansive courtyard in the middle. "This place is huge," Brittney said, her own words sending her off to panic mode.

"We'll find them. Ah!" Emily spotted a security guard standing off by one of the hallways. "Excuse me, do you know where the Patriarch Room is? We're late for my friend's wedding reception."

Huh. A week ago Brittney would've had to order food for Emily if they were out for lunch. Now here she was approaching strangers and eliciting information. All without the slightest hesitation. She probably wasn't completely cured, but her harmonica performance last night had helped her dig up some confidence.

"It's down the hallway to your right," the security guard said, pointing to the hallway across from them.

Emily flashed a smile. "Thanks."

They turned and started toward the hallway.

"No, no," the guard said, stopping them. He rubbed his chin. "It's left. I'm sure it's a left." He pointed down the hallway he stood by. "Down this way."

"You sure?" Brittney said. She placed a calming hand over her heart palpitations. If the people who worked here couldn't figure this place out, what chance did they have?

The guard shrugged. "Sorry. I'm new. Just got this job yesterday, and I'm still learning the layout."

Oh, great. Just what they needed.

The guard pursed his lips, looking up at the ceiling as if he could see the Liberty Grand's floor plans there. "I'm sure it's a right. It has to be." He pointed down the hall. "Go right."

Brittney and Emily nodded at each other, both saying at the same time, "Right it is."

They strode down the right hallway, their heels clicking on the marble floors. Chatter and music sounded distantly but grew louder the closer they got to an arched doorway that led into a foyer with a fountain in the middle. Past the foyer, they found the banquet hall.

The reception was in full swing. Groups of people huddled by the two bars on either ends of the hall. Mixed drinks in their hands, people stood away from their tables and talked with friends and family. A live band played dinner music in the background, no words, just melodies. Kids raced each other across the dancefloor illuminated by chandeliers above.

It was a big wedding. Easily three hundred people.

"Do you see him?" Emily said.

In this small village? Probably not. She looked everywhere. Her gaze turned, her head spun. She recognized no one. Didn't see Josh or Vanessa, and Vanessa should be the easiest to find in her wedding dress.

Then she spotted him. It was him, all right. A guy with a beard and a lousy fitting suit. Even wore sneakers instead of black shoes. An air of I-don't-care-what-people-think in the way he stood. Typical Guy. She went up to him, his back to her, touched his arm, and turned him toward her.

"Hi—" Her words caught in her throat. Her heart dropped down to her stomach. "You're not Guy."

He was just a guy. Not her Guy.

#

Guy sat in his assigned seat at the long table reserved for the wedding party. As best man, he sat next to Josh.

His leg bounced up and down, his finger tapping the back of the cue cards in his hands. He skimmed over his best man speech. He'd gone over it a dozen times, and yet the words didn't stick. Even as he read them now, the words blurred. He blinked to clear his vision. No luck.

Nerves, just nerves.

"You ready?" Josh asked, sitting beside him, a slight, sadistic smile on his face.

"Can't we skip the speeches?" Guy said.

Josh tilted his head, making it seem as though he chewed over Guy's request. Then his face broke out in a huge grin. "Nah."

Guy's eyes narrowed. "I hate you."

"You're going to do great." He put his hand on Guy's shoulder and squeezed. "You look the part at least."

Guy took a deep breath. He tugged at his tie a bit. How did Josh wear this noose around his neck every day? "Okay. I'm ready. I think."

"Just don't screw it up, okay? Vanessa will kill you."

Vanessa was making the rounds to each dinner table, resplendent in her wedding dress. Radiant. Her smile brightened the hall up. She was the happiest Guy had ever seen her.

He gulped. "No pressure."

#

The Guy-imposter's eyes perused Brittney from the top of her blond hair to the tips of her pedicured toes, smiling at her lecherously. Where Guy sometimes looked lazy and sloppy, this guy reminded her of a cockroach. Brittney stepped back, hugging herself, feeling like she needed a shower with disinfectant.

"You bastard!" A woman stampeded toward them, hiking up the hem of her bright pink outfit with her white elbow-length gloved hands, a brooch on her left breast. One of Vanessa's bridesmaids. She had fire in her eyes and held a champagne glass. "Is this her? You told me this was over."

Brittney's eyes widened. She'd been caught in a case of wrong place at the wrong time with the wrong guy with a history of cheating. "I think you have the wrong—"

Champagne splashed in Brittney's face and all over her blue dress. The alcohol stung her eyes, and she yelped. Caught off balance, she teetered back on her heel, heard a snap, and tripped, falling down on her tail bone.

An audible rip sounded, and her form-fitting dress felt a whole lot looser.

She blinked and wiped her face. The bridesmaid came after her with the emptied champagne glass. The intent on her shrieking, red, angered face was clear: that champagne glass was now a weapon. She lifted the glass up over her head and brought it down.

Brittney steeled herself, lifting her hands up like a shield.

A tattooed fist flew right across the bridesmaid's face, knocking her to the side, the champagne glass soaring across the room and smashing on the dancefloor.

"Oh, my God! Emily!" She had come out of nowhere with her tiny fists of fury flying. She held out her hands and helped Brittney stand up. Mouth agape, Brittney couldn't believe Emily—her shy, nervous, anxious Emily—had done something so rash, so out of her comfort zone, so… totally bad ass.

"That hurt more than getting tattooed on my butt." Emily waved her hand, grimacing. "We're in the wrong wedding. You gotta get out of here!"

A crowd had gathered around the downed bridesmaid, helping her up. They were distracted for the time being.

"But what about you?" Brittney asked. They were supposed to

infiltrate the wedding, find Guy, and talk to him. Instead they managed to crash a wedding they never intended to attend. The result was one ruined dress and one black eye.

"I'll hold them off and catch up with you later."

"Since when did this become a mission?"

Emily shoved her. "Just go!"

Eyes turned toward the two of them, the crowd registering what had taken place. She couldn't waste any more time. Emily sacrificed herself so that Brittney could find Guy. "I won't let you down," Brittney said to Emily. She slipped her heels off and ran out of the banquet hall.

Her bare feet slapped against the floor, air rushing through her hair. She ran down the hallway and into the main entrance. Passing the guard, she said, "Wrong hallway!"

"Really?" the guard asked. "Hey! You all right?"

"Peachy."

As Brittney ran down the other hallway, she expected someone from the wedding she'd inadvertently crashed to come after her. She found a small alcove where a statue stood. She slid in and behind the statue, put her back to it, and pulled in the ripped hem of her ruined dress to cover herself. She held her breath, squeezing her eyes tight.

She waited and heard nothing.

"Phew." She slid down to a crouch, dropping her shoes and hugging her knees to her chest. She was a sweaty, tired mess. Sticky from the champagne. Makeup ruined. Heel snapped on one shoe. Dress ripped, stained, and the opposite of elegant or beautiful.

And worse, she still hadn't found Guy. She put her head down between her knees. Maybe she should go back, find Emily, face whatever consequences they'd have to face, apologize profusely, and then leave.

"And now," a voice called, and Brittney lifted her head up.

"Before we invite the bride and groom to their first dance, I'd like to invite the best man to say a few words."

Brittney stood up. Another reception was just across from where she'd been hiding. She poked her head out from the alcove and looked both ways. No wedding party from hell in sight.

She walked into the reception, one hand holding the straps of her shoes, the fingers of her other hand crossed.

"Please welcome the best man, Guy Moraine."

Brittney's heart paused in her chest.

Applause erupted, and there was Guy, standing in front of a podium atop a stage.

She had found him.

And now the real struggle began—how to keep him.

Chapter Seventeen

Even from where she stood at the back of the reception, Brittney could tell Guy looked different. Not at all like the guy she had mistaken him for at the other reception. She stayed in the back where no one could see her. She'd wait until he was done with his speech and then try to catch him when he was alone or not preoccupied with something else.

Guy cleared his throat and leaned against the microphone. He scanned the banquet hall, making sure everyone was ready. All eyes were on him. Silence filled the room.

"I know what you're all thinking—since when was the wedding photographer part of the wedding party?" He snickered at his own joke, but his audience was hushed. Brittney winced; it wasn't his best joke, but he was warming up. "The truth is I've known Josh since we were in diapers and sucking on our thumbs. I grew up with him, watched him become the man he is tonight standing beside the woman he was born to be with. But decades of knowing each other wasn't the reason he chose me to be his best man.

"Josh and I met Vanessa in university. We had a humanities course together, something about ancient mythology. We were in a group assignment, became friends, and started hanging out together. But just friends, or so I thought. But as the months went by, I had the sneaky suspicion that Josh and Vanessa were dating, or at least were thinking about hooking up. I had no way to prove it except through my photography.

"So I snapped a photo of them together. This photo."

A screen behind him flashed a photo of Josh and Vanessa, both in their late teens, at some coffee shop, looking at each other with a slight smile on their faces. But it was the eyes that gave it away. Love really started with the eyes. It made love tangible.

Brittney had seen this photo before in the collection Guy had hidden away. It was one of her favourites, too.

"They didn't know I'd taken it. I'd been late meeting up with them that day, and they hadn't seen me come in. But I saw them, and I was compelled to take their picture. That day they looked in love, as crazy as that sounds. When Josh finally told me they were dating, I simply told him I already knew. And when he first kissed her and he wanted to tell me how amazing it felt and how amazing she was, I told him I already knew. And finally, when six months had rolled by and he told me he loved her and was going to tell her that night, I told him, well, it's about time you told her.

"Then he told me, all right Mr. Know-it-All, how do you know? And I showed him this photograph. I told him I knew they were in love from that first moment. And the sucker believed me. So you're welcome, Vanessa." He winked at her, and laughter followed.

"The truth is, I'm guilty of creeping on their relationship, documenting their ever-growing love ever since." He clicked a controller he held in his hand. A collage of all the photos he had taken of Josh and Vanessa popped up on the screen, from their days in university, all way to the present. One of the photos had even been taken at the gallery. Then he switched to the next slide, this one showing a picture of Josh and Vanessa today, on their wedding day. "And I'm continuing that tonight. Yes, I slipped this one in last minute before doing this speech." He chuckled softly, shaking his head. "This is going to sound silly, but Josh and Vanessa, thank you for falling in love and letting me document it. Josh was the one who said I had this talent to tell the story of how two people fall in love. The *love spark*, he called it. It sounded absolutely ridiculous because I've never said the words myself to anyone." He stopped abruptly, looking out in the crowd as if he were searching for someone. Was it her? Was he thinking of her? Searching for her? Or was this just a dramatic pause? "Scratch that. I have said it to someone. And recently." Brittney's stomach tightened—he had meant her. "And it's through Josh and Vanessa, watching their love grow, that I could see it for myself. So raise your glasses everyone, and let's hope we all find a love as inspiring and as fulfilling and as strong as the one Josh and Vanessa have."

Everyone cheered, raised their glasses, and sipped.

"Now let's freaking dance!" Guy screamed into the mic, fist in the air. Josh and Vanessa shot up from their seats, Vanessa giving Guy a look he couldn't miss. "Oh, right." Guy smiled sheepishly. "I forgot the bride and the groom still have to do their first dance, and then the parents are going to say something. Sorry, everyone. My bad. No dancing yet."

Everyone laughed once more. To them, this was part of the best man speech. But she knew Guy had gotten carried away by the moment.

Guy stepped down from the podium and started toward the bar. Brittney followed him, ignoring the stares from the people she passed. She came for one person, and she had found him. At the moment, he had her back toward her as he talked to the bartender.

She closed her eyes, took a breath, then opened her eyes. She had her shoes in her hand and a ruined dress, but she had come to talk to him with her words, not her appearance. "Guy."

It sounded like a whisper, too low for him to hear.

She tried again, this time stepping closer to him, projecting her voice. "Guy."

He stiffened. Slowly, he turned around to face her. "Brittney? What are you—" His eyes took her in, then bugged out. "What happened to you?" He went up to her.

"You look…different," she said, ignoring the concern in his eyes and his tone. Instead, she focused on his clean-shaven face, his hair cut and gelled, his fitted tuxedo, the smell of his aftershave. He was so handsome. She ran her hand over his smooth cheek. "You shaved."

"And I nicked myself," he said, pointing to a pink spot under his chin. "What are you doing here? We should sit down. Did you like go through the shrubs outside or something? Why are you so sticky?"

"I have to tell you something." She laid her hand on his chest. "I have to tell you something right now."

He furrowed his brow. "What?"

Her eyes heated up with tears. "That speech was beautiful."

"Did you come all the way here, looking as if you outran hellhounds, to tell me *that*?"

She shook her head. "No, I…I came to tell you I'm sorry. Sorry for the things I said to you yesterday."

"You don't have to—"

"Let me finish."

"Okay."

Silence. Brittney bit her tongue.

"So?"

"Just give me a minute," she said. "I didn't really think this through." She'd been too busy trying to figure out how to get to him than worry about what she'd do once she found him. Not only that, but a fair bit of people stared at them as opposed to the bride and groom on their first dance. "Everyone's staring."

Guy noticed it, too. He extended his hand to her. "Follow me."

She took his hand, and he escorted her out to the foyer.

"Better?" Guy said. They sat by the fountain's ledge, listening to the streams of water spill into a pool.

"Did you mean what you said?" she asked. "In your speech? That you'd never said it to anyone?"

"If by 'it' you mean 'I love you,' then yes, I haven't." He snorted. "Which, in hindsight, makes the exhibit that much more ironic. The only person I ever said it to was you. And I was surprised at how easy it was."

"Easy?"

"Yeah. Like it felt natural. Like why hadn't I said it from the first day I met you?"

"Because you would've looked like a psycho?"

"Most definitely." The corner of his lip curved up. "Was it nice to hear? Has any other guy—an imposter Guy—said it to you?"

Imposter Guys didn't use the word love. They preferred a different "L" word: lust.

"Guys don't usually say *I love you* to me."

"I find that hard to believe."

"I mean, they do. But they say it about the way I look or what I'm wearing or a part of my body. Or my whole body. It's never about me. They never love me for me. They never saw past what I looked like. All they saw was a pretty blond girl. They never saw what I could become. Unlike you."

"I guess that makes me something of a gentleman?" He considered it, tugging at his tie and brushing pretend dust off his suit jacket. "Never been called that before."

"You saw who I wanted to become before I even realized it, and it had nothing to do with being smart or getting into business school." She focused on her hands in her lap. "I saw the gift. The photos you took of me. Thank you. I needed those."

Guy took her hand in his. "You're all those things. All the things in the photos, all the things you want to be. Smart, clever, capable. But you're even more than that. Sometimes we have a hard time seeing what we're like deep down. No one knows that better than I do. I had no clue who I was deep down. All I saw when I looked in the mirror was someone without direction. A drifter. I wanted to be a photographer, but I didn't even know what direction I was going with that, either. My photos were a mess, just like the rest of my life. Then I met you. You saw the potential in my photography, in my pictures of couples in love. You pushed for it. You pulled the director card and demanded it for the gallery. You built a path for me, set me on a course. No one has ever believed in me as strongly as you have. No one would've ever taken that risk for me. That leap of faith. And for that, I thank you. And for that, I love you."

"It isn't just for my looks?"

"It's not why I love you."

"And what happens when I get old? What happens when this beauty fades?"

He put his hands on her waist. "You'll be as beautiful to me when we're old and grey as you are now. True beauty, the kind of beauty you have both inside and out, never fades. I'll always love you. From now until we're eighty. Wrinkles, crow's-feet, bunions—bring it."

"I'm not getting bunions."

"The point is, you don't have to be afraid of me falling out of love with you. I know what love is because of you, and for so long I was too afraid to understand it. So I ran away from it. I ignored it. I thought I'd end up like my parents. But you opened my eyes and showed me the truth of what I was convinced wasn't there."

Brittney put her hands on his chest, felt his rapid heartbeat. She didn't meet his gaze. "I'm sorry for all those things I said. You weren't just using me as a means to an end. As some kind of tool. If anything, I was using you to get ahead."

"We used each other." Guy shook his head. "No, not used. We never *used* each other. That's the wrong word. Couples don't do that. Couples in love don't do that."

He meant them. They were a couple and were in love. She liked the sound of it. It was so mature, so invigorating to hear, to know, and to accept.

"We supported each other," Guy said. "We were there for each other. We didn't give up on each other. Okay, granted, we had a bump on the road, but we're here now together."

Hearing him refer to them as a "we" felt good in her stomach, in her heart. She'd felt alone for so long, even with all her Instagram followers, even with Ackerman and Derrick. Ever since her father had left. But she realized now it had never been about getting her father back. He had abandoned her and made her feel like she had to become someone others liked. What she had really wanted was a "we," had wanted to be part of someone's life and for them to be part of hers. She wanted a team, a partnership, a lover. She had that now with her mother, with Emily, and now with Guy. "You're sounding very romantic right now."

"That's not all. Apparently, I can also see when couples fall in love."

"Oh?" she said, playing along. "What do you see when you look at me looking at you?"

He gave her his deep, unwavering, photographer's stare, where the lens focused on one object in the frame and blurred out the rest. "I see capital L love."

She smiled, her heart pounding so hard in her chest she was convinced he could hear it, that it was louder than the music blaring from the banquet hall. "Well, Guy Stumps Moraine," she said, using the nickname she'd given him that first day they had become a team, "I capital L love you."

He squeezed her hips. "I'm going to kiss you now."

"You better."

"And I'm never going to stop kissing you."

"What if we need to breathe?"

"Air's overrated."

"So now I give you life, is that it?"

He replied with a kiss, a kiss that wasn't born from trying to make someone else jealous or born from explosive, untethered passion. This kiss was purposeful. It meant something, symbolized their connection and love, and above all else—it felt damn good.

"You gave me a life," he said, "that I can love not only because of the path you set me on, but because you're in it."

"Kiss me again, Stumps."

And he did. Again and again, until they were both out of breath.

Chapter Eighteen

"I've never danced so much in my life," Brittney said back at Guy's apartment. After fixing her makeup and wiping off the stickiness as much as she could, she'd become Guy's plus one at the wedding. She had to be careful with the ripped dress and made sure not to flash her underwear unsuspectingly to anyone on the dance floor. With her one heel broken, she'd been barefoot the whole time, too, and had become known by everyone as the Shoeless Girl.

"Best. Wedding. Ever," Guy said, putting his camera on the kitchen counter.

"It was fun." Emily and Jeff had joined up with them, too. Emily had been unharmed, and no charges had been pressed against her for delivering a Mike Tyson special to the bridesmaid. They had kept her captive for a bit, had threatened to call the police, but Jeff, who seemed more savvy and street smart, had come to her rescue. The wedding had been more enjoyable with the man she loved in her arms and with her best friend beside her. "Josh and Vanessa are perfect for each other."

"It's almost criminal."

"Think we'll ever get there?" she asked, then wished she could grasp those words and shove them back into her mouth. Sounded a bit needy.

Guy gave her a lopsided smile and kissed her on the neck. "I'm going to make sure we do."

"Me, too."

The apartment felt different. Still dirty and a mess, but the last time she'd been here, she had been in a fight with Guy, and it was here where she had found the pictures that set them on this journey. Back then she'd been so angry with Guy, convinced they couldn't work together, convinced it would all backfire.

Huh—a lot had changed in a month and a half.

"You may not have known this before you told me you capital L love me," Guy said, scratching the back of his neck, "but as of next week I'll be homeless."

"I know, and I still love you." She could've paid him the money owed from the exhibit, but it still wouldn't be enough to keep this place afloat. Maybe for a few months, but then he'd be right back to where he started. "Guess we'll both be moving back with our parents."

Guy groaned.

"It'll only be temporary," she said, fixing his tie and suit jacket, even though neither needed fixing.

"Do you have a plan?"

"I think so." She'd continue to work at the Collar Gallery with her mother and gain more experience. She needed time to figure out her next move. Business school wasn't for her. She had wanted it for the wrong reasons. Maybe she could combine her experience as a model with what she learned working at the gallery. Something to do with fashion, maybe? And marketing? "What about you?"

Guy sighed. "I need a job. Any job, really. Something to pay the bills while I start my own photography studio."

"Your own photography studio?"

"I was thinking of calling it the Love Spark Studio. Maybe I could do wedding photos?"

"You did it tonight."

"And I liked it. Who knows? Maybe I could do photographs of people and their relationships, document couples and families and friends." Chuckling, he shook his head. "If only the old Guy could hear me now."

Brittney smiled. Guy's camera sat atop the kitchen counter next to the empty pizza box. She picked it up and fiddled with all the gimmicks and settings in the back. Even though she'd spent most of her life posing in front of cameras, she'd never operated one herself. "Does this thing have a timer on it?"

"Of course. Why?"

"We've never taken a picture together."

"I see," Guy said, smiling boyishly, hands on her hips. "You want a pic of me and Brittney?"

"Maybe you'll see the love in us."

He took the camera from her and fiddled with it. "I'll set the timer." He set it down on the kitchen counter. "Okay, you ready? It's gonna go off in thirty seconds."

He took her by the hand and positioned her next to him, standing far enough away from the camera. The futon bed would serve as their background.

She stiffened, feeling uncomfortable. What was she thinking suggesting taking a photo now? It was three in the morning. They were both exhausted, and it showed. She must look like a scandal worthy of TMZ: hair frizzy, eyes dark and baggy, face gleaming with sweat, dress torn and stained.

Guy, on the other hand, ran a hand through his hair and was ready. He held her hand in his, facing the camera.

"Shouldn't we be looking at each other?" Brittney said.

"Nah, let's take a traditional portrait."

Brittney rolled her eyes. "Boooo-ring."

He tugged on her hand. "It's almost thirty seconds. Smile at the camera."

"I know how this works, Guy. I was a model."

"No duck lips."

She elbowed him in the side.

"In ten, nine, eight, seven, six…"

Guy dropped her hand and ambushed her with tickles. She bent forward, laughing out loud.

"What are you doing, you maniac?" she said, holding onto his wrists to stop him.

He stopped, cupping her face with his hands so she looked right at him. "This."

Then he kissed her, and the camera flashed.

Your Starter Library is Waiting for You!

It's important to me that I build a strong, close-knit relationship with my readers. It helps with my writing and lets me know what you'd like to see more of. I occasionally send updates with details on new releases, special offers and other exclusive, bonus content. By signing up, you'll be the first to know about everything related to the books, characters, and worlds I loved to create and I hope you love to read.

And if you sign up, I'll send you **two free books** to get your George Kayde library started. Those books are:

Table for Two – a romantic comedy set in Toronto about a sassy restauranteur and a savvy business consultant.

Knight in Training – a fantasy romance set in the Kingdom of Rowanark about a squire hellbent on becoming a knight and a village girl with a hidden past. This book also happens to be the prequel to the Rowanark Tournament series.

You get these two books **for free** by signing up at http://georgekayde.com/free-books/.

Enjoyed this book?
You can help make a difference!

If you've enjoyed this book, I would be forever grateful if you could spend just five minutes for a review (it can be as short as you like). Readers have more power than any publisher, publicist, or marketing firm. Thankfully, I have the best thing there is: **dedicated and loyal readers.**

Your honest review would make a difference because it helps bring my books to the attention of other readers.

Please leave review on the book's Amazon page.

Thanks very much. You rock my socks because you've taken the time to better my career and get more books to you in the future.

Acknowledgements

A huge thank you goes out to my editor, Donna Alward, of Red Pen Coach. Without her, none of this would be possible. I am glad I found her when I did and she is a joy to work with. I admire her patience, her advice, and her talent. She's a writer of contemporary romances herself, so if you liked *Pix of Me and You* then make sure to pick up one of her books, too. You won't regret it. I personally recommend *Someone Like You.*

I'd also like to thank Christa Holland of Paper and Sage Designs for the gorgeous cover, and Jennifer Litteken of the Killion Group for the fantastic book blurb.

I'd like to thank my wife, Catherine, for giving me the time, the space, and the support to write books. She's my super fan, and the first to hear all my story ideas. My parents, brother, goddaughter/sister-in-law (don't ask) and friends also deserve a shout-out for listening to me throughout the years go on and on about the writing.

And last, but definitely not least, I'd like to thank God. The Almighty always has my back.

About the Author

George Kayde lives in Toronto, Ontario, where he works his day job as a city planner for the City of Toronto. When he's not writing fiction or studying architectural plans, you can find him buried in a book, seated in the back row at the cinema or annoying his wife with improvised songs.

George writes love stories from the here and elsewhere. His stories take place in contemporary settings and in worlds dreamed up in his head. Regardless of where and when these stories take place, romance, love and relationships are always at the heart of them.

You can learn more about George Kayde in the following ways:
Website: www.georgekayde.com.
Facebook: https://www.facebook.com/georgekayde/
Twitter: @kaydegeorge.
Email: george@georgekayde.com.

www.ingramcontent.com/pod-product-compliance
Lightning Source LLC
Chambersburg PA
CBHW051442050726
47593CB00005B/1889